GW01086339

Skullduggery

SKULLDUGGERY

A NOVEL

SILVIA FOTI

CREATIVE ARTS BOOK COMPANY
Berkeley • California

Copyright © 2002 by Silvia Foti

No part of this book may be reproduced in any manner
without written permission from the publisher,
except in brief quotations used in article reviews.

Skullduggery is published by Donald S. Ellis
and distributed by Creative Arts Book Company

For information contact:
Creative Arts Book Company
833 Bancroft Way
Berkeley, California 94710
1-800-848-7789

ISBN 0-88739-412-4
Library of Congress Catalog Number 2001097453
Printed in the United States of America

To Mom

Acknowledgments

My thanks to John Camper, the Chicago mayor's press secretary, who graciously answered my questions on what goes on in City Hall. And to Chandu Bhakta, M.D., an expert on broken wrists, as well as Martina Hough, anthropology administrative assistant at the Field Museum. Also Arthur Velasquez, president of Azteca Foods, Inc., for giving me a tour of his tortilla factory–where none of the shenanigans described in this book would ever occur. Although I've never met them, (but hope that I will) I thank Alice Bryant and Phyllis Galde for writing their inspiring book "The Message of the Crystal Skull," Llewellyn Publications, 1989.

I'm also deeply indebted to Robert Gover, author of "One Hundred Dollar Misunderstanding," my creative writing mentor. I give my special thanks to my friend and cheerleader Jill Sherer, my devoted brother Ray, who's quite the expert on auto PCs, and my husband Franco for his boundless and unconditional support. And finally, a big thanks to Beverly for helping me unearth myself.

Skullduggery

Chapter 1

I was on my back with the Chicago mayor sprawled on top of me. I was having trouble breathing. Pain radiated along my left arm. Above me, a collage of faces, aghast, quickly assembled.

A woman leaned over. She was so close, I smelled her cleavage. Her bra was midnight blue, a perfect match to her gown. Her face contorted like one of those twistable squishy dolls. And then she shrieked.

"He's dead! He's dead! The mayor is dead!"

This wasn't my fault. I thought he was drunk or something, the way he was acting.

I looked over to my right, past the mayor's left ear. He had three long black curly hairs sprouting from his helix. Something was missing. What was it? I searched through my mind.

"The skull," I gasped. "Crystal Skull is missing."

If I had that skull in my hands this very minute, I'd smash it to pieces. It has been nothing but trouble for the past six weeks. That was when my editor, Alyce Brownlee, first told me about it.

"You're my best reporter on occult phenomenon," she said, after assigning me the story.

That's because I don't believe in half the stuff I write about, I wanted to answer. But I didn't. I was close to maxing out on another credit card and didn't have another source of income.

My assignment was to follow the skull, get to know it, understand its history, and research its meaning. Alyce promised to make a big splash of it in *Gypsy Magazine*, her national monthly on supernatural happenings.

"Just picture your byline over a full-color shot of Crystal Skull," Alyce said, gesturing wildly. "Alexandria Vilkas in fourteen-point bold."

Seeing my byline in print always excited me, but even for a 36-pointer, I knew that this story wasn't worth it.

And here I was on New Year's Eve with the Chicago mayor sprawled on top of me. *Jesus! When were they going to get this guy off me?* I squirmed under his weight.

"Don't move!" a policeman ordered. "Someone will be here right away."

Hey, where was I going? My timing sucked.

It couldn't have been more than fifteen minutes earlier that I'd spotted the mayor and his wife coming toward our table. They made a complementary Mexican couple. He was big and thick, and she was small and thin. At any rate, I was not in the mood to deal with them. It was near midnight on New Year's Eve, and I was tired.

I was with my date at The Crystal Palace, another new theme restaurant in River North, and it was filled to capacity. This eatery had a mystical motif with dancing gypsies sashaying between tables, astrological charts of famous people adorning the walls, and big, jagged crags of crystal hanging and twirling from the ceiling, ricocheting light. It was an elegant end-of-the-year bash with streamers and balloons. On the face of it, it was just a New Year's Eve party.

But it was also much more than that.

All of the guests received specially engraved invitations to this grande affair. The guest list included, besides the mayor and his wife, the Windy City's wind-up well-to-do's. You had your aldermen, your actors, your bankers, and their significant others. Some even came with their wives. The host was Edgar Sheldon, billionaire tycoon, who had his finger up everyone's business. Including mine.

Like I said, I was here on an assignment for *Gypsy Magazine*, but I wasn't getting any material for my story. I mean, who wanted to talk to a reporter at a New Year's Eve party?

"Just absorb the atmosphere," instructed Alyce, who was seated at my table. I worked on absorbing the champagne. At ten minutes to midnight, my trouble began.

I looked over to Juan Guerrero, my date. He was the mayor's press secretary. It was clear the mayor and his wife were heading our way. Juan sprung from his chair like a jack-in-the-box clown. He tried very hard to have all the right moves.

I gulped down my champagne, grabbed my white linen napkin, dotted my lips, and stood up alongside Juan.

"Mrs. Morales, you look absolutely stunning," gushed Juan to the mayor's wife, as he reached over to shake her hand. She held his hand and wouldn't let go. The floor was filled with dancers swaying to the Big Band sound. Still in the clutches of the mayor's manicured wife, Juan was compelled to ask her to dance. Both looked at the mayor. He nodded. They walked into the dancing crowd.

Juan threw a look back at me. I let him know with the glare in my eyes that I was not pleased. He knew this look of mine. Then, for the sake of the mayor standing next to me, I pasted a wide grin on my face. Very wide.

"You look beautiful tonight, Alexandria," the mayor said.

"Oh thank you," I answered. "I wasn't exactly sure what to wear."

He scanned me. He was going over every nook and cranny. Was I enjoying that? What was I supposed to make of his brazen stare?

Maybe I asked for it. I was wearing a long black, body-hugging gown that revealed my entire back, from the neck to below the waist, with only one thin black strand connecting the back of the dress at my shoulder blades. I had my hair piled into a dozen twists and twirls.

I had barely eaten. But I'd done some serious drinking. Whoops!

My ankle collapsed, causing me to lose my balance, and I fell right into the mayor's arms.

Mayor Bernardo Morales had fine features—thick black hair that was slightly longish, a squarish jaw, penetrating brown eyes, and delicate, yet large, sensitive hands. I always noticed men's hands. When he ran for election four years ago, women in Chicago swooned. He was the first Mexican-American to run Chicago.

"I'm so sorry," I said, trying to compose myself.

As I regained my balance, Mayor Morales grabbed my arm and steered me toward the dance floor.

I was in a jam this time. I was going to have to waltz with the mayor.

As I lifted my right arm in preparation for the waltz, I looked over the restaurant. The theme was crystal, and pieces of crystal were everywhere. Big colorful pieces were perched in the center of the guests' round tables, surrounded by white candles. Some crystals were carefully polished while others were rustic and jagged. Small fragments were embedded into the walls, reflecting a magical luminescence.

The grandiose decorative centerpiece of this evening, however, was Crystal Skull. I had been covering it so intensively that I began to think of it as a person. I didn't actually name it, but I called it, well, Crystal Skull. Anyway, "it" looked over the crowd from a plexiglass pedestal. Not too far from the entrance. In fact, I touched it on my way in. For luck. Crystal Skull added a special sparkle to the evening.

When was this waltz going to end? One, two, three. One, two, three. I moved to the sedate beat. The mayor fixed his eyes on me. He started to grope me. *Quite the lady's man!* I took another deep breath and held it.

"Are you enjoying yourself?" asked the mayor, looking a little strained.

"Why, yes, immensely, sir," I stammered, letting out my breath. *Politicians and their libidos.*

"So, you came with Juan tonight," the mayor said, as he held me even more tightly by the waist. *He already had a mistress. What was he squeezing me for?*

"Yes, sir, we both went to journalism school together," I said, avoiding the impulse to squirm.

"So I understand," said the mayor, breathing quickly and heavily. "Juan can't stop talking about Miss Alexandria Vilkas and her talents."

One, two, three. One, two, three. I looked down and saw a sea of pumps and flat heels graze the floor. The waltz continued.

"Do you like to dance?" the mayor asked.

"Yes, I love it," I lied.

One, two, three. One, two, three. The waltz finally ended, and the countdown to usher in the New Year was about to begin.

"Perhaps you should look for your wife," I suggested.

"Oh, there's plenty of time for that," he answered, grabbing hold of the inside tender part of my upper arm. He was starting to look sweaty. Was that a little twitch?

Ten!....Nine!....Eight!...There must have been a thousand people chanting the last seconds backward as the New Year was about to launch. The lights dimmed. Seven!.....Six!....Five!...I was feeling giddy thinking about my pillow. Four! ...Three!...Two!....One!

Happy New Year!!!!!

Here we were, well into the twenty-first century. Cigarettes still weren't outlawed, but they cost a small fortune. The band blared "Auld Lang Syne." Streamers descended from the ceiling, confetti snowed down, and the mayor bent toward me. It was going to be the kissy-kiss.

He threw his arms around me, clutching me. He buried his lips into my neck. It was sort of a slobber, really.

This man will stop at nothing, I thought, taking a step back.

But then he began to feel heavy. I mean, really heavy. In fact, I was holding up his entire weight. On top of everything, I had to deal with a drunk mayor. *What was that twitch? When will those lights go back on?*

I put my arms around him to hold him. I lost my balance. I

fell backward, trying to hold him up with my right arm. I broke my fall with my left.

Ouch! My left arm! I felt and heard a crack.

The mayor fell right on top of me. People stopped kissing each other.

The music stopped.

"Turn on the lights! Turn on the lights!"

The lights came on.

There I was on the floor with the mayor sprawled on top of me, his legs spread over mine, his arms folded around me. I felt his hand lodged between my back and the floor. His face looked ashen, sweaty. He smelled like fish. I shook him with my right hand. My left hand was killing me.

"Mr. Mayor, Mr. Mayor, are you all right?" I asked.

He wouldn't budge. His eyes were wide open.

I tried to squirm my way out from under him.

A woman in a midnight blue gown leaned over. She shook the mayor. A sea of faces crowded around. I was having trouble breathing.

"He's dead! He's dead!" shrieked the woman. "The mayor's dead! The Chicago mayor is dead!"

Chapter 2

The next morning, I was drifting in and out of sleep in a bed at Northwestern Memorial Hospital, recuperating from surgery. My mother, known to everybody else as Irene Vilkas, was at my side, telling me everything would be all right. She looked as fresh as a newly poured bubble bath, even though I knew she must have been up all night. Not a blond hair was out of place. Her bun was as tight as ever.

I looked at my left hand. A plaster cast stretched from my fingers to about three inches past my left elbow.

"You broke your wrist," said Mom. "While you were trying to break your fall, apparently. We were afraid you had a concussion too."

I barely heard her. Visions were appearing. I felt as if I were drowning in a whirlpool, being sucked into its depths and swirling around and around, unable to grasp onto anything tangible. Just dark water. If I could just open my eyes again, I'd feel better. A nurse came to check me.

That entire night, every hour or so, somebody came to take my temperature or read my blood pressure. The visions wouldn't stop. A burst of stars, like the Milky Way in a blanket covered me. The twinkling. The shimmering. Then a big black spider appeared to weave a web. There was a wooden stage, dusty with time and furnished with empty chairs. A spotlight shined on the stage, expectantly waiting for players to appear. Nobody came. Instead, the spider wove her web in an intricate design, filtering a desolate light.

I opened my eyes again. Sunlight from the window filtered through some curtains. It was a bright light. January in Chicago. If it was sunny, it must be after eight o'clock.

"How do you feel?" asked my mother.

"Like shit," I said. "Did I pass out? I barely remember anything. Were you here all night?"

"Yes dear. Actually, it seemed like the entire city was checking up on you last night. You do remember what happened, don't you?"

How could I forget?

"Uggggh! This did not happen to me," I moaned. The sun was too bright.

"I'm afraid it did, dear," she answered in that special tone she used only for me, her only daughter. That tone that indicated she was the only person in the world who could possibly show me the errors of my ways.

Maybe it was just a bad dream. Maybe the mayor didn't really die.

"How's the mayor?" I asked. "Is he all right?"

"No dear, no he's not," she answered. "He's dead. Died right in your arms. How could you let that happen?"

I loved that about my mother. Blaming with a question, as if allowing me the favor of indicting myself.

"Do you seriously believe I had any control over that?" I shouted.

A man in a white coat walked in. My mother stopped talking. I felt so grateful. The doctor was young, clean-shaven, and had wavy blond hair.

"You've had quite a night, I understand," said my hero in white.

I was still trying to piece together what happened. I lifted my left arm and winced.

"That won't hurt so much in a couple of weeks," the doctor said, standing next to me. He had small hands with thin, bony fingers. "You had open-reduction surgery a few hours ago."

"Huh?"

"To put your wrist bones back together again," he explained. "You broke two of them—the radius and the ulna. A colles fracture. It happens when you try to break your fall while going backwards."

"How long do I keep the cast?"

"You should be as good as new in about eight weeks. Are you right-handed?"

I nodded.

"Well then consider yourself lucky." He smiled. A very nice smile.

"Will I be able to type?"

"I would take it easy for about two months."

Two months without typing. It would be like cutting off my lifeline. *What would my editor say? My story on the mayor. It was due next week. And the one on Crystal Skull. It was due the week after.* I felt a knot form in my stomach.

The doctor walked to the foot of my bed and placed my chart in a metal sleeve. He folded his arms. Then he scrunched his eyebrows together.

"There's a couple of detectives outside who want to talk to you. I've been holding them off as long as I could, but I told them they could come in after you woke up. Are you ready for them?"

The knot in my stomach got bigger and tighter and fouler. I shook my head no.

"Maybe another twenty minutes or so," he said, shrugging his shoulders. "I'll tell them to come in after your breakfast is delivered—which should be any minute. You'll be released from the hospital in a few hours."

He wrote something on a piece of paper and held it up. "It's a prescription for pain killers," he said.

I looked at my left arm again. Blacks and blues flared out from under the cast. The only skin I could see was my shoulder.

I grabbed the prescription with my right hand. The piece of paper felt like a ticket. If I could just get it stamped, maybe this whole episode would expire. After the doctor walked out, I faced my mother.

"Well?" Mom asked. She took the prescription from my hand, opened her purse, and stuffed it in there. She managed to keep her eyes on me the whole while.

"Well, what?" I snapped back. She was always there to watch the worst times of my life.

The phone rang. Mom sighed with exasperation as she picked up the receiver.

"Yes?" she lilted.

She handed the phone to me.

"Hello?"

"Alex, thank God! I was so worried about you!"

"Juan!" I turned to my side so I could ignore my mother's rolling eyes.

"How did you know where to find me?" I asked, trying to keep my voice low.

"The whole frigging town knows where you are for God's sakes. Haven't you turned on the TV yet?"

"No, Juan, I've been a little busy this morning. And thanks for asking me how I feel."

"Okay, okay," Juan said. "I was going to get to that. How do you feel?"

"I have a broken wrist."

"Does it hurt?"

"Yes, Juan. It hurts."

"You know, I wanted to go with you to the hospital last night, but I had to come into the office and start dealing with the press."

The press. He was the mayor's press secretary. I could only imagine what kind of a night he'd had.

Shifting my body back over again, I looked for the remote control and switched on the TV.

"So, do you know what happened to the mayor?" I asked.

"Nobody has any idea. I hear they're going to do an autopsy.

His wife is freaking."

Autopsies aren't pretty. I witnessed one and almost threw up while watching the corpse being turned inside out. An autopsy involves an internal dissection of the body and a toxicological examination of body fluids. I imagined the mayor would be examined from head to toe. I mean, a mayor doesn't just drop dead out of the blue. People would need to know every detail of his body to determine what happened. Morales would be cut from one shoulder to the other, from the lower tip of the sternum down to the pubis in a big, open "Y" shape. He would have his heart, lungs, esophagus and trachea removed, weighed and examined.

To me, an autopsy was the ultimate indignity. Murder was bad enough. But an autopsy was like another mutilation. Morales' death cut the life out of his body. His autopsy would insult it.

But it had to be done.

"How much longer do you get to keep your job?" I asked. If Juan's boss was dead, his career was probably killed as well. Chicago politics. I figured Juan would never work for another Chicago mayor again. He was known as Mayor Morales' right hand man. Some even called him the mayor's Mexican conscience.

"That's a good question," he answered. "The vice mayor took over this morning, and I guess he'll end up running in the primary, but I'm as good as yesterday's leftovers." He sounded upset.

Flipping through channels, I was looking for news of the mayor's death. The timing was very suspicious. He was running for his second term as mayor. The primaries were next month. He was considered the favorite, although it was no secret he had enemies. Plenty of them, as a matter of fact. Particularly Alderman Robin Dryad of the 23rd ward. He recently launched his own mayoral campaign, and although he was considered to have an uphill climb, he did have a fighting chance. He also happened to be my mother's boss.

"Alex?"

"Yes, Juan." A station looked like it was covering the story.

"What are you going to do about your story on the mayor?"

Now my blood pressure was rising. "Is that why you really called? Just to find out about my story on the mayor?"

"No, Alex, you know I care about you. We talked about that before. But he had his last interview of his life with you."

It was true, come to think of it. Just hours before the mayor died, I interviewed him in his home. I expected to be hounded about that too. My mood darkened.

"He had his last *dance* of his life with me!" I said. "Which, by the way, wouldn't have happened if you didn't leave me alone with him. Remember?"

"I know. I know. But back to your story. I'm getting all kinds of questions about what his last words were to you."

"Are you coming to visit me, or not?" I knew I'd be released in a few hours, but it was important for me to know Juan's answer.

"Babe." Pause. "I don't think I'll be able to see you today, honey."

Asshole. I just let him talk.

"I'm totally swamped. There's no way I can break away. I've got the press crawling all over. I promise I'll make it up to you. Tomorrow, I promise. But can you please, please tell me something about your last dance with him?" He was begging.

I was wide awake now. I sat up in my bed, flipped my legs over to the side and stood up. I wasn't even feeling dizzy. I slammed the phone receiver into the cradle. I felt better.

Now my mother raised her eyebrows.

I lay back down again.

"Well?" she asked. That tone. With her arms refolded.

The phone rang. I let it ring ten times. Then it stopped.

Mother was still looking at me.

"Well, what?"

"What the hell happened last night?"

Chapter 3

"Or am I going to be the last one to find out?" she asked.

"Mom, I truly wish I knew what happened. Honest, I know just as much as you do. I was dancing with the mayor, and the next thing I knew, he conked out. I thought he was drunk."

"You're going to have a lot of questions to answer, you know."

Breakfast interrupted us. It smelled so good.

I lifted the stainless steel lid and eyed the scrambled eggs, bacon, toast, butter, coffee, packets of sugar, salt and pepper, two-percent milk, orange juice, and peach slices.

"Want my bacon?" I had been abstaining from red meat for the past few months.

Mother shook her head. "If you don't mind, I think I'll take a walk to the cafeteria and get something for myself. I'll also get your prescription filled while I'm at it."

Out went Mom and on went the volume of the television.

After propping myself up, I stabbed my scrambled eggs with my fork. I didn't realize how hungry I was until I slid them around in my mouth. I turned the volume up even louder to hear a reporter interview a curator from the Field Museum.

"I understand the mayor asked you to examine the Crystal Skull a few weeks before he died," said the reporter. It was probably twenty degrees outside, but the reporter was doing the interview outdoors. The Field Museum was in the background. As if it were the White House, or something.

"Yes, the mayor was interested in having that skull displayed at our Field Museum someday, and he had gotten the skull owner's permission to have it examined," said the curator. The words "Jerome Gelding, chief curator of the Field Museum" appeared on top of his chest, typed in simultaneously during the interview. Late breaking story effect.

"Can you describe that skull for us?" asked the reporter.

"It was worth an estimated twenty million dollars, and was considered to be a most unusual artifact. According to legend, there were twenty-two skulls created more than four million years ago that were placed by the Planet's Masters in strategic points across the earth to help humanity advance. Said to hold positive energy and a strong force to advance civilization, Crystal Skull's powers are acutely felt near the millennium throughout a fifty-year period, from twenty-five years before the millennium and twenty-five years after."

"That's very interesting," said the reporter. "Do you really believe that?"

"Truthfully, I'm not sure," answered Gelding. He looked over his shoulder, toward the museum. He had a braided ponytail that flung toward the camera. He turned back to face the camera. "But that doesn't really matter. What does matter is there are a lot of people who do. And there is no question that Crystal Skull is very valuable."

"Do you believe the skull's disappearance is linked to the mayor's death?" asked the reporter.

"I have no way of knowing that," he said. He started looking around again. Then he faced the reporter again. "But the timing is remarkable."

"Is there something wrong?" asked the reporter.

"No, nothing's wrong," said Gelding, looking over his shoulder again. "It's just that...you know...the skull... " He buttoned and unbuttoned his coat.

"What about the skull?" asked the reporter, shoving his microphone closer to the curator.

"You have to be careful around it," he answered, taking a step closer to the reporter and looking straight at him. "It makes you think crazy things. You know what I mean?"

The reporter paused, seemed to listen to his earphone. "Well, sir, I understand we're running out of time," he said. He took two steps to his right and the camera followed. His face filled the screen.

"And so there you have it. About eight hours ago, the mayor of Chicago fell to his death at The Crystal Palace. Minutes later, someone noticed that a crystal skull, a valuable featured artifact at this restaurant, had disappeared. Are the two events connected? We don't know. We do know, however, that the mayor adopted this skull as one of his pet projects, and that it was a symbol for the mayor. Ever since this city elected its first Mexican mayor, the city council has been split in half. Oddly, that split was reflected in this skull. The mayor's supporters want this skull displayed here at the Field Museum. The mayor's detractors wanted this skull smashed. More later. Back to you, John."

Taking my last piece of toast, I wiped up the last juices from the eggs. The coffee was nothing to write home about, but at least it was still hot. I pushed away the empty tray and rearranged myself in my bed. I wish I had better coffee to think with. What did happen last night? How did the mayor die? I began to wonder if it was murder, but I hadn't ruled out natural causes. What kind of a story was I going to write now? I would have to talk to my editor. What was going on with that skull? Did the person—or persons—who took the skull kill the mayor?

Jesus! What was I doing? I was conflicted about getting involved any further. If I jumped into solving this mystery, I'd have to cover a lot of territory—some of it personal and emotional. I wasn't sure I wanted to deal with all that.

I already knew as a journalist that I'd have to cover a lot of history to make sense of the present. I'd have to re-analyze events from a fresh perspective to better understand what had transpired. For every two steps forward, I'd have to take one step backward. I'd have to interview people and ask them to recall events with the mayor and Crystal Skull. Shit. There was so much work to do.

I'd also have to journey back in time myself, practically relive some of my key moments with the mayor and Crystal Skull. Some of them I didn't really want to revisit. I shuddered. Yet I knew I had information no one else had. If I didn't do this, I'd....I'd what?

I was a natural at denial. The Queen, in fact. I could just pretend nothing of note had happened. That it was just a coincidence the mayor died in my arms.

Damn! How many more things was I supposed to stuff inside myself? There was no more room! I was on overload!

I knew I'd have to take this on. I'd have to take this on to purge, to unblock, to clear the way. But for what?

I'm not sure. I think it might have to do with that teeny, tiny me, covered by layers and layers of denial.

I took a deep breath. I knew I'd have to get involved. This time, I couldn't turn my back.

I began to organize the key events in my mind.

I had been researching Crystal Skull since it first appeared in Chicago the day after Thanksgiving, just six weeks ago. I remembered that day very well. That's where this story really began, I thought. And I had to piece it all back together if I was going to make any sense of what happened last night.

Chapter 4

Six weeks ago it was Friday, the day after Thanksgiving. Archer Avenue, one of the main streets on the South Side of Chicago, was in a gridlock, with construction causing a bottleneck of traffic that stretched for two miles in either direction. Yellow hard hats and orange vests were all over the place. I shifted back down into second gear, and vowed that my next car would be an automatic. All stick shifts should be banned from Chicago because construction on all major streets was constant—a yearlong event. It's like someone in City Hall just threw a pair of dice and this year, they landed on Archer Avenue. Move all the Caterpillar cranes to Archer! And don't forget the cute little construction workers! Last year, the dice landed on Cicero Avenue. The year before they landed on Southwest Highway. It didn't matter. All I knew was that every year, I was screwed. In fact, I was practically conditioned to driving through construction. Chicago patronage at work. Without construction jobs to hand out, politicians couldn't repay their favors, and they had plenty of them. I should know. I've heard all about city politicians and their favors from my mother who worked for Alderman Robin Dryad as his executive secretary for the past eighteen years. Jesus, who could work for the same guy for so long? Most women couldn't even stay married to the same guy for that long.

Finally. It took me thirty minutes to drive down a mile. I should have walked. There it was. The white-walled psychic studio. It would have been nice to park right in front of the place, but there was no parking with the street being ripped out. Another deep breath. "I am calm. I am not stressed," I muttered. "This is just a job."

Like I said, it was Friday, the day after Thanksgiving when half the people were still in their pajamas downing bottles of Maalox. The other half were on the road congesting the streets to start their Christmas shopping. I found a spot about a block away. But no, this psycho had to have an opening the day right after Thanksgiving. When my car door slammed, the tail of my coat jammed in the door. The door had a bad lock. I've been meaning to get it fixed. Rrrriiiipppp.

"Damn!" Nobody heard me. Everybody was inside—except for the city construction crews. Off went my coat. I opened my car door, which would not lock, and hurled the ripped Claiborne into the backseat. Slammmm.

Another deep breath. I grabbed the two lapels of my sweater and crossed one side over the other. The air definitely had a chill to it.

I couldn't believe I was doing this assignment—an ongoing series on crystal. And this super psycho put a full-page ad in the *Daily Southtown* inviting the entire frigging city to see his crystal skull. And of course it had to be on the South Side of Chicago, which made it my beat at *Gypsy Magazine*. Not that I wouldn't have had to cover it anyway—even if it meant a trip to San Francisco. But putting it right in my backyard. Jesus. That look from Alyce Brownlee, my editor. There was no way I was going to get out of covering this psycho's opening, no matter what day of the year it was. I researched the stuff, I interviewed experts on the stuff, and then I wrote about the stuff. Which got published. The subject was hot. It was practically mainstream. My own grandmother was always talking about her dreams and what they meant. My Polish girlfriend's mother went for psychic consultations more often than she went to church.

But I still didn't believe in it. Whatever. It was a legitimate magazine with a national circulation of 650,000. I got bylined, some exposure. What else did a working reporter want?

Don't ask. When I went to journalism school, I aspired to be an international reporter covering the world's major political events, jetsetting from one country to another, filing reports on wars, fallen presidents, disasters. You know, the good stuff. Instead, I got stories on crystal, acupuncture, the tarot, astrology.

But I had to admit, this crystal story was getting to me. In fact, most times I couldn't get it out of my mind. It was like I was walking to the edge of a cliff, peering over, and trying to find an answer to a question I didn't even ask.

I shuddered and turned to walk down Archer Avenue. How many times had I walked down this street—a wide, diagonal road that sliced through the city's southwestern edge and screeched to an abrupt halt just before approaching the North Side. As if it wouldn't dare offer passage to Chicago's richer, snobbier self. You'd have to take State Street for that.

But I was comfortable on the South Side. It was grittier, more real. Most people who lived here actually grew up in this neighborhood. And nobody liked change around here. I couldn't help but snicker, because this was the way to Alderman Robin Dryad's office, where Mom worked. I could just imagine what they were saying about this psycho moving in right next to them.

In fact, this whole thing was weird. Number one, the guy chose to open an office right next to a city politician. Number two, the guy was a guy. You just don't see guys doing this in this neighborhood. All the other psychics around here were women. Mostly Mexican women. Curanderas. Brujas. Witches.

There it was. White stucco walls. Pretty door with a major-looking stained glass window. It looked new. He must have spent something on that. The sign said it all. "South Side Psychic Studio." His store-front window was draped in white.

Wonder what was behind that curtain? I half expected Mom to pop out of Alderman Dryad's office to take a look for herself, but oh, yeah, it was the day after Thanksgiving, and Mom was probably busy scrubbing the pots right about now. Scraping off the black crust from her potato casserole cake that stubbornly clung to the pan. And to the lining of my stomach. Jesus.

Another deep breath.

Empty your mind of everything you know, and pretend you don't know anything. That strategy usually worked best when I was interviewing sources for a story. The last thing sources wanted to do was talk to someone who actually knew more than them. It scared them too much, and then they would clam up as if they were on stage in front of a crowded auditorium. This, of course, was the exact opposite of what I learned in journalism school. I spent a lot of time unlearning a very expensive education. No matter how many psychic studios I walked into, every single one was my first one. I got a lot more information that way. I treated all my sources like my first love—virgin territory.

As I opened the door to the studio, I gagged from the stench of cat urine. It was so strong, I could barely breathe. Taking a moment to get used to the smell, I looked around for cats, but didn't see any. Otherwise, the place was immaculate. The carpet had recently been vacuumed, with the rows of vacuuming marks still evident. The waiting room had a full-sized sofa with plump pillows covered with a zebra pattern. Two walls were mirrored. Now that was interesting. A long glass case was filled with crystal objects of various sizes. Some were spheres. Others were three-inch hexagonal columns. The colors ranged from blue to rose to orange to clear. Many were meditation pieces that could fit in the palm of a hand "to help users harness their own God-power and focus their vision on the Creative Force," stated the descriptive sign on the glass case.

A sixty-something-year-old man with long white hair walked out into the waiting room, rubbing potato chips off his greasy hands.

"Are you the South Side Psychic?" I asked.

"Christopher Warlick." As I extended my hand to shake his, I tried to ignore his hand's slippery feeling. "Or you can call me Mr. Wizard." He chuckled.

He had a slight accent. Sounded European. I could just picture the article I would write: "Wizards of the Windy City." He reminded me of the fat nun who was my high school geography teacher—jovial, talkative, and opinionated. It always struck me odd to see fat religious people because I assumed their spiritual appetite should overshadow their physical hungers, that their desire for food should be diminished to make room for their divine prayers.

"I called you a couple of hours ago for an interview about your skull for *Gypsy Magazine*," I began, looking around for anything resembling a skull. "Is this still a good time to talk to you?"

"Yes, yes, yes," he said. "It is good timing, as a matter of fact. For the unveiling. Go out in front of the window. You will have a better look." He was pointing emphatically.

I was just starting to feel warm again, but out I went. This was work.

Whoosh. The white curtain glided away to reveal an intricate window display—a fanciful motif that looked like a magical fairyland. Blue velvet draped the ceiling, sides and floor. Crystal-colored stalactites hung from the ceiling. A crystal fairy godmother dressed in a shiny silver outfit held a little crystal wand that pointed toward the skull. There it was. Crystal Skull. The godmother's wings fluttered to and fro in a mechanical fashion. Little figurines of gnomes dotted the floor. The skull was placed on a pedestal before a three-way mirror so that all sides of the skull would be reflected.

I giggled. *Marshall Fields, eat your heart out.*

I watched Warlick, the Wizard, crawl inside the window box to adjust the display. He looked like he was greeting an old friend. As he touched the skull, he smiled widely, as if he were imbibed with a tremendous amount of energy. He looked back at me through the window and nodded his head as if he heard the skull say something. Then he closed his eyes and stood very still, perched next to the pedestal with his left hand resting on the skull's crown. I thought of an old nursery jingle "I'm a Little Teapot" as I saw the wizard transfixed in this odd position.

The skull was about eight inches high and six inches wide. It was very realistic looking; even its eye sockets were not identical, but were slightly offset, like a normal person's eye sockets. I wondered how much it weighed.

People were starting to gather around the window display. Warlick came outside and began to speak. I rummaged through my purse, looking for my tape recorder.

"Quartz is a special stone because it can exist anywhere in the universe in its original form," he told the crowd. I tried to blend in. "It is the only material in the universe that can be transported anywhere—from earth to sun to another planet to another galaxy, and even to other dimensions."

"What about the skull?" someone asked.

"This skull is more than four million years old," the wizard said. "It holds the wisdom of humankind. It's time for Crystal Skull to be revealed again so that its message will be heard. The message says: Persevere. It is possible. Uncover and you will see the crystal clarity of your mind. Use it for the development of the human race."

"And how did you get hold of this skull?" I asked.

"It has been handed down to me from my grandfather in the old country. It has been in our family for centuries. I am a descendant of a long line of wizards. My family left Europe and came to America. Now I am here in Chicago with Crystal Skull. The skull goes where it is needed, where it can help the most. Its course is closely monitored by Masters from other universes, who use it to watch the earth, and also to transmit what perhaps should be happening on earth."

"How do they do that?" asked a man near me. This was where I was starting to disbelieve. That happened to me a lot in my line of work. But I kept my tape recorder on. All I had to do was quote the guy. Nobody said I had to believe him. That was called objective journalism.

"The Masters work from a similar skull in their presence and use their own skull to transmit their message to this one on earth. Crystal Skull could be understood by a select individual or it could be heard by the masses."

Chapter 5

Two police detectives walked in. I was so startled, I spilled coffee over myself. Good thing it wasn't hot anymore. The cops didn't look friendly. In fact, I didn't like the looks on their faces at all.

"Mizzzz Vilkas?" asked one of them. It was practically a sneer. "I'm detective Joe Burke, and I've got a few questions for you." He flipped open a notebook. I felt strange being on this side of an interview.

"Do you own a twelve-year-old beige Toyota Corolla that was parked outside of the Crystal Restaurant with license plate number TUS 061?"

"Yup, that's mine."

"We found the crystal skull in your car."

"But that's impossible!" My mind was racing.

"Where did you park your car last night?"

I had to think back. It seemed so long ago. "Actually, I don't know how I was so lucky. I was going to valet it, but then there was a spot right on Orleans, a little north of Ontario. I mean, you know, just steps away from the restaurant. I pulled in right after a car pulled out."

Even to me, the story sounded farfetched. Finding an open parking space on the street in that area was like spotting a four-leaf clover in the dead of winter. Things like that just don't happen. But that whole day was filled with one strange, serendipitous incident after another. My dress was on a major sale. My hairdresser took me without an appointment. The mayor had his interview with me. And then that spot just waiting. Upon reflection, I was due to have my luck run out.

"Yes, Miss Vilkas, that's exactly where we found it," Detective Burke said. His tone was getting a little gentler. "As we began to canvass the area, we noticed the crystal skull in the front seat of your car. Do you have any reason to know how it got there?" His voice became softer.

"No, none at all." I was beginning to feel like I wanted to help him.

"I understand you're about to be released from the hospital. Would you mind coming down to the station with us to answer a few questions?" He seemed so friendly now. He was sort of trying to relax me, I think, because I was very nervous. That was nice of him.

"No, officer I wouldn't mind at all. I just need to get my things together." My heart was pounding and I was scared. But I kept telling myself that everything would be alright. The rest blurred by like a videotape on fast forward. I signed my release papers. I got dressed. All I had was my black dress from yesterday. My mother came back and argued with me for agreeing to go down to the police station. But it was a sure bet that if she told me not to do something, I was even more inclined to go ahead and do it. I told her I'd call her when I got back. She handed over my pain killers.

Detective Joe Burke and the other guy, I forget his name, escorted me to their car. I half expected them to handcuff me or something. They took me to 11th and State Street. When I walked in the station, I noticed a few other policemen look at me kind of funny, but I didn't think anything of it at the time. I was probably quite the sight—hair all over the place, long, black dress under my black coat. I couldn't put my panty hose on with my bad wrist, so I was bare-legged with pumps on New Year's Day in Chicago. Open-toe pumps, on top of it. Which were wet because of all the snow on the ground. My tootsies were frosted, but I didn't want to say anything. They escorted me to an interrogation room and asked me to sit at the table. They asked me if I wanted some coffee. I said no thanks. They asked if they could take my coat, but I didn't want to reveal my bare-backed dress to them. And they left me there by myself. They walked out of that room and locked the door. I got up to check the door, and for sure, it was locked. I sat back down, and started to think. My wrist was hurting and my heart was pounding. I think the adrenaline rush just pushed out most of my thoughts about my pain. It seemed like I was by myself for a while.

The door opened again, and Detective Burke walked in with his sidekick following. He had this look like he really meant business. He was short and stocky with closely clipped hair. He had pock marks on his face like he had a lot of acne when he was a teen-ager. I was starting to regret being here.

"Can you explain why the crystal skull was in your car?" he asked.

"Like I said earlier, I have no idea."

"How do you explain your fingerprints on it?"

I had to think for a second. "I know that skull. I was working on it. And so when I saw it at the restaurant, I touched it. I thought it would bring me luck."

Detective Burke raised his eyebrows and then he turned to his buddy. "Did you hear that? Luck." He was getting sarcastic. His buddy was writing everything down in a notebook.

"What do you mean by working on it?" He shifted in his chair and cocked his head to an angle.

"I'm a reporter for *Gypsy Magazine*. Have you ever heard of it?"

"Sorry," he said, raising his voice an octave. Actually, I didn't think he looked like a typical reader of occult phenomenon.

"I've been working on a story about crystal and Crystal Skull for a couple of months," I said.

"So you knew that it was worth a lot of money."

"Yes, of course I did."

"And that's why you stole it."

"No, I didn't take it. I couldn't have. I was dancing with the mayor." I was starting to feel somewhat flustered. This was my first interrogation, and now it sounded like he was accusing me.

"That's another thing I wanted to ask you about. Can you explain to me how the mayor died in your arms?"

"No, I have no idea. Actually, I thought he was a little drunk at first, but then he just sort of...slumped."

"Slumped?" Detective Burke looked at his sidekick again, who continued to write in his notebook.

"Well, like he went...limp."

"Did you notice anything else unusual?"

"He was sweaty. And there was this twitch that I kept noticing. It seemed like he was a little confused, or dizzy. He was kind of breathing funny too. Actually, I remember him having a fishy smell. And the next thing I know, he just conked out on me."

He stared at me. But I didn't have anything else to add.

"So what do you believe is the cause of the mayor's death?"

I'd been wondering about this all day. "Maybe he was poisoned. What did the autopsy say?"

"How did you know he was going to have an autopsy? That information hasn't been released yet."

"My boyfriend told me."

"Who's your boyfriend?"

"Juan Guerrero. He's the mayor's press secretary."

"How long have you known him?"

"We first met in journalism school. At Northwestern. We were in the master's program. That was about six years ago."

"And that's when he became your boyfriend? Two privileged kids falling in love at a fancy college?" He turned to his buddy. "Make sure you write that one down."

"No, no, not at all. We were friends for a long time. We're both from the South Side. We stayed in touch, even after we graduated. Then about six weeks ago, it started getting more serious."

"How serious?"

That was a confusing question to me. "I don't know..." I started.

"Let's go back to the skull for a second. If you didn't put the skull in your car, who did?"

"I have no idea."

"Who else has the keys to your car?"

"Well, no one else. But, really, anyone could have put it there. My lock is broken. It doesn't close well. I've been meaning to get it fixed, but I figured, the car is kind of old and beat up anyway."

"You drive a car in Chicago that doesn't lock? They'll give a degree full of shit to anyone. You think we're stupid or something?" He slapped his sidekick. He was laughing too. "Come on. What's the story?"

"That *is* the story. That's the truth!" I was starting to get a little worried for myself. That wasn't the first time I ran into that attitude about my degree either.

"So how was it that the mayor of Chicago was dancing with you anyway?" He leaned back into his seat and tilted it. All he needed was a bowl of popcorn on his lap.

I'd been trying to figure that out all day too. "That morning, I had an interview with him. So he sort of knew me. And that evening, I was sitting next to Juan. I guess the mayor just came to our table to talk to his press secretary about something. But then the mayor's wife felt like dancing, so she grabbed Juan. That left me alone with the mayor. Then he just asked me to dance."

"You had an interview with the mayor? What was the interview about?"

"It was about astrology. You know, his belief in astrology? That certainly was no secret."

Detective Burke rolled his eyes. I'm sure he knew what I meant though. It was a big scandal. The mayor's enemies found out that he used an astrologer to map out his strategies, and when that information hit the press a few weeks ago, his election campaign was rocked. My mother's boss, as it so happened, was the one who leaked the information.

"What else did you talk about?"

"We talked about Crystal Skull."

"Did you tape record your interview?"

"Yes, and I took notes too. I take lots of notes. I barely use any of them, but I have to take them. It's kind of part of the ritual of writing."

"Perhaps we could take a look at your notes?" He clasped his hands together.

I just laughed. He asked it so simply, like it was no big request at all. "I don't think so. Reporters are kind of funny about sharing their notes with the authorities. Or haven't you heard?"

"Oh, I heard alright," he said. Then he stood up and leaned over me. I didn't like being that close to him. "Look, we have your fingerprints on the skull and you were the last person to be with the mayor when he died. Tell us how you killed him. We're going to find out during the autopsy anyway. If you admit to it right now, we'll see what we can do to lighten the sentence."

"My sentence? Wait a minute. What's going on here? Should I have a lawyer?"

"Only guilty people need a lawyer," he said.

"Am I under arrest? Do I have to stay here?" I watched Detective Burke and his buddy walk out of the room and lock the door again. I felt like crying, but I knew he'd be back soon, and I didn't want to give him the satisfaction of seeing me broken down. I was innocent. I had nothing to worry about.

He came back. "We're going to let you go now. Unfortunately, we don't have enough evidence to keep you today. But we'll get it, and when we do, we'll bring you in, and we'll book you. Let me tell you one thing, Mizz Vilkas. You're our number one suspect. We know where you live, and we'll be watching you. Don't even try to leave town. In two weeks, you're going to have a little talk with the D.A."

"The District Attorney?" I asked.

"Looks like you do understand some things," he said.

"But why? I didn't do anything."

"The mayor of Chicago is dead. Somebody's guilty. So far, you're our best suspect. Now get outta here."

I was starting to shake. "Where's my car?"

"It's impounded for evidence."

"How am I supposed to get home?"

"You got a fancy degree from a fancy college. You figure it out."

Chapter 6

I walked out onto State Street, looked to my left and saw a bus stop on the other side of the street. It was on Twelfth Street, also known as Roosevelt Avenue. There was no bench. There was a stairway going down to a subway station. I took a seat on the top stair. I had to decide between taking the bus or the El.

I was very upset. I didn't have to be treated that way. As if I were a criminal. "The number one suspect," he called me. *Asshole.* I looked into my purse and saw the painkillers. I took two, swallowing them with my spit. The lumps slid down my throat slow and sure, like two programmed missiles.

It was New Year's Day, and the likelihood of a heated Chicago Transit Authority bus coming my way was about as remote as this city firing employees who failed to show up for work. If I took the El, I'd still have to take another bus to get home. I decided to call my editor. I didn't feel like dealing with my mother and I was still pissed off at Juan. Another deep breath. It was close to noon, and Alyce Brownlee had been up for hours. She had a condo in Streeterville, which was about two miles north of where I was sitting. With the lack of traffic, she would be here in less than ten minutes.

Alyce hired me two years ago, when I was filing stories for a weekly newspaper on the South Side. That was when I was making nothing and still lived at home with my mother. But when I started to write for *Gypsy Magazine*, my finances improved. I could afford my own apartment. I was still earning next to nothing, but I was on my own. I got that job through my own merits, which made me feel good.

Writing about occult matters and New Age spirituality wasn't what I had in mind for myself. It didn't seem, well, very journalistic to me. I mean the facts were difficult to check in the traditional sense. If someone told me a piece of crystal helped him concentrate better, how was I supposed to disprove that? It's not that I didn't believe in God, but I was skeptical about the authenticity of soothsayers. I was fine if I didn't try to analyze it too much. But I couldn't help myself. I was antsy. I wanted to move up in my career; I just didn't know how.

A cabbie pulled up and honked. I was about to wave him away, but then Alyce rolled down her window from the back seat. "Hop in, kid!"

Alyce personified the female, brash editor. Maybe not with her looks, but definitely her personality. If cigarettes were still cheap, she'd be a smoker. She chewed a lot of gum. In fact, I think she had to quit smoking when taxes on cigarettes went sky high several years ago. She was forty-six-years-old, had thick, short, brown hair with generous streaks of gray. Today, she was wearing a gray wool business suit. She rarely wore makeup, maybe a little mascara. I think I saw clear nail polish on her once.

My feet were numb. I hobbled into the cab. The heat inside felt so good.

"I could have called a cab myself, you know."

"Don't worry. I didn't feel like driving. I still have a hangover."

Always practical and sure of herself, Alyce was my mentor. I looked upon her as my career mother, someone who I could always turn to when I was troubled with my work. She was pretty good with advice when I was troubled with my personal life too, but I didn't want to wear her out.

I gave the cabbie my address in Garfield Ridge and told him to go down Archer Avenue, all the way to Central Avenue. Then it would be a few more blocks west. We drove past China Town, Bridgeport, Brighton Park, and a diner named after Midway Airport.

"So you've gotten yourself into a fine mess this time, kid. What the hell happened?"

I burst into tears. It was just all too much. Maybe the pain killers were finally taking effect too.

"The police think I stole the skull and that I killed the mayor," I sobbed. "They found the skull in my car. It had my fingerprints on it. I'm their number one suspect. I see the D.A. in two weeks."

"If I ever heard anything so ridiculous, this is it." Alyce pulled out a packet of gum and offered me a piece. We both chewed gum in silence. I was starting to settle down.

"Obviously you didn't do it, so we'll start from there," Alyce said. "That means somebody else put the skull in your car. All you have to do is figure out who put the skull in your car, and you're home free."

"But there were a thousand people at that party, Alyce. Anybody could have done it. And Morales had a million enemies." Hyperbole was best when I didn't know the exact numbers.

"That's true," Alyce said, cracking her gum. "You know what, kid? You're already writing a story about Crystal Skull and the mayor. I want you to get on this case to solve the murder. That's going to be the ending to your article. Everything's connected, and there's some evil lurking in this city that's trying its damndest to suck out its spiritual soul."

She was starting to get very excited about her vision of this story. That worried me. When she got like this, it always meant a ton of work for me.

"For God's sake, Alyce! The entire city police force is investigating this case. How am I supposed to solve it?" The task seemed too insurmountable. "I'm just a journalist. In fact, I don't even believe half the stuff I write. And besides, I can't type now with my broken wrist."

"That's the least of your worries. Your right hand is fine, isn't it?"

I just stared at her. She was always after a story. No matter what.

"Do it the old-fashioned way. Write it out long-hand. In fact, this is the type of story that needs to be written slowly. Your brain needs to synthesize different types of information—police procedures, spirituality, and politics. You have to connect a regular old-fashioned murder with a New Age twist. Writing it out long-hand is the best thing for this. It'll make the whole process more organic."

Alyce was a writer's writer. Some editors got to where they were without ever having to write much. They were hand-picked for their managerial abilities by people who thought the actual writing part of a publication wasn't that important. As if that got done by itself. I really liked the fact that Alyce could write. That was crucial to me. That made it easy for me to respect her. But there were times like this that I wanted to look for a bottle and smash it on top of her head.

"I don't even write letters to my friends in long-hand. Forget it! I want an extension on my deadline. The doctor said I won't be able to type for almost ten weeks." There was no reason to let her know the doctor said only eight.

"That's fine. That's fine. Take as long as you need. This story is too important. I'll use some of your other stories that are backlogged for the next two issues. You've got ten weeks."

Ten weeks was as long as I needed, according to Alyce.

"Thanks, Alyce. You've got a big heart." I really meant that, though. We had been parked in front of my apartment for several minutes already, and the meter was running. It showed that since Alyce got in the cab, she traveled thirteen miles.

"Now get going, kid. Get some rest. Take a few days off. Come in early next week, and let me know where you are in the story."

I watched the cab drive down my street. Then it screeched to a halt and went in reverse until it stood in front of me again. Alyce rolled down her window.

"I almost forgot. I want you to cover the mayor's funeral, kid. Watch the news to find out when it's scheduled."

This time, she drove away for good.

Chapter 7

I turned around and faced home. It was the first-floor apartment of a white-brick, three flat built at the turn of the millennium. My rent included two bedrooms, a kitchen, a living room, a dining room, a porch, use of a washer and dryer, a backyard, and a garage. Rows of three-flats lined my street, and mine didn't look much different from the other buildings on the block.

This was where I spent my nights and weekends. This was the South Side. Sometimes I thought my soul was like the city, split neatly in half, with neither side willing to acknowledge the other. The South Side of me liked cheap rents, fast food, and the more practical wide-open spaces, where there was some elbow room to stretch out and park a car. But I hated the rampant racism and clannishness. The North Side of me liked the expensive restaurants, the allure of cultural substance, and the deep lake. But I hated all the show-offyness.

It was cheaper to live on the South Side. My landlord was a recent Polish immigrant who bought the three-flat with cash shortly before I moved in. He didn't believe in mortgages, which kept my rent low. If I helped rake the leaves, shovel the snow, and clean the backyard, he gave me an additional break. Although I didn't think I'd be shoveling snow in the near future with this wrist.

Inside, everything was just as I had left it. A big mess. I was too tired to care. It was three in the afternoon. I took a long bath and changed into my pajamas. Skipping the blow dry, I put a towel around my shoulders to protect my jammies from my wet hair.

Time to eat. When I opened my refrigerator, I noticed a lot of old leftovers and wilted vegetables. Once, potential meals, but now trash. The canned vegetable beans looked pretty good. I had a packet of tortillas from Tortilla King. Dinner was served.

I switched on the TV to the Chicago All-News channel. It was all about the mayor's death. As I bit into my twice warmed over tortilla, the anchor detailed the results of the mayor's autopsy. Mayor Bernardo Morales, the first Mexican mayor of Chicago, had died of nicotine poisoning. Traces of nicotine were found on his hands and his face, which when absorbed through his skin, had lead to his death.

Death by nicotine was somewhat ironic, I thought, because the mayor was known for his clean-up campaign against the illegal cigarettes that have been infiltrating the city.

The TV showed his family grieving. He was survived by his wife, three children, and both parents. There was going to be a public vigil in City Hall in three days.

The police investigation continued. The chief of police announced he officially believed the mayor was murdered. He said it could have been political or it could have been personal. He wasn't sure whether the theft of the skull was linked to the mayor's death.

My dinner started to gather in my throat.

I saw a photograph of myself on the screen. I choked on my vegetable beans. They teletyped my name under my face. They even spelled it right. Alexandria Vilkas. They picked up the picture that ran every month in *Gypsy Magazine*.

Now the entire city knew the police found Crystal Skull in my car. I turned off the TV. I took two painkillers and looked for my wine.

The phone rang, but I didn't answer it. I'm sure it was my mother.

I had already eaten two tortilla rolls, but I was still hungry. Half a bag of stale chips. Peanut butter and jelly after that. I was very upset. I went into my bedroom and sat on my bed.

Everything needed to be quiet, very quiet. In this stillness, I could think and gather my thoughts. What to do? What to do? How do I get myself out of this? Why did I let myself fall into this? Was this in any way my fault? Was this a set-up, or was it an accident? Who killed the mayor? Why did he have to die? And why did it have to be in my arms?

I hadn't meditated for a few days. I looked at the meditation chair in the corner of my bedroom. Time to reconnect. God would help me. Or my Higher Self would get me out of this. Whatever. All I knew was that this actually helped me in some mysterious way. Maybe I was feeling so desperate, I was just begging for a way out of this mess. In a way, it didn't matter. I needed to see the white light to calm down. I walked over to my chair and sat in it. I closed my eyes and placed my hands, palms up, on my knees. My mind was a chatterbox and I couldn't command it to be still. I was very new at meditating and had heard that people could do this, draw their mind to a blank and feel a tremendous sense of bliss.

Deep breath in. Hold it. Count to twenty. Deep breath out. Hold it. Count to twenty. Deep breath in. Count to twenty. Deep breath out. Count to twenty. As I exhaled, I felt the familiar heat rise along my spine and converge at the base of my skull, the medulla oblongata, the body's recipient of cosmic energy. I let my mind fall deeper and deeper into the great white light until I thought of nothing else but peace, tranquility, and love. I felt like a wave on an ocean of God, moving in tandem with the divine natural rhythm. Then my mind wandered for a moment, and I pictured an ant carrying a bread crumb through the desert sand storm of life's illusions, persistently walking toward the light despite the raging storm winds tempting me with their fury.

My mind wandered further. I tried to bring it into check. It was so hard, like controlling the gales of a blizzard. Some men spent twenty years in a cave until they got this right. I couldn't fight my mind's meanderings, so I decided to ride them out and then usher myself back to my task of meditation later.

I was remembering a conversation I had with my mother several weeks ago. Maybe it was that Sunday after Thanksgiving. We were in a restaurant in Chinatown. The chatter around us was loud, but it added to the festive atmosphere. The smells of shrimp, lobster, and soy sauce mingled with the aroma of hot mustard, steamed vegetables, and fried won tons.

"Today was a humdinger of a day," my mother said to me. "You wouldn't believe what these men have concocted. I was there, and I still don't believe it."

"You really love the dirty political underbelly, don't you?" I asked, relieved that I was finally getting food into myself.

"Dirty underbelly is rather harsh," she responded, biting into a fried won ton. "'Cunning maneuvering,' maybe, or 'having a talent to create favorable circumstances' is more like it."

I couldn't believe how much my mother enjoyed all the intrigue in the high-society and political circles.

"Don't you think it's a big waste of time?"

I watched my mother stare back at me, as if she were wondering what planet I just fell off.

"Alex, I try so hard to lead you down the right road, but you just don't seem to click into the more important aspects of life."

"My work is the most important thing in my life for now," I answered. My mother always told me she just wanted to be friends, but it always turned out that she had a lecture for me about how she would live my life. Were all mothers that way?

Mom rolled her eyes and twirled her fork.

"You call writing about ghosts a job?" she asked.

"Why don't we talk about something else?" I tried.

Mother repositioned herself in her seat, and said, "Alright. You haven't heard about what happened in the office today."

"Yeah, what was going on?" I asked, relieved she changed the subject.

"Robin is going to kill Bernardo Morales," she said, grinning from ear to ear.

"Yeah, how so?"

"He's got his election strategy all figured out, and it's rather wicked, if I do say so myself."

"Well that's no surprise, if you're talking about Alderman Dryad. How do you even have the stomach to work for him?"

"Actually, this is sort of connected to your line of work, now that I think about it. It seems our beloved Mexican hero has made a habit of consulting the stars."

This was a double whammy for me, and I couldn't believe how my mother could be so adept at throwing these psychological curve balls, one right after the other. First, she insinuated that Mexicans were beneath her, knowing full well I was dating Juan Guerrero. Second, she demeaned my job again with her tone of voice.

But I ignored it all, not even knowing where to begin responding. I just continued the conversation.

"What do you mean by consulting the stars?" I asked.

Mother lowered her head and her voice, and said in a hushed tone, "The mayor has an astrologer."

I watched how much she enjoyed this gossip.

"What?"

"Actually, I don't know why I'm even whispering," she said. "It's going to be in the newspaper tomorrow."

"That's what you were talking about when you were on the phone with the *Chicago Tribune*?" I asked.

"MMM-mmmm," she said, keeping her lips pursed together in a smug smirk.

"Astrologer, what astrologer?"

"The poor creature's name is Maria de la Cruz," she said. "She's been giving the mayor all sorts of advice, and he's been making many of his political decisions based on the positions of the stars. Can you believe that?"

"No," I said. I really couldn't. This was too much.

"It seems this has been going on from the very beginning of his campaign. And here's something else, dear. In fact, this part is the real secret: We're saving this bomb for a later day, maybe just before the primary."

My eyes were wide open. My mother was so cold and calculating. Yet I was mesmerized, drawn to her like a bug to a fancy, sticky Roach Hotel. It all looked so comfortable on the outside.

"The woman is extremely beautiful," went on my mother. "It seems our handsome and debonaire Bernardo couldn't resist her. He's been having an affair."

"No way. I don't believe it."

"But it's true," she said. "Robin had an investigator follow him."

"How long was he doing that?" I wondered whether that was even legal. Wasn't that an invasion of privacy?

"Several weeks, it seems. Apparently, someone tipped him off. And once he found out Morales really was visiting Maria de la Cruz regularly, he became more confident about launching his own campaign."

"So, now it's official," I said. "Alderman Robin Dryad is running against Mayor Bernardo Morales."

"Yes, and with the news of Morales' immoralities, Dryad's chances of winning are much better. Don't you think?"

"What did you tell the *Chicago Tribune*?"

"That Morales is not as perfect as he looks. He has a lovely wife and three beautiful children. But he regularly calls an astrologer—sometimes three times a week. She has a home in Bridgeport and they often meet at a hotel."

"Which one?"

"The Stouffer Riviera on Wacker Drive."

I still couldn't believe this.

"So that's all it takes to become a candidate in a mayoral election?" I asked.

My mother just smiled and shrugged her shoulders. "That was some meeting today. I'll be spending the next two days writing up the minutes."

"Can I see a copy?" I asked.

"Now dear, you know those minutes are confidential."

At the time, I didn't think it mattered.

Chapter 8

I took a deep breath in. Held it. Blew a deep breath out. Then I opened my eyes. Sitting in my meditation chair, I thought about that conversation with my mother and wondered how it was connected to my predicament.

Since I was the number one suspect in the mayor's murder, I felt I should play a hand in my own fate. I could try to solve this murder mystery the way I did an investigative story. I'd start with research, do interviews, analyze the information, organize it, then write it. I had to find the link between Crystal Skull and the mayor's death.

I decided I would start interviewing those closest to me and widen my net of information from there. First thing tomorrow morning, I'd go to my mother's house. Feeling better, I went to bed.

At 7:30 the next morning, I readied myself for my first official interview on this case. It was good to feel productive, like I had a purpose. My mother lived about six blocks away from me. Without a car, I'd have to walk.

Before leaving, I called my car insurance agent to see what my policy said about cars being impounded for evidence in murder investigations. I wondered if I were entitled to a rental. No answer; I left a message.

My boots had thick rubber soles. They came up about four inches above my ankles and had a rim of fake fur. The snow crunched beneath them, glistening in the morning sunlight. The cold was invigorating and I enjoyed hah-hahing into the air to watch my steamy breath. It was proof I was alive.

Before I knew it, I arrived at my mother's house. I rang her doorbell, but there was no answer. I rang again. She couldn't be gone. Just as I was walking toward the back yard to see if I would have better luck with the back door, the front door swung wide open.

"Alex! Dear! What are you doing here?" my mother asked. That was odd. It was after nine, yet she still had her robe on. And she was barefoot.

"I just came for a visit," I said. "Surprise! Did you miss me?"

"You could have called to warn me," she said, wrapping the robe more tightly around herself.

"What's the big deal? You just live to see me anyway."

She clucked and gave me the once over. "I tried calling you yesterday, but there was no answer. Come on in. It's chilly out here."

I kissed her on her cheek and after walking past her, stamped the snow off my boots, removing them in the foyer. I tossed them into the nearby pile of shoes, comprised of several pairs of women's shoes and, oddly, one pair of men's cowboy boots.

"Whose boots are those?" I asked. I'd never seen them before. Alligator leather, quite worn out.

"Oh, um, they belong to a friend of mine," my mother said, avoiding my eyes. "He must have left them here the other day."

"What friend?" She was allowed to have friends, but I didn't want her to date. No one could replace my father. Even if he died nineteen years ago, when I was just ten.

"Oh, um, I'll have to tell you about him another time. I wouldn't want to bore you right now."

This was worse than I thought. She could have made anything up, I suppose, to make me feel better. But outright evasion was bad news. Very bad. A mother was supposed to be wise, all-knowing, and most of all, unsexual. I debated with myself. Should I press the point or let it go? Then I saw the ashtray with the cigarette butt stubbed into it.

She was on her way to the kitchen. "Have a seat, I'll get us some coffee," she said over her shoulder.

I took a seat next to the ashtray and stared at it like it was an alien object that emerged through a time warp. Bending down close to the ashtray, I took a cautious sniff to smell the tobacco ashes. What a monster ashtray. It was a green marble disc, about eight inches in diameter, that was raised about six inches high by a figure of Hercules. He had a face carved in stress from bearing the weight of the green orb on his shoulders.

What was that doing here? Near the turn of the millennium, the number of class action suits by smokers against tobacco companies mushroomed. The first suits were isolated incidents, but once judges began awarding million-dollar compensation packages to the smoking victims, it became a free-for-all, and no Congressman took any money from a tobacco-interest company ever again. Then it became a festival of tobacco bashes. Smokers had less sympathy from the public than child molesters. Even though Congress didn't succeed in officially outlawing cigarettes, they did make them unaffordable by raising cigarette taxes. Today, a carton of ten costs as much as my car was worth.

"Whose cigarette is that?" I asked when my mother came back with two mugs of coffee.

Again the evasion. "Why, um, it's mine," she said, pushing a strand of her blond hair behind her ear. Usually her hair was swept away from her face, swirled neatly into a tight bun. "One of Robin's friends gave me a pack at the office the other day. Um, you know."

"No, I don't know. Tell me more."

She took a sip of her coffee, crossed her left leg with her right, and started to gently swing her right calf up and down, pointing her toes to the floor. She had her slippers on. "What! I can try one if I want, dear!" She shrugged as if I had asked the silliest question in the world.

Yeah, right. She obviously didn't want to talk about this. I took a sip of my coffee. Mom wasn't known for her good coffee, either.

"So, what's going on, dear? I saw you on the news last night." She wasn't communicating to me in her usual outraged outbursts. In fact, she was unusually subdued. But I had bigger problems to solve.

"Oh, it's horrible," I said. "I have no idea who put that skull in my car, but I want to find out. I think it might lead me to the mayor's killer. And that's why I'm here."

"Oooooh?" Her voice climbed high as she stretched out the word.

"I want to ask you about Alderman Dryad's campaign strategy. Who's been visiting him, what he's up to. The mayor's enemies. Can you tell me?"

She held her cup of coffee in midair and froze herself in this position for a couple of seconds. "I'm still not following you, Alex."

"The police informed me that I'm now their number one suspect in the mayor's death. Since I'm the only one who seems to be sure that I didn't kill him, I feel like I need to find the real killer to get myself off the hook. The mayor's murder might be political. It might be connected to Alderman Dryad's campaign. That's where you come in to help me."

She looked at me, her coffee cup to her lips, shielding the bottom half of her face like a veil. Yet her eyes were very expressive. They were a glimmering green and were wide open, as if she saw a ghost. Then she stood up, walked past me, back into the kitchen and into her bedroom. She came back out holding a manila folder, which she handed to me.

"I think you'll find everything you need there. They're my minutes from that meeting."

"The meeting you said you couldn't tell me about?" I asked. "The one that was so confidential?" I reiterated, remembering how secretive she was during our dinner in Chinatown.

"Yes."

I opened the folder and saw about twenty sheets of paper

filled with single-spaced type. Nobody ever complained about my mother's organizational skills. She was privy to so much information in this city that she was known as a walking file cabinet.

"Wow! What the hell happened there?" I asked.

"Shhhh. Not so loud," she whispered. "Just put that away for now, and read it at home."

"Why?" I asked. "What's the big deal?" She was acting very funny.

"I, um, I have a headache, and I want things to be quiet."

I looked again through the manila folder.

"I just met with Robin yesterday to go over them, so they're all in order," she continued in her hushed voice. "You can keep that set, just don't let anyone else see them, if you know what I mean."

I knew what she meant. "No, what do you mean?"

"Not for Juan's eyes." The way she emphasized Juan. Like he had leprosy. Like he wasn't part of the family, never would be, and wasn't worthy enough to be trusted with anything confidential.

"Of course not," I said, struggling to contain my venom inside. I took the folder and tried to leave before saying something I'd regret.

"And, how is Juan doing?" she asked.

"He's fine." I was at the doorway putting on my boots.

"What's the story with you and Juan anyway," she asked. "The only good thing about him was that he was well-connected. And now he's managed to lose that."

Now she was scrutinizing again. It had become a little easier since I moved out of her house, but even these periodic microscopic check-ups were enough to keep me inhibited in my relationships. When I lived at home, I was under her watchful eye every moment and I thought I was going to suffocate. How would I ever have any chance of meeting a guy without her intrusions, questions, insinuations, and psychological grills?

"For now, we're just friends, Mom. He's a very nice man and

we enjoy each other's company." I didn't want to give any more details. She would just store the information as a piece of ammunition to be hurled at a later moment.

"But...." she said, then pursed her lips.

Unfortunately, I already knew where this was going.

"His skin," she whispered. "It's...it's... brown." She rubbed her own skin on her forearm back and forth and looked up at me.

"So?" I asked.

"And his eyes. They're brown too," she said, pushing back another strand of hair.

"Very good mother. Two points for excellent observation. Did you have anything else to add?" *Did she talk to her friends that way, or was it just to me?*

Mother took a sip of coffee and shrugged her shoulders. "I'm just trying to help you make a good decision on who you should marry."

"Marriage? We're not even close to that subject."

"You're twenty-nine-years-old dear," she reminded me again. "Thirty is just around the corner, and it's time for you to really start thinking about somebody to marry. You know, it doesn't get any easier when you're older."

Was this really the woman who gave birth to me? Was I the spawn of her belly? My words escaped me, uncontrollably.

"Mom, I haven't lived at home for two years, I'm supporting myself, and I'm happy in my career. I don't need a man to define myself."

She put down her coffee mug on the cocktail table in front of her.

"Besides, look at you," I continued. "You're lecturing me about finding a guy, while you haven't been with a man since dad died. That's a little twisted, don't you think? You know, you're almost fifty-five years old. Time's a wasting. Chop. Chop." I banged my cast against the wooden doorway twice, containing any winces that would betray my pain. I was beginning to think I should do this more often.

It was then that I heard it. A cough. Another cough. A distinct male, low alto cough. The kitchen door opened, and in walked a man naked from the waist up. He was wearing mom's bath towel from the waist down. I knew this man. I just didn't recognize him. In fact, it took me a couple of more seconds to register the fact that it was Alderman Frank Messina. He was smiling. Laughing. Tilting his head back. He thought this was just hilarious.

"Frank!" my mother yelled. "What are you doing?"

I looked back at her. I was ensnarled in an aspect of my mother's life that I wish I knew nothing about.

"Mom! How could you?"

This was just too much for me. I grabbed my coat, jerked my boots on, and ran out.

Chapter 9

The image of Alderman Frank Messina standing practically naked in my mother's house blazed before me with such an intensity that I followed it all the way home. He continued to taunt me.

How long had he been having a relationship with my mother? Was he the only man she ever went out with? How could she do this to my father? What right did she have? The snow crunched under my boots while I held the manila folder. After another block, I folded it in half and scrunched it into my tote.

Maybe he was the killer. I had seen him in Alderman Robin Dryad's office several times. He was Italian and part of the Old Boys European network that once ruled Chicago. He usually wore alligator shoes. He wasn't very tall, maybe my height, about five-foot-seven. I was eyeball to eyeball with him when I had to shake his hand. Like shaking an old leather shoe. His face had a worn, reptilian look.

From what I could surmise, Alderman Dryad had sort of become Alderman Messina's mentor, taking him under his wing. Especially after Bernardo Morales became mayor. Fifty aldermen made up the city council. Under most administrations, they rarely made the news because they were programmed to vote along with the mayor and his Democratic machine. But Mayor Morales was different. He was emotional, an orator. Votes came to him without the machine, as if by magic, drawn by his charisma and magnetic powers with the public. After he was elected, the city didn't function the way it used to. It became unpredictable.

Alderman Messina was one of the aldermen who was against the mayor. That put him on my list of likely suspects. There were also those rumors about Messina's involvement in an underground cigarette movement—in which cigarette sales were just a fraction of their real cost. I would have to do more research on this. And it was no secret that Mayor Morales was against any untaxed cigarettes in this city. His raids on cigarette silos in Pilsen—where tax-free cigarettes were often stored– made the front-page of all the newspapers a few weeks ago.

My coat was still open and I was cold. I noticed a police car drive by. *Were they watching me? Well, screw them. I didn't do it. I'm living my life the way I want to. I'll show them who killed the mayor. In the next thirteen days. I'll show my mother and her new boyfriend too.* I tried to button my coat, but it was hard with one good hand. I continued walking.

Maybe I should dig deeper into this tax-free cigarette angle. The mayor's death was caused by nicotine. Was that a message by this underground tobacco movement? Give a lethal dose of nicotine to choke the mayor who was cramping their style?

I was just a block away from home when I saw another police car sitting directly across the street from where I lived. A policeman in the car was holding a cup of java while dunking a doughnut. I walked right up to his car and knocked on his window.

"See anything interesting around here?" I asked.

"No, ma'am. Just watching the scenery. Detective Joe Burke's orders." He answered with a mouthful of doughnut.

It wasn't even ten in the morning. I was already exhausted. I flopped onto my couch and listened to my phone ring. After it stopped ringing, I punched in my pass code to retrieve my voice mail. There were eight messages. One was from my mother from yesterday. No need to call her back. One was from my editor, who had another idea for my story. One was from my insurance agent about the car. Five were from Juan, including the last one. He was worried about me; he wanted to see me; could I please call him back. I'd let him leave a few more before I got back to him. That was the only empowering aspect I had in our relationship.

I called my insurance agent. She informed me that I was not entitled to a rental, which upset me. This was costing me more than I bargained for. My next call was to a rental agency at Midway Airport. I wanted a compact—any color but red.

My life was slowly getting back in order—considering my mother was having sex with a man who wasn't my father, I was the number one suspect in the mayor's murder, and my relationship with my boyfriend was about as steady as a spinning top. If I keep moving at top speed, everything's fine.

Except for the fact that I didn't feel like doing anything. I needed some mental hibernation. I put on Silvestre Revueltas. He was a Mexican composer who studied violin in gangster-era Chicago. He died of alcoholism in 1940. My favorite was "La Noche de los Mayas"—Night of the Mayas. It was music to wake the dead.

For the next three days I lived on pain killers, wine, and junk food.

On the first of those three days, I thought about my father.

I'm sure if I ever went into therapy, which I was thinking about a lot lately, I'd be told that I had a problem with men because I was afraid they would abandon me the way my father did. He was a violinist. He was twenty years older than my mother, and was always traveling giving concerts. During those rare moments when he was home, he would put me on his lap, whisper how much he loved me, how I was his favorite musical chord in the symphony of his life.

He hoped I would be a violinist someday. He fantasized how we would travel together performing concerts across the world. I started taking violin lessons when I was three-years-old. But when my father died, my passion for playing died with him. He died of a massive heart attack right on stage during a concert in Germany. Up to the very end, he was doing what he loved most. After that, my mother changed; she became harsher, stricter. She said she was left a sum of money from his insurance policy, and that got us through one year. Then she needed to get a job, and that's when she met Alderman Dryad.

On the second of those three days, I thought about Crystal Skull.

I wasn't sure what to make of the stories I had heard about it, but for some reason I needed to see that skull again. I went over my notes.

It was one of twenty-two planted throughout the earth at strategic points. If you diagrammed those points, the picture would form an eight-pointed star. Crystal Skull holds a holographic memory of the collective conscious and unconscious knowledge and experience of our planet. It has been infused with languages, symbols, and numerical systems, which have been revealed to people when they had become advanced enough to comprehend this information. Crystal Skull directly influenced our planet's progress.

Crystal Skull represented a particular cycle of growth on earth. Like the other skulls, this one was programmed for healing, attunement and energy. Crystal Skull participated in the growth of humanity by providing mental power-surges. Most interestingly, it had the power to place itself where it was most needed.

Why was it here in Chicago? What was its purpose in this city? And how was it linked to the mayor's death?

About every hour or so, I looked out my window. The police were taking shifts with me. I usually saw two cops sitting in a car. Once in a while, I saw only one. I still couldn't figure out how often they switched. I turned my thoughts back to the skull.

Crystal Skull had been used in religious rituals and placed in temples of worship. Millions had witnessed these magical skulls in their lifetimes, and they were familiar with their vibrations. In fact, they were drawn to a skull repeatedly over many lifetimes to feel its power and invigorating energy.

Jesus. What did I feel?

Crystal Skull had a certain magneticism to it. I remember when I first touched it. It was the day after Thanksgiving when I interviewed the wizard. When I first layed a hand on the cranium, a chill ran across my spine, and my mind spun with questions. Was it just my imagination or was I having problems breathing? I remember feeling claustrophobic.

Then I remembered my dream, the one I had that night after interviewing Christopher Warlick. In my dream, I looked at Crystal Skull. It expanded until it ballooned out to fill the entire room. It pushed me against a wall. It started to hum softly, then louder. It was not entirely unpleasant. The sound tranced me. I numbed. It squished me against the wall. I thought it was trying to give me a message, but I didn't know what it was saying.

On the third day, my editor called.

I was still in a grog and had to get back to life so that I could attend a funeral.

Chapter 10

That morning, four inches of white, powdery snow blanketed Chicago. A relentless cascade of snow clumps floated down from the sky, adding their gentle weight onto this city's shoulders, flake by flake.

"I really don't feel like going Alyce," I was telling my boss over the phone. "What difference will it make?"

"You're a writer, aren't you?" she challenged.

"Why can't I just watch it on the news?" I asked. "I'll take notes from the comfort of my couch."

"I want your story to live, breathe, and recreate the death of this Mexican mayor who believed in astrology and the magic of Crystal Skull," she said. "After reading your story, your readers will resurrect his spirit. They'll be inspired by his life and his convictions."

"Alyce, can I ask you something? What the *hell* is in your coffee?"

"Look, kid. You're not just doing this for the magazine or for me. You're doing this to make sense of your life and your role in the mayor's death. I know you like I know myself. You *need* to write. You need to write the way a wounded animal licks its own blood. Get out in the middle of this snowstorm, talk to the people, and bear witness to the mayor's vigil."

I had to admit. She knew how to inspire me. *Like an animal licks its blood?* Even if I could never live up to her expectations. But like I said, Alyce was my career mother. I couldn't let her down. In fact, I lived to please her.

"How many writers have you given that speech to?" I asked.

"Never mind about that, kid. You do what you need to do, and I expect a hell of a story from you. Don't let me down."

Off, she clicked.

Well, I was starting to feel more confident about confronting my world again. I decided to take a shower. I had to wash off three days of self-pity. The hot water streaming down my body felt good, and I spent a few extra minutes breathing deeply under the steady, pulsing flow of water onto my breasts, and down my back.

I blow dried my hair, found my favorite faded jeans and was relieved I could still zip them up. I took a big plastic garbage bag out from under my kitchen sink and went around my apartment picking up the litter: pizza boxes, newspapers, styrofoam containers, brown paper bags, empty potato chip bags, plastic forks, spoons, empty bottles of red wine. Actually, I filled up two garbage bags. Already, the place looked better. Then I went around the apartment picking up all my dirty clothes, towels and bed sheets and stuffed them into my laundry basket. I separated my whites from my coloreds, and took my white load down into the basement. Two cups of bleach and the load was washing. I liked the familiar bleachy smell.

I made a strong cup of coffee, then applied my make-up and quick-drying nail polish. Next, I organized my purse. It was black leather with a zipper, big enough to hold a newspaper and several folders of information. I checked my supply of pens, the batteries in my tape-recorder, my reporter's notebooks, and aspirin. The manila folder my mother gave me was still in there. I made a note to myself to read that soon.

My television was on. It reminded me how congested the traffic was. I looked out the window and saw a police car across the street. It looked like another cop from the one I saw the other day. I waved to him. He waved back. Maybe he could drive me to the mayor's vigil? At least he'd be doing something useful.

Never mind. My rental was already filled with a thick layer of snow. I might as well just take the Archer bus all the way in. I put on an extra pair of socks, found my ski mittens, a black, wrap-around wool scarf, applied petroleum jelly to my lips, put on my boots, another thin sweater for the layer effect, buttoned my coat, and pulled the hood up over my head. I was ready for a Chicago winter day.

At the bus stop, I waited twenty-three minutes. There were still a couple of empty seats on the bus. I took the one next to an old, white lady. She looked safe.

"You goin' to the funeral?" she asked, just seconds after I sat down.

"Yes." *It was really a vigil, but whatever.*

"History just seems to repeat itself, don't it?"

"I'm sorry?"

"Why, I was just about your age when I went to the funeral of Harold Washington, the first black mayor of this city who died just when he was gettin' really strong. Did you ever hear of him?"

"I think I was about ten years old when that happened." The comparisons were constantly being made on the news stations. Both were the first men of their minority races to run this city. Both men were charismatic and had become very popular. Both men had divided the city council. Both had become legends just after their death.

But there were differences. Mayor Morales was murdered, and I was the number one suspect. A police car was following my bus.

"It's just not meant to be," she said.

"What's not?"

"Change. We done had a dynasty run this city, and if anyone tries anything different, they die."

"You think someone killed Harold Washington?"

"Honey, those rumors are never gonna die. This is Chicago, ain't it?"

"This is Chicago," I said, not sure what I meant when I agreed with her. But for the rest of the trip we rode in silence. The bus made the turn onto State Street and rode north until Van Buren. That's where I got off and walked the rest of the way. I wasn't the only one. Thousands were here, so many more than I ever saw at a St. Patrick's Day parade.

Everything was going to start at 10:30 A.M., so I had about half an hour to get into position somewhere.

The line began forming at the LaSalle Street entrance of City Hall yesterday. There was going to be a vigil procession down State Street, beginning at Adams Avenue to Washington Avenue. Then it would turn west toward Clark Street and end in City Hall, where Mayor Morales was lying in state. Mourners would enter through the LaSalle Street entrance.

A procession was organized by the Mexican community to commemorate Mayor Morales. City Hall doors would open at 10:30, when the public viewing of the mayor would begin. The vigil would end at midnight in two days.

This was history in the making, and despite the weather, thousands of families with their small children were there to witness the final departure of their mayor.

People were organizing themselves along the route. Near City Hall, the crowd was six to eight people deep. I started interviewing people, asking them why they came, what Mayor Morales meant to them.

A Mexican-looking man walked by wearing a billboard that read "Mayor Morales wasn't just for anyone who was anyone. He was for everyone."

I came up to several men dressed in colorful Mexican costumes. I picked a smiling guy who looked easy to talk to.

"Excuse me sir, I'm with *Gypsy Magazine*. Would you mind telling me why you're here?" I had my tape recorder out.

"Aztec gods demand human sacrifices," he said.

I stuffed the tape recorder back in my purse. It never failed. I always hit the looney birds. I tried to walk away to find a quote I could actually use, but he grabbed my arm.

"Huitzilopochtli, whose name means Hummingbird Wizard, needs these sacrifices to triumph over the God of Darkness." He had a scary look in his eyes. Like he was in a panic.

"Was Mayor Morales a human sacrifice?" I asked.

"The Hummingbird Wizard speaks through Crystal Skull. He demanded a sacrifice."

"You think Crystal Skull told the murderer to kill the mayor as a sacrifice to your Aztec god?"

The man smiled and walked away. I didn't even have a chance to ask him his name or what neighborhood he lived in. Rather than chase him for the attributions, I dismissed what he said and looked for someone else to quote. Someone normal. I walked up to Alderman Enrique Diestro from Pilsen, the first original Hispanic community in Chicago.

"Excuse me, Alderman Diestro, I'm a reporter from *Gypsy Magazine* and I'm working on a story about Mayor Morales. Would you mind telling me what he meant to you?"

"Did you bring your camera?" he asked. I could tell he just loved himself.

"No sir, this is just a print interview," I said. I clicked my tape recorder a few times.

"Hey, you look familiar," he said, leaning closer to me. "Aren't you the one who was dancing with the mayor when he died?"

"Yes. Do you mind if we continue? The procession will begin soon."

"No, not at all," he said. "Latinos are the second largest minority group in Chicago, yet they are barely represented by Latino aldermen in the City Council. While they make up twenty-six percent of this city's population, they account for less than fifteen percent of the full-time city payroll. When Bernardo Morales became mayor of this great city, to the minorities, he brought balance. But to the Great White Majority, he upset the balance. Until Bernardo Morales took over, Latinos were isolated from the political mainstream. He united us, inspired us, and ignited us. What did he mean to me? He was a trailblazing Mexican who electrified the city with his soul. He defied the entrenched white political power. That's why he died."

I nodded and smiled. This wasn't the first time I heard this speech. I heard several versions of it from Juan. But it was representative of the Latinos. It was good for me to have a quote like that for my story. Alyce would love it.

The procession began. It was like a parade with solemnly marching musicians, aldermen, policemen, firemen. Sad music played. It seemed surreal to commemorate death. There was Alderman Robin Dryad.

"Who do you think killed the mayor?" I asked Alderman Diestro, knowing I couldn't print his answer. *Gypsy Magazine* could be sued for defamation of character, unless I had my facts completely straight. Which at this point, I didn't. For now, this question was part of my own internal investigation.

"Is this for the record?" he asked.

"No. Off the record. What's your opinion? Speculatively speaking."

I turned off my tape recorder.

"There's no doubt in my mind that Alderman Dryad was behind this," he said. "That's what most of us think. He has the most to gain. The election is his now. I don't know how to prove it, but I'm keeping an eye on him."

Then he excused himself and joined the procession. He got in step behind Alderman Dryad. I thought about Dryad and his likelihood of becoming mayor now. He certainly came from far behind.

His Romanian father settled on the South Side of Chicago. Robin was practically born into his job, the way he explained it. He used to accompany his father, a precinct captain, as he knocked on neighborhood doors to register voters. Sure, he'd tell them it didn't matter who they voted for. But everyone knew it mattered. Everyone was registered a Democrat. Everyone respected the Machine. Robin was a Machine guy.

I watched him in the procession. He had steely blue eyes

and a long, hookish nose. To me, he looked like a killer. He'd be just the type to plant Crystal Skull in my car. I had a feeling about this. He was always so diplomatic. You never knew what he was really thinking. In fact, I don't think he even knew.

He had been alderman of Garfield Ridge for twenty years. That was a long time. Nobody saw him leaving soon. Unless of course, he became mayor. That was the beauty of Chicago politics. Once you got in, you stayed in. The only way you left was in a coffin or in handcuffs.

I was in one of two single-file lines. I crossed the LaSalle Street doors and looked at the red carpet under my feet. It lay over the hall's gray marble floor. To my right hung a wall of bouquets, wreaths, and huge horseshoes of flowers. I was closer to Mayor Morales in his coffin.

I saw a table filled with burning candles, rosaries, crucifixes, and Madonna statues. I walked slowly, watching the people before me pay their respects. Occasionally, I looked up at the rotunda's ceiling. Camera crews hovered near the coffin. Reporters interviewed entertainers and politicians who had tears in their eyes. Juan was up there too. I debated whether I should talk to him.

Finally, I approached the coffin draped in the city flag and surrounded by blue bunting. I kneeled down in front of it, made a sign of the cross, and closed my eyes. I prayed to God I would find the person who killed the mayor, figure out who dumped Crystal Skull in my car, and get myself off the hook. I also prayed this city would heal. And, oh yeah. May Mayor Bernardo Morales rest in peace.

I stood up and stared at Juan. Maybe I should talk to him. He left me eight messages. I walked toward him. Then, suddenly, I was surrounded.

Cameras.

Microphones.

Lights.

"Alexandria Vilkas, you were dancing with the mayor on New Year's Eve when he died in your arms." I was looking at a man who I know I should have recognized from Channel

Seven. "Can you please describe your last moments with him?"

I couldn't describe the mole on his nose.

"Ms. Vilkas, isn't it true you were the last reporter to interview the mayor?"

I nodded.

"What did he tell you during his last interview?"

I was paralyzed.

Then a blond TV reporter approached. She asked, "And what about Crystal Skull? How did it show up in your car?"

I shrugged my shoulders.

Juan stepped in. He put his arm around my shoulders.

"Miss Vilkas has no comment," he said to the crowd.

I looked at him. I wanted to throw my arms around him. He grabbed my right hand and walked me to the elevator. He gave me a key and told me to get to the fifth floor and sit in his office. In a few minutes, he'd come up and sneak me out and take me home.

My hands shook. I never expected anything like this. I walked into his office through a side entrance to avoid walking past the twenty-four-hour policeman guarding his front door. Once I entered Juan's office, I sat down and hyperventilated.

About thirty minutes later, Juan picked me up. He took me to his car to drive me home.

Chapter 11

This cannot be. *This cannot be.* I kept saying that to myself, as I buckled myself in the passenger seat.

I had this fantasy that there was a man out there, who understood my every thought and mood. I wondered if Juan was the one. I know I hoped he was. And I know I hated the not-knowing that he wasn't.

It was snowing again. Juan stared intently at the road, fidgeting with lights and wipers. He turned on the radio, then switched the channel. I knew his routine. He could be very quiet. I didn't feel like talking.

What did Juan mean to me?

I was afraid that if I ever fell too deeply in love, I would have no need to continue doing anything else. That the relationship would paralyze me—like those blinding TV camera lights at the vigil—freezing me in time and causing me to lose my separateness.

But I was twenty-nine, that do-or-die age. Maybe I really should be married by the time I turned thirty. It wasn't just my mother who was telling me this. It was the rest of the world too. Even though they tried to be more subtle about it. Like inviting me to be a bridesmaid for the tenth time. Like having me drive behind a minivan stuffed with kids, foam surf boards, and beach towels. Like bringing me to the movies to watch a romance where the point was to have the unlikely pair overcome all obstacles to meld into each other.

I didn't normally explore this territory. I preferred to avoid it, walk around it, surround it in big, fat, yellow police tape emblazoned with the word "Caution." It must have been this story about Crystal Skull. I was touching old soul scars.

"I guess I should thank you for saving me from that mob back there," I said.

"They were like a pack of wolves around you," Juan said. "I was worried about something like that happening."

"I never saw it coming."

"I could have warned you about that, but you never returned my phone calls."

The snow fell hard now. The whiteness glittered through the street lights. Juan pulled back his shoulder-length black hair behind his right ear. I wasn't sure how I felt about the silver loop hanging from his lobe. I recognized this as a South Side prejudice. His nose was jagged from a gangers' brawl years ago, broken and rearranged. I liked how his straight black hair hung over his six-foot-three-inch frame and how his bronze skin made him look like an Aztec burning with wild purpose under his business suit.

I was hungry.

"I have no food in the house," I said. "Can we stop at the grocery store?"

Juan pulled into the Dominick's parking lot. A police car pulled in right next to us. This was getting annoying. Juan waited in the car while I did my grocery shopping. Lots of microwavable food, fruits, and salad stuff.

Finally, we were home. Juan carried in my six bags of groceries. He helped me unpack, found two wine glasses, uncorked the red wine and poured. I wasn't sure I felt like drinking it at the moment. But there it was.

"So," he said, handing me the glass. "Why didn't you call me back?"

We were in the living room. All of my furniture pieces were hand-me-downs from my mother or discoveries at garage sales. The style was eclectic. I also called it a music room. My father's violin was the focal point. It rested on a custom-made shelf on the wall. Underneath it, my stereo system stood with my collection of classical music.

I didn't feel like answering Juan's question yet. My eyes were glued to my father's violin. Juan followed my gaze.

"That's nice," he said. "Your father's?"

I nodded. "He died when I was ten."

"At least you knew him for ten years."

"What does that mean?"

Juan shrugged his shoulders.

"What's your father like?" I asked. "I've never heard you talk about him."

"I don't have one. He knocked up my mother, then disappeared."

I sipped my wine slowly. "Is your mother bitter?"

"She managed."

Juan downed his glass and poured himself another. "You never answered my question."

"About why I didn't call you?"

He nodded.

"I was going to, but I didn't think you could help." The wine tasted good. "I had to start figuring things out."

"Like what?"

"Like who killed the mayor."

"What have you come up with so far?"

"Well, I know it wasn't me—even though half the city seems to think so."

"Yeah, I saw that on the news," he said.

"I'm the number one suspect since Crystal Skull was found in my car."

"What happened after that?"

I told him of my voluntary interrogation at the police station, how I was being followed by the police all the time, and how my editor wanted me to write a story about the mayor and his fascination with astrology and crystal.

"I'm obsessed with solving this murder mystery," I said, looking intently at him. I took a long, slow sip of my wine. "You're about the only one I could cross off my list."

"I didn't know I was on it," he said. He refilled my glass.

"Everybody and their mother is on my list. And that includes *my* mother. God!"

"So how did I get so lucky?"

"I know you, Juan. You worshiped the mayor. Like he was your own father. You waited your whole life to work for somebody like him, a politically-connected Mexican. The death of Bernardo Morales is like the destruction of Mexico in Chicago. And besides, now you're out of a plum job. So, at this point, you're about the only one I could trust."

"Okay," he said. "I guess that's a relief. What's your plan?"

"I'm going to interview everyone I meet, ask them what they know about the mayor, and follow my hunches." I was circling the rim of my wine glass with my index finger. "Want to help me?"

"How can I help?" He stood up and poured himself another glass.

"You must have plenty of theories of who killed the mayor. You were one of his closest confidants."

"He kept a lot of secrets from me. I didn't know everything about him." He was taking his tie off and unbuttoning the first button of his shirt.

"Got any guesses?" I asked. I kicked off my shoes. Juan started rubbing my feet.

"Always," he said. "I'm just not sure what they amount to." He pressed down hard on my right calf and worked his way to the sole. "I was with him the night he broke up with Maria de la Cruz," he said.

"The astrologer he was having an affair with?" He went to my left leg.

"The one your mother's boss used to launch his election campaign."

"Hey, I was never a fan of politics," I said. I really didn't feel like talking about my mother now.

"That was the beginning of the end for Bernardo. That really crushed him."

"Did you know about the affair before then?"

He stopped rubbing my feet, then crossed over to the chair facing my couch. He planted his legs in front of himself. His knees were about a yard apart from each other. He leaned into the space, resting his elbows on top of his knees with his half-empty glass dangling in between.

"I've known Bernardo for many years," he said. "He was always having an affair with some woman or other. Sometimes more than one. But with Maria, he got caught. That's what killed him."

I couldn't tell if Juan admired Bernardo's ways with women. It bothered me that he might.

"What do you mean?" I asked.

"Maria got in the way of his power plays, so he had to get rid of her."

"What happened the night he broke up with her?"

"You know, it's funny you should ask. I've been thinking about that night a lot. It was the day after the story broke in the newspaper. The same night after Maria went on TV. I knew something strange would happen. He asked me to drive the limo."

"I remember Maria on TV," I said. I invited Juan to lunch at Berghoff's that day. We watched the interview together, standing at the lunch bar. That was actually the day our relationship officially began—six weeks ago.

"Yeah, right," he said. "Well, that night he asked me to drive him to the Stouffer Renaissance Hotel."

"The one on Wacker?"

He nodded.

"He asked me to wait for him in the hotel lobby. About an hour later, he returned. Maria followed him."

I raised my eyebrows.

"I know! Right in the lobby! She starts screaming, 'You bastard! Because you love me so much, you need to stop seeing me? Just like that? For ten years, we've been meeting, and I've been listening to your promises about you leaving your wife. It's all bullshit! You owe your career to me.'"

"What did she mean by that?"

"I guess all her astrological forecasts."

I crossed my legs under me, adjusted a pillow and leaned back. "So then what happened?"

"Then Bernardo turns back to her and says, 'Maria, please, let's not end it like this.' Then she says, 'How would you like me to end it? Like a librarian who checks the expiration date on a book you returned? Thank you sir, hope you enjoyed it!'"

"At least he had the decency to tell her it was over."

"Believe me. Sometimes, it's best to end it without saying anything."

I needed some potato chips. I walked into the kitchen, pulled out a bag of chips, poured them into a bowl, and walked back into the living room. I grabbed a handful.

"So then what happened?"

"Then Bernardo tried to calm her down, saying something like 'But you must understand why it needs to end. You must see the logic behind it.'"

"Twisted politician's logic. Dick before brain. But whatever." I grabbed another handful of chips as I listened to Juan continue his story.

"So she goes really crazy. 'Understand? Understand?' she says to him. 'I understand perfectly. You've gotten your fill of me. Now it's inconvenient and it's time to throw me away. I loved you, Bernardo! How could you do this to me?'"

"I always wondered about women who dated married men," I said. "What did she expect?"

Juan looked like he was trying to muster an answer.

I let him off the hook. "Never mind. So that was it?"

"She had a videotape of them together."

"She what? That was ballsy of her."

"For insurance," Juan said. "She was going to use it to blackmail him. If he wasn't going to get back together with her, she would show the media the videotape of them having sex together and ruin his career."

"When did she have time to do the videotape?"

"Apparently one of the times they were together, they video-taped themselves."

I let that sink in. Jesus. This town was nuts.

"You know," I said. "This guy deserved to die. Where did he get off being the mayor of Chicago and having himself video-taped while doing the nooky nooky with a woman who wasn't his wife?"

"He totally screwed himself over with that," Juan said, shaking his head. "But he wanted that tape back."

"I bet he did. Did he ever get it?"

"No, not as far as I know."

"So Maria must still have that tape."

I stood up to start dinner. But then Juan grabbed my right wrist. I knew what he wanted. I wasn't sure that I did.

Chapter 12

It's been a long time since a man paid so much attention to me. It was a like a flame was being lit inside my stomach that burned with an intensity that could consume me. I wondered what it was like being on a man's mind morning and night, what it was like to cause a man to lose sleep and his appetite. My connection with Juan was getting stronger. Maybe this was the night we would really click.

Juan stared at me. I became self-conscious and looked away. My cheeks burned.

He pulled me down alongside him on the couch. He laid his hands on my shoulders and pressed me back as he moved on top of me. He came to me like a swift, silent warrior. I let him lead, still bewildered over how I felt about him, about being with him. For six weeks, we just talked. But tonight was different. He kissed me on one cheek, then the other. His hair fell over my face. I pushed it back behind his ears. I ran my fingers through his hair and felt their long, silky threads stroking my arm.

I still wasn't sure I wanted to do this. I pushed myself back up to slow things down, to allow myself time to...to.....But he would have none of that. He kissed me firmly on the mouth holding my face in both his hands. I responded to his take-charge roughness.

I was twenty-nine-years-old. I needed to get married soon. I kissed him back. He liked that. He positioned himself on top of me, keeping his left leg on the floor for support. His right knee was in between my legs. I had to keep my left wrist out of the way. I tried to be careful about not having my cast interfere.

His right hand slid underneath my blouse, clasped my waist, then slid to my back to unsnap my bra. I arched my back to accommodate him. When my bra unsnapped, his hand came to my left breast, which filled his palm. He buried his head in my chest and I heaved, wondering if I would feel the wild thing. Juan had a dangerous, untamed look.

I ran my right hand through his hair. When Juan raised himself and looked downward, I knew he wanted me to unzip him. He stood up to allow me to pull his pants down, then his white bikini briefs. In the meantime, he had undressed me. By this point we were on the floor. He looked into my eyes as he found his way into me. I hoped to feel something, but I didn't. I don't think he noticed.

I watched his face scrunch up, his eyes open wide. He hit ecstasy. He threw his head back. He heaved and rolled off me. I rolled onto my stomach. He slapped my butt.

We both sat back up on the couch. He kissed me on the cheek. I was grateful for that.

"I'm hungry," he said. He rezippered himself.

I put my clothes back on too.

"I was just about to make some dinner," I said. I wasn't hungry anymore. But I knew he loved Tortilla King tacos. I microwaved them for him. He poured more red wine. We were at the kitchen table. We ate and we drank. We watched the news on TV. It was repetitive information about the mayor's death. We were quiet. Juan stood up with the bottle of wine and his glass and walked back to the living room. I washed the dishes with one hand. I felt empty. I felt like crying. But I had no one else to be with. Juan's okay. What else did I expect? Besides, he just lost his job. He needed me.

I went back into the living room. Juan was asleep on my couch.

Chapter 14

Since I couldn't sleep, I went into my office. I was saving newspaper clippings about the mayor's death. Now I felt like reading the official version about it. I took notes of all of the facts that were unquestionable.

This was my Objective Fact List.

He died at midnight on New Year's Eve at the Crystal Palace while dancing with me. When he and his wife entered the restaurant at 11:30 P.M., the room was filled with about a thousand people. He asked me to dance. Juan was with his wife. The mayor died in my arms.

Within seconds of his death, Crystal Skull vanished. The mayor had launched a campaign around the skull, igniting the city to follow its spirit. He called Crystal Skull the city's new inspiration. He had been meeting with the wizard, the skull's owner, to have the artifact displayed at the Field Museum.

The mayor's detractors were lead by Alderman Robin Dryad. They were threatened by Crystal Skull. They intended to save the city from its ruinous spell. They called the skull "the city's nest of vipers." They met with the wizard to have the artifact destroyed.

Crystal Skull became a touchstone to city council members. Those who liked it were in Mayor Morales' camp. Those who hated it were in Alderman Robin Dryad's.

On New Year's Day, the police found Crystal Skull in my car. I was recuperating from surgery. My fingerprints were on the skull, as were many others. Although I wasn't under arrest, the police marked me as a suspect until the case was solved.

After the mayor's autopsy, the coroner announced the mayor had died of nicotine poisoning. Nicotine can poison by inhalation, skin absorption, ingestion, or eye contact. The coroner found traces of nicotine, a pale-yellow liquid, on the mayor's skin, particularly on both of his palms and cheeks. The coroner ruled it was absorbed through the mayor's skin. Depending on the nicotine's dose, the mayor had died within five minutes to four hours of his skin absorbing the poison.

I read the coroner's interview and copied the key quote.

"Symptoms of nicotine poisoning include initial burning of the mouth, nausea, confusion, twitching, disturbances in hearing and vision, headache, dizziness, breathing difficulty, rapid heartbeat, and incoherence," said Tom Hall, chief medical examiner. "Death usually results from respiratory failure due to paralysis of the muscles. Nicotine is usually used as a pesticide and is readily available. It's a pale-yellow to dark-brown liquid with a slightly fishy odor. It poisons by inhalation, skin absorption, ingestion, or eye contact."

I thought back to when I was dancing with the mayor. I remembered how much difficulty he had breathing, how confused he seemed. He seemed drunk, even lewd. In reality, he was probably dizzy from poison. I remembered his twitches too.

The mayor recently propelled a campaign against the illegal cigarettes that infiltrated the city's bars and street corners. His investigation uncovered cigarette silos in Pilsen, where the Nicotine Ring stored tax-free cigarettes.

This concluded my Objective Fact List. Now I needed to find a motive. Soon I had three to choose from.

Here was my Subjective Fact List.

The Nicotine Ring may have sent a message via the mayor's dead, nicotine-laced body. The message was to stop meddling in their tobacco enterprise. Maybe the Nicotine Ring had individuals in an official capacity like politicians or even police officers.

Half the city council repeatedly stood against the mayor's initiatives. The most vociferous alderman was Robin Dryad who announced his candidacy for mayor in the upcoming primary, now just six weeks away. When he first made his announcement just after Thanksgiving, he had an uphill battle. Most people liked the mayor. Even after the disclosure about him having an astrologist. It made him look human, everyone said. That meant Mayor Morales was not going to go away soon. If he would have won the next election the city could have been under his rule for four more years, perhaps completely erasing the European Sodabread Guard. There were many boys who were tired of heartburns caused by the Mexican Taco Guard. Perhaps one of them would have killed the Mexican mayor to clear the path back to power.

Finally, the mayor's personal life was a mess. He may have publicly stayed on the straight and narrow, but privately his path cut a wide swath. How many women had he dated during his marriage? Did any of them have his children? Clearly, Maria de la Cruz was very upset when he ended that relationship. Did his wife ever suspect? Maybe she would have killed her own husband from the humiliation that she had to bear from his public philandering.

I was getting tired. Juan was still snoring on my couch. I left him there. Even though I gathered a lot of information that day, I still didn't feel any closer to solving the mayor's murder.

Chapter 14

It was a rough night. I tossed and turned, unable to find my way to a good night's rest. Juan's smell was still on me. What was the name of his favorite cologne again? Imprimatur. It seemed to be everywhere.

By seven o'clock, I was relieved I could get out of bed and hoped the day would engross me to distraction from my worries. I looked for Juan, but he was gone. Good.

I went over my notes again. I called my editor to check in.

"How are ya' kid?" she asked. Her cheeriness was like a splash of cold water.

"I've been better, Alyce."

"I saw you on the news again, kid. You're becoming a regular celebrity."

"That's not exactly what I had in mind for myself."

"So, where are you on the story?"

Conversations with Alyce never strayed far from whatever story I was working on. She was one of those single-minded editors who worked around the clock, having no other life.

"I'm still collecting information."

I told her I had the motive narrowed down to three theories:

It was either a politician who didn't want Morales to win the next election. Or someone in organized crime to stop him from raiding cigarette silos. Or it was personal revenge, like a mistress jealous with rage.

"Not bad, kid," she said. "And where does Crystal Skull fit in?"

"I don't know yet. But I was thinking of visiting Christopher Warlick. I thought he might have a theory or two."

"Okay, kid. Stay out in the field today. Go visit the wizard. Organize your notes. And tomorrow, I want you in here for a full debriefing. We'll go over everything you've got, and come up with a working outline for your story."

She was getting worried about my making the deadline. She was low on copy too, which made her even more edgy.

"Don't worry Alyce. I have a ton of notes. I'm sure I can pull it together." I just wasn't sure I could do it by the deadline. But it wouldn't have been the first time. I did what I always did: Told myself that somehow, someway, it would all work out just fine.

When I hung up, I took a shower and looked at myself in the mirror. I needed a workout. I hadn't stepped foot in a gym in over two weeks. I skipped breakfast.

I found my workout bag and stuffed in my black leotards, socks, water bottle, and gym shoes. I tossed in shampoo, a towel, and moisturizer. I didn't forget clean jeans.

My new rental car had been sitting in front of my apartment for two days. It had all of the latest equipment, including an auto PC that could give me directions where to go. The woman from the agency told me the PC would warn me when the car needed gas or oil or a tune-up, and that it would heat and cool the interior according to my preference. What a neat little car computer.

Unfortunately, it couldn't shovel the six inches of snow that it was buried under. I went into the garage and found a broom. It took me twenty minutes to shovel off all the snow with one hand. The car didn't have an ice scraper. I dug out a credit card and scraped the ice off my windows.

Finally, I hopped in. I turned on the heat, tried the radio and wipers. I said hello to my PC. It answered me, "Good morning." This was too weird.

A police car followed me on my way to the gym. I swear it was inches behind me. I felt like slamming on my brakes, so it would crash into me. But I didn't. I just took a deep breath.

I made it to the gym minutes before the next aerobic class. Once on the floor, the loud music vibrated my body with energy. I stood close to a speaker to feel the effects of the music wash over me. It pushed out my panic. I mimicked the instructor's movements, exercising past the dull ache in my body until I felt it no more, past the heavy tiredness I carried from the past weeks until my heart pounded with renewed vigor.

By the time I cooled down, stretching my body to the beat of slower, gentler music, my mind wandered. I thought of the wizard and his skull. In retrospect, he had said a lot of things that didn't make much sense.

"In the past, civilizations misused Crystal Skull," the wizard said to me on one of my prior visits. "It was the catalyst of chaos and destruction. When man became too strongly attached to material attractions and failed to heed nature's warnings, society disappeared through volcanic upheavals, tidal waves, and earthquakes."

"Did the skull cause the natural disasters?" I remember asking.

"No, but it helped channel them," he said.

"Through what power did the skull operate?"

"The skull drew its power from the Creative Force, from the strength of The Mind," Warlick said. "Crystal is derived from the Greek word crystallos, or 'clear ice.' Crystal endures forever as it neither ages, oxidizes, or decays. Crystal mirrors the wholeness of creation, expressed as an orderly structure of atomic particles in distinct patterns."

My cool down ended and my mind snapped back to the gym. I walked into the steam room and sat on a bench. I wanted to know more about the properties of crystal and the skull's significance. I made a mental note to myself to follow up with more questions. I changed back to my street clothes and drove to the South Side Psychic's Studio. One of Chicago's Finest was right behind me. I waved to him on my way in.

When I walked through the door, a tinkly bell rang. I smelled cat again.

"Alexandria, Alexandria, how good of you to come," Warlick said, coming into the room with a bag of sour cream and onion potato chips. He shook my hand, leaving some chip grease. I wanted to wipe my hand somewhere. In walked a white, fluffy angora. I crouched down to pet it, stroking its back several times while it arched up and slowly swayed its tail.

"I was wondering where your cat was," I said.

"She normally does not come out for visitors," he said, dipping his hand into his bag and pulling out a chip. "I am amazed she made an appearance for you. My wife is allergic to cats. She is begging me to give this one away. She is a very good, quiet cat. Do you want it?"

I stood up. The cat nuzzled itself against my legs.

"Oh, I don't think I could," I said. "You know, I'm so busy with my job and all, I couldn't spend any time with her."

"Do not worry about that. She is very independent. Like you. I am sure you two would get along." He really wanted me to have this cat, I could tell, and was pushing it on me like a long-distance phone rep. How could I tell him I wasn't crazy about owning a cat? The smell, the cans of cat food, the litter box. I shuddered.

"You know, I'm not sure my landlord would let me have any pets." The cat scrammed into the back room.

Christopher sat down on his zebra-patterned couch and patted a spot next to himself.

"Please take a seat," he said. He laid his open bag of chips on the table in front of him. "I was wondering when I would see you next."

"Oh, Mr. Warlick, my life is a mess," I said. "I feel like I'm on the verge of a nervous breakdown. And it's all because of Crystal Skull. I must talk to you."

"I am so sorry, Alexandria. Of course, I will help you. My

skull. Yes. Quite a skull. I do not know what to do about it."
He looked confused.

"Did you hear about how they found Crystal Skull in my car?"

"Yes. Yes. The police called me."

"I didn't take it," I said. "You've got to believe me. I would have never done that."

"Yes, Alexandria, I believe you." He stroked my back. He sighed deeply and looked at his empty window display. "The police will give me my skull back soon."

"Why, that's wonderful!" I said. But I was bewildered by his expression. "What's the matter?"

"I do not know what to do about that skull. It is causing many problems. I have much to think about." Then he looked back at me. "But tell me, Alexandria, how can I help you?"

"Actually, I wanted to ask you some questions." I dug through my bag and pulled out my tape recorder. With my broken wrist, I didn't feel like taking notes. "Do you mind?" I said, waving my tape recorder. "I need to finish my article."

"No, not at all. Do you want a potato chip?"

"No, no thanks. First, I want to go over the special properties of crystal."

That was my interview technique. Start slow and simple, then build up to tough questions.

"Crystal is the perfect jewel, a symbol of purity, the length of space that never ends," he said. He stood up, grabbed a round crystal sphere and showed it to me. I looked into it.

"The Age of Aquarius is known as the Crystal Age," he continued. "Crystal is the mineral symbol of Aquarius. This is a grand age. The age of advanced communications. Quartz can store, release and regulate energy. It has been the revolution of electricity. The chemical name for quartz is silica, or silicon dioxide. That is the main part of all computer chips."

"So you think Crystal Skull is like a computer of our civilization?" I asked.

"Alexandria!" he said. "That is very good! I like that!" He put the crystal ball back into its stand and picked up his bag of chips. He crunched for a long while. Maybe he was hormonal and needed his fix of salts.

"Crystals are known for keeping records," he said. "In spiritual matters, crystal helps guide our search for the meaning and importance of being here. Chemically, crystal is made of silicon and oxide, the same elements that humans are made of. Each cell of our body is a universe of atomic forces, an exact duplication of the original forces that began with creation. We began inside the Creative Force. But through our wills, we explored the path of our silicon and oxide vibrations. We came to the point farthest away from God—the material world. To return to our spiritual origins, we must follow crystal vibrations back along the same path."

"We must follow the crystal vibrations back?" I asked. I said it but I didn't understand it.

"Yes," he said.

"You think Crystal Skull can show us our way back?"

"Yes, but it is not easy."

"How are we supposed to find our way back?"

"We are here to learn lessons. Earth is a classroom. Everything is as it should be. Events unfold to teach us something, to lead us back to the path. Often it is a path we want to avoid, because it has a razor-thin edge, and it is the path of most-resistance. The razor edge bites, but eventually events always lead us back on that path."

Okay. Uh-huh. I checked my tape recorder.

"Friends leave unexplainably, perhaps, and this hurts," he continued. "We learn the friendship evolved to its end for a purpose. Then we think and wonder about the mystery. We are supposed to do that. The immortal answer is to find our way back home—back to the bosom of Beginning, back to where we were born, back to the place we left."

He must have noticed the puzzled expression on my face.

"This makes no sense to you, right?"

"Right."

"Events seem out of logic, right?"

"Uh-huh."

"You notice such an event. It frustrates you because you have no power over it, right?"

"Something like that."

"The event is not yours to manipulate. Yet you are forced to watch and wonder why it is happening. What does that mean?"

"I have no idea."

"The answer is instructional. Remember, everyone is where they need to be in the evolution of their soul. They are where they are as a result of all of their previous actions."

"Really?"

"For example, you may be in a position that is over-whelming—like being a murder suspect."

"I'm with you so far."

"You think you suffer as a result, and this may be true. You may wind up convicted of a murder you never committed."

"You're not making me feel any better, here."

"But you are continuing your evolution. You learn you are on your own. People come into your life who you will want to worship, who you will want to believe have all the answers. These people come with many faces. Usually they are friends, relatives, bosses, a lover. Perhaps a psychic."

What was he trying to tell me?

"You will give these people great power over yourself. You will allow their every action, their every word to rule your life. If they take a wrong step, you will not see the misstep, for you will be blinded into believing they can do no wrong, that they know more than you. Eventually, however, you will be disap-pointed and disillusioned."

"Are you trying to cheer me up? Because really. My mother tries to cheer me up this way too."

"Yes, Alexandria. This is where you learn to trust yourself, your instincts, and your gut."

He pointed his index finger into my gut.

"You hold the only lantern to help you find your way back to your path. Work on polishing your lantern. Work on build-ing reserves to keep that lantern burning. Work on your ability to hold your lantern high so that you can find it when events turn dark around you."

"What lantern was I supposed to polish? What reserves was I supposed to build?" I burst into tears and felt the cat rubbing itself against my legs. I was scared of what lay ahead. "Oh, Mr. Warlick! I don't know what to do! I don't know how to get out of this mess! How am I supposed to solve this murder?"

"Think. Why are you here?"

"I'm here because of Crystal Skull. Is that the lantern I'm supposed to polish? The one that will guide me on my path to solving this murder?"

"Perhaps it is," he said. He walked into the adjoining room. He returned with a new jumbo-size bag of sour cream and onion potato chips.

"The day before the mayor died, he came here to talk to me," he said.

"He came here? The mayor? On the South Side? To your studio?"

"Yes."

Chapter 15

The red light on my tape recorder flashed. *Damn!* Low battery. I had a spare, but why did this have to happen in the middle of an interview? The wizard crunched on his chips as he watched me change my batteries.

"So you say the mayor was here the day before he died?" I asked, once my tape recorder was in order.

"Yes, Alexandria, yes." He crunched some more. He was fast working his way through that bag.

I decided to wait him out, watching him eat his chips, listening to him crunch while he was deep in thought. I used the time to calm down from my battery episode. This was the only aspect of my life where I had developed a keen sense of patience. I was trained to let sources fill the silence. I knew how to keep quiet. Among reporters, it was almost like the blinking game. Whoever talked first lost. Finally the wizard spoke.

"Someone else came here too," he said.

I waited.

"It was Maria de la Cruz."

"What! The mayor and his mistress were here, both on the same night?"

"Calm down, Alexandria. Calm down. I will tell you every-thing."

"Do you mind if I have some chips?" I asked. We soon had a routine, taking turns dipping our hands into the bag for handfuls.

"It was the day before New Year's Eve," said Warlick. "I had just received a call from Edgar Sheldon, inviting me to his party. He told me he heard about Crystal Skull, and he wanted to show it at his restaurant. He said he thought it would really add a special touch. I told him I could not part with Crystal Skull, that it was like a child to me."

Our hands bumped into each other as we both reached for more chips. I let him go first.

"But then he offered me $50,000."

"He what?" Crunch. Crunch.

"He said money did not matter to him, that he had a hobby collecting unusual artifacts."

"Really?" I never knew that about him. You'd think I'd know something about my publisher. I needed more chips. I picked up a handful. One had a hole rimmed in green. I wanted to throw it out. I thought of putting it back, but instead, I ate it.

"I told him Crystal Skull was not for sale," he said.

I nodded, waiting.

"He told me he didn't want to buy it from me. He wanted to rent it. He said I could visit Crystal Skull whenever I wanted."

"How long were you going to let him rent it?"

"He asked for six months."

"So what did you say?"

"The temptation was too great for me, and I agreed to take the money. It was a very bad decision." He shook his head and dipped in for another chip.

"It's not your fault," I said. I needed to wipe my hands. No napkins. "Anybody would have done that for all that money." *I certainly wouldn't have had any problems.*

"When Mr. Sheldon came to get Crystal Skull, he wrote a check for $25,000 and said he would give me the other half in six months. I still have not cashed that check. I just knew it would be too dangerous to let Crystal Skull go. And now look what happened." He spread his arms out and then let them drop. "The mayor of Chicago has died."

"You think Crystal Skull had something to do with the mayor's death?"

"You do not know how powerful Crystal Skull is." He was pointing his index finger at me, shaking it.

I shook my head.

"I have lived with Crystal Skull all my life. It is like an extension of me. It feels what I feel and sends it back. When you focus on Crystal Skull, your emotions amplify." He waved his hand in a circle to help explain.

That was true. Whenever I looked at Crystal Skull, I began to feel something. But my problem was I didn't want to investigate those feelings.

"Just touching or viewing a powerful, positively charged crystal can set off a chain reaction in your subconscious that can affect you very deeply," the wizard continued. "Crystal Skull can influence you to do things."

"What kind of things?" I asked. My hands were still greasy. I couldn't find a napkin, so I took another handful.

"Things that were deep in the back of your mind, but that you never bothered to bring forward because it was too much trouble," he said.

"Like what?"

"Anything. Your childhood, your parents, your relationships, your job, your future..." He trailed off and seemed to look a little misty-eyed.

"What if you have evil things lurking in your mind?" I asked.

"That is just my point. Murder. If you feel like killing someone, you may go through with your plan."

I still had a hard time believing all this. That skull was just a big hunk of glass, as far as I was concerned. I studied a chip. It had ridges. It was one of those big, long ones, the size of a giraffe's tongue.

"So are you going to cash that check now?" I asked.

"I have sent that check back to Mr. Sheldon after Crystal Skull disappeared. I told him if Crystal Skull were ever found, I wanted it back, that it was no longer for rent." He looked at his display window.

"So tell me about the mayor's visit."

"Yes, of course. Shortly after Edgar Sheldon called, the mayor rang and asked if he could come visit Crystal Skull. I said yes. The mayor was here in a few hours."

"He was alone?"

"He drove up with someone in his big black limousine. He had two police officers with him."

"So what did he want?" I asked.

"The mayor was very polite. He sat down and we talked about many things, which are confidential. He was here almost two hours. I can tell you he was a very spiritual, believing man."

I knew Mayor Bernardo Morales could be charming. My interview with him about his beliefs in astrology left me no doubt he really believed in the stuff. I nodded for the wizard to continue.

"He told me he heard this skull was very old and special, that it would be a good idea to have it at the Field Museum to be shared with the rest of the city."

"He wanted it displayed at the Field Museum?"

"Yes, but then I had to tell Bernardo that I just agreed to rent it to Edgar Sheldon for six months to be shown at his restaurant for fifty thousand dollars."

"And?"

"The mayor was shocked. Then he was silent for a few moments. He said he would pay me for the skull as well, that the museum was prepared to purchase the skull."

"What's the asking price?"

"Twenty million dollars."

"Twenty million dollars! Jesus! Why does everyone want your skull all of a sudden?" I still didn't get it. The bag had only crumbs at this point.

"Oh, Alexandria. It is very special. You do not know."

"Why wasn't someone from the museum making you an offer then?" I asked. Now I was really done. I wanted a napkin. I purposefully rubbed my hands, hoping I could pass the hint. Maybe the cat would walk by again.

"He told me he knew someone at the museum very well, and that they would do what he asked them. I told him I would think about it."

The wizard didn't notice my silent plea for a napkin.

"What did he say?" I asked.

"He asked me if he could take Crystal Skull to the Field Museum for one day to have it looked at by an expert. He told me the expert would write a full report, which could be used as proof to authenticate it. I wanted that, some legitimate proof from a real expert about what Crystal Skull really means."

"Did you ever get that report?"

"Not yet. But I have the name of the man at the Field Museum who took the skull."

He stood up and rummaged through some papers on the counter displaying his other crystal pieces. He came back and handed me the note. I resisted the impulse to wipe my hands on it. It had the name Jerome Gelding written on it. I knew I would have to talk to him next.

"So what about Maria de la Cruz?" I asked.

"Yes, yes, just as the mayor was leaving with the skull, Maria de la Cruz came."

"That sure was some night!" I said. "Did they see each other?"

"They were very surprised to see each other. They barely talked to each other, however. The mayor kissed her on the cheek. She asked him to stay, but he said he had to go."

Sure, why would he stay just because his old girlfriend asked him to?

"Why did she come here?" I asked.

The wizard suddenly looked very pale. I was wearing him out. Plus those bags of carbs must have made him sleepy.

"Did you want to continue with this another time?" *Please say no. Please say no.*

"Yes, Alexandria. I think that would be a good idea. I am very tired all of a sudden."

God forbid, a source should ever complete his entire story for me all in one shot.

"Of course, Mr. Warlick. I totally understand. I'll call you tomorrow, maybe?"

"Yes, that would be a good idea."

Chapter 16

I walked to my car, found my gym bag, and wiped my hands on a towel. I stared at the note the wizard just gave me with Jerome Gelding's name. I decided to call him from my cell phone. First I called information for the museum's number. Then I got through their operator who only wanted to give me the museum's hours. I explained I needed to talk to Mr. Jerome Gelding, who was part of the museum staff. No, I didn't know his title or what department he worked in. She gave me another number. I hung up and tried that number. I was transferred to the wrong office. When I tried to explain what I wanted, I got cut off. I tried again. This time I got through. After two rings, I was prepared to leave a message.

"Jerome Gelding speaking."

"Mr. Gelding?"

"Yes."

"My name is Alexandria Vilkas, and I'm a writer for *Gypsy Magazine*. I'm working on an article on Crystal Skull, and I understand that you wrote a report about it at the request of the former mayor?"

I waited for his confirmation.

"Yes."

"Do you mind if I come over and talk to you about the skull?"

"I'll be free in about two weeks," he said. "I'm very busy right now. I'm under a lot of pressure to finish a project."

Hey, bud! I'm under a lot of pressure to write my goddamn story! But I knew that wasn't going to work with him. He wouldn't give a hoot about my deadline. Instead, I tried begging.

"Look, Mr.Gelding, I can totally understand how you're so busy. But at this point, I'm at my wits end. The Chicago Police Force has me fingered as their number one suspect in the mayor's death."

"That's you?"

"Yes, that's me, unfortunately. So I'm not just writing an article. I'm trying to solve the mayor's murder. And I believe your knowledge about Crystal Skull will help me prove my innocence. Is there anyway you can fit me in for about twenty minutes?"

"I guess I could spare that long," he said.

"Oh thank you, Mr. Gelding. You don't know how much this means to me. I'm so grateful. Really."

"Can you come right away?" he asked.

"I could be there in less than half an hour."

"Perfect. I'll be expecting you. In fact, I'll meet you at the front of the museum. I know what you look like."

I was on the Stevenson Expressway, heading north toward Lake Shore Drive. I drove under the McCormick Place Bridge and past Soldier Field. The second turn-off to the right on the Drive was the Museum Campus. I pulled into McFetridge Drive, otherwise known as 14th Street. After I paid the parking lot attendant, I found a spot that faced the lake, now a thick sheet of ice that stretched into the hazy horizon. Thigh-high piles of snow were mounded along the parking lot's perimeter, which I thought I'd have to climb over to reach the sidewalk, but I finally found an opening I could walk through.

Walking up the steps to the Field Museum of Natural History, I tried to remember the last time I was here. It must have been in third grade.

A tall, gaunt man met me halfway up the staircase. Jerome

Gelding was bald on top. At the bottom of his neck hung a three-foot, dirty-blond braid. His forehead had a deep furrow about an inch above his eyebrows. It rounded back at such an angle, I thought his head resembled an egg. He had close-set eyes, thin lips, and was noticeably nervous. He wore tattered jeans. He was probably more comfortable peering through a microscope.

I extended my right hand. "Mr. Gelding, I presume."

His handshake felt as lifeless as a dead fish.

"Follow me," he said. "We don't have much time."

He turned around and climbed the stairs, two at a time. I could barely keep up with him.

"Where are we going?" I shouted when he was about three yards ahead of me.

"My office," he said, turning his head back. "Hurry up!"

Once inside, I saw from a distance the seventy-five-foot long Brachiosaurus. From my third-grade field trip, I remembered that it was forty feet high. Gelding didn't slow down, and I fell further behind.

"Hey, is that Sue?"

He nodded. She was in the main hall, as well.

"Who's bigger, Sue or the other one?"

"Sue is the most complete and best preserved Tyrannosaurus rex fossil yet discovered," he answered. "The Brachiosaurus is eighty-five tons and is still the largest dinosaur on display in the United States."

"Oh."

He flashed his I.D. card as we walked past the cashiers toward the south-end staircase.

"Follow me," he said, as he bounded up two flights of stairs.

I was breathing heavily by the time we reached the third floor. I watched him open a door with a key. It was lunchtime, and the place looked abandoned. We were walking down a long hallway with old-fashioned wooden doors.

"So many windows!" I said.

"It was all built before electricity," Jerome explained, as we walked past several rooms filled with museum pieces.

"What's all this stuff up here?"

"The museum contains more than twenty million objects, yet only one-fifth of one percent of the Field Museum's collections are on display at any given time." He wasn't nervous anymore. "Up here, we catalogue and analyze everything."

"Fascinating," I said, walking past a room filled with Native American art.

"Is this where you analyzed Crystal Skull?"

"In that lab over there," he said, pointing to a door down the hall.

"Can I see?" I asked.

"No!" He looked around nervously. "Just come to my office." We walked past another door, until we came to one with his name on a piece of paper taped to it. He walked in ahead of me, and asked me to shut the door. Once inside, I didn't know where to turn. The office had stacks and stacks of papers everywhere—on the floor, on the desk, on the guest chairs, on the shelves, on top of the computer, on the file cabinet.

"Take a seat," he said, pointing to a chair with two stacks of paper.

"Where should I put these?" I asked, pointing to the stacks.

"Just pile them on those on the floor."

I did as he suggested and sat down. The space between my toes and his desk was filled with more stacks.

"Why are you in such a hurry?" I asked.

"I've got a big project to finish."

I waited, hoping he would continue. Instead, he took off his coat and tossed it over the back of his chair. I followed his lead, careful not to let my coat brush any nearby stacks. He rummaged through them, looking for something. He looked at the tops of the stacks on his desk, in front of his desk, on the floor next to him.

"Aha!" He picked up a report on the stack on top of his computer. "This is it." He handed it to me.

It said "Crystal Skull....An Analysis by Jerome Gelding." I leafed through it and saw several diagrams with numbers written all over them.

"Is this for me to keep?"

"God, no! I just wanted to show you that I did it."

"What are you going to do with it?"

"I don't know. I haven't figured that out yet." He grabbed the report out of my hands. "The mayor asked me to do this, you know."

"Yes, Mr. Gelding, I heard. The wizard told me. Does anyone else know about this report?"

"Just my boss. We both decided to hold onto it for a while, in light of the recent events."

He held the report close to his chest, crossing his arms over it. He rocked back and forth in his chair, cradling it.

"Mr. Gelding? Is everything alright?"

"Is everything alright? Is everything alright? No, everything is not alright. I haven't slept since I looked at that damn skull. And now the mayor's dead. Who knows what else will happen." He slapped the report, like a child having a tantrum.

"Do you think the skull had anything to do with the mayor's death?"

"Yes, I'm sure of it."

"How can you be so sure?"

"It's a good thing the skull is with the police now. That's all I can say."

I decided not to let him know the wizard was about to get his skull back.

"Why do you say that?"

He opened his report and showed me a diagram. It looked like a blueprint of the skull with diagonal lines crossed over it.

"You see that? You see that?" He was pointing to the diagram. "That's why."

"I don't understand, Mr. Gelding. You'll have to explain."

He held his head in his hands, dragged them over his face, pulling his cheeks down until his lower lids drooped, revealing their inner red flesh. He swung his head back and grabbed the back of his head.

"It's too much, it's just too much," he said.

"I'm sure you're very overwhelmed Mr.Gelding. But please

try." I pulled out my tape recorder and put it plainly in his sight.

"Describe to me how you analyzed this skull, Mr. Gelding."

"He's got a name, you know," he said.

"A name?"

"Yes, his name is Mr. Skull. Sometimes, I just call him Skull, but usually I'm more formal." He giggled and looked around.

"Mr. Skull," I said. "Okay, how did you analyze Mr. Skull?"

"I used photographic equipment with polarized, infrared, and ultraviolet sources. I also used an X-ray machine and a microscope. Mr. Skull is very, very unusual. He has incredible optics of a very sophisticated nature. Halfway back in the roof of his mouth, he has a broad, flat plane, similar to a forty-five-degree prism. This surface refracts light from beneath the skull into his eye sockets."

"Why is that significant?"

"Well, for example, if Mr. Skull were placed on a stone altar with a fire underneath, the flickering flames could be reproduced visually as being alive in his eye sockets."

I tried to picture the skull with the flames in its eyes.

"The back of his skull is formed as a beautiful camera lens," he continued. "It can gather light from anywhere in the rear and direct it into the eye sockets. The zygomatic arches are carved in relief, beside the cheekbones, just like in a human skull."

He began to look around him nervously. "Did you hear that?"

"No, I didn't hear anything." We both waited another moment.

"Before we go any further, can you tell me what your title is?" I asked.

He started to laugh.

"What's so funny?"

"I used to be the chief curator around here."

"Until when?"

"Until last week." He was laughing again. He stopped abruptly and looked around. "Did you hear that? That was really clear."

"No, I didn't hear anything."

He banged on the report with his fist three times. He kept looking around.

"Yes! Yes! I heard it," I pretended. "I clearly heard it."

He relaxed and smiled.

"What happened last week?"

"They asked me to move into this office, away from everyone." He kept looking around. "Nobody wants to hear my story."

He took my tape recorder and screamed into it, "Nobody wants to hear my story!"

I practically jumped from my seat. I was having second thoughts about this interview. Nobody knew I was here.

He gently laid the tape recorder back down. "They told me to delete everything from my computer, but I tricked them. I printed everything out first, and then I deleted the documents." He pointed to the stacks on the floor.

"Why did they want you to delete your records?"

He lifted the report about the skull. "Because of Mr. Skull."

I took a deep breath, and wondered if I should continue. I think it was more out of a sense of politeness that I stayed riveted. *Think. Think. Another question.* I couldn't think of one.

"You're probably wondering why they just didn't fire me, aren't you?"

"Now that you mention it."

He leaned over, and said in a stage whisper. "Keep your enemies close to you. That's why." He sat back down. He flipped the report to another page.

"I remember my first night with Mr. Skull. I thought it was just another job. Like any other job. We were together all night, from seven o'clock on. All alone. I submerged him in a bath of index-matching benzyl alcohol to view him under a polarized light. That's when I noticed he was cut without regard to the axis and he was made from a single piece of crystal. His jawbone was from the same piece of crystal. The exquisite workmanship and high gloss of the finish makes him look brand new. But, it's obvious there's no one in this world today who could possibly produce a crystal skull of comparable quality. No way. Mr. Skull is very, very, very old. When I had him under the microscope, I studied his surface scratches and grinding marks. Mr. Skull has gone through at least three major changes—probably by three distinct and separate civilizations."

"You miss him, don't you?"

"I haven't been able to sleep since he left." He laughed. "It's like I'm obsessed with him. I can't stop thinking about him. I don't even try anymore. He's just there in my mind."

"You would do anything to get him back, wouldn't you?"

"Anything."

"Murder?"

He sat still.

"Were you at the Crystal Palace on New Year's Eve?"

He nodded.

"Would you kill the mayor to distract the crowds so you could steal the skull?"

The door flew open.

"Jerome! What are you doing?" A man with a name tag I couldn't read walked in. "Who are you?" he asked me.

"I'm Alexandria Vilkas, a reporter for *Gypsy Magazine*. I'm doing an article on Crystal Skull."

"And you've been interviewing Jerome Gelding?"

"Yes."

"Did you know he's just the museum's messenger boy?"

He could have slapped me in the face, and I probably would have felt less of a shock.

"Wasn't he the chief curator until last week?"

Now *this* man was laughing. "Don't feel bad. He fooled a TV reporter too, except that was on live television, and last I heard, that reporter lost his job."

My face reddened. "And that report?"

"Oh, that report's authentic. It just wasn't authored by Jerome Gelding. It was written by a team of experts."

"Can I interview one of those experts?" I asked, hoping I could salvage some of my time here.

"Maybe in a few weeks."

"Can I have a copy of the report?"

"You'll have to get a copy from the skull's owner. We just mailed him his copy today." Gelding laughed.

"So, who is Mr. Gelding?" I asked again. "Didn't he have *anything* to do with the skull?"

"Yes, he brought it over to the museum. He's our messenger boy, aren't you, Jerome? He's a very bright man. Even got into college and studied anthropology. He helps with some of the analyses. We humored him with this office. But he's just a little..." He twirled his index finger in the air near his temple.

My tape recorder was still running. I clicked it off and jammed it into my bag. *Shit. Shit. Shit. Shit.*

I almost walked out the door before I remembered my job again.

"Excuse me sir, could I have your name, please?"

"Sure, it's Steve Viking."

"And your title?"

"I'm the chief curator around here."

Gelding giggled.

"You think that's funny Jerome?" asked Steve Viking. "You shouldn't be fooling those reporters, you know. That's very nasty business." He was shaking his index finger at Gelding. "You've been a very, very bad boy."

Chapter 17

I was fuming. How could I be so stupid? I trusted the wizard and didn't even bother to verify who Jerome Gelding was. I made a total fool of myself. That's what I get for blundering ahead without thinking things through. I didn't double-check my source or my information.

I took another deep breath. Well, at least it wasn't live television. I empathized with that poor TV reporter. I remembered watching him from my hospital bed. Come to think of it, he had interviewed Mr. Gelding in front of the Field Museum rather than from an office. As I recalled, Gelding seemed abnormally nervous then too. He kept looking back over his shoulder, probably wondering how much more time he had on live television before someone from the Field Museum would rush out to stop the interview—the way mine was cut short. How did Gelding fool that TV reporter? Did that reporter take the same route I did, first through the wizard, then through his false lead?

I walked to my car, turned it on, but kept it in park. It was snowing again, a light snow. In front of me was the lake. Calmness. It was like applying a strong ointment that could penetrate my aches.

A deep breath. What just happened? Was anything I heard believable? How could I find out? I took out my cellular phone and called the Field Museum.

"I'm trying to verify the title of a Mr. Steve Viking at your museum. Could you please help me?"

I was put on hold for about thirty seconds. Then I was transferred.

"Yes, I'm trying to verify the title of Mr. Steve Viking. Can you help me?"

I was told he was the chief curator.

"Was he in charge of the report about Crystal Skull?" I asked. *Bonus point. Bonus point.*

That information was confidential. I hung up. When would I get a break?

Somehow, I'd have to get a copy of that report. I'm sure it would list the authors of the document, the team experts. Once I had their names, I'd know who to interview. Steve Viking said it was mailed to the skull's owner today. I'll have to call Warlick for a copy.

What now? It was about two in the afternoon. I was hungry. There was a policeman in his car about three lanes away from me. He was eating a hamburger. At that point, even meat looked appetizing.

As I was putting my cellular phone back in my bag, I saw it, like I saw it for the first time. The manila folder that my mother had given me.

The report! Of course! It was there for days. I still hadn't faced the fact that my mother had a boyfriend—that's why I'd blocked on this folder. It was a sharp reminder of the day I saw Alderman Frank Messina practically naked in my mother's living room. I took it out as carefully as if it were a Swiss Army knife that was rigged to whip out its utensils all in one shot.

As I opened its contents, I felt like I was in confrontational therapy, facing aspects of my mother's life that I didn't want to believe. She worked for a politician. She enjoyed it immensely. She fed on gossip. She thrived on duplicity. To her, it was just a game. She loved running the show, but since she didn't, she tried to run everyone else's. She made Alderman Dryad utterly dependent upon her. She led him to believe he couldn't exist without her.

But she was my mother.

Read. Just read. Be objective.

These were minutes from a strategy session. I tried to picture the setting. It all took place on Sunday morning, three days after Thanksgiving. It occurred in Alderman Dryad's office on Archer Avenue. I had been in his drab office many times to visit my mother. The view from his second-story front window looked down upon Archer Avenue. Across the street was a vegetable and fruit store, next to a Polish delicatessen. On the other side was a small clothing store. A picture of Dryad hung in the front foyer. He stood next to the former mayor, who was Irish. My mother told me one of Dryad's constituents painted it for him after he got him an extra garbage can. Favors knew no bounds on the South Side.

That Sunday morning, Dryad called a special meeting. I'm sure it took place in the adjoining room that had a long oval table, battered from years of wear. I looked at the minutes. My mother even listed the breakfast items on that table: Vegetable quiche; cheesy, potato hash brown casserole; sausage patties; an assortment of bagels and muffins; and a fruit tray.

The self-serve coffee pot was probably plugged in at the back of the room, and I'm sure my mother served the coffee and took the minutes.

I noted which aldermen were present: Dryad, O'Hara, Chiappetta, Messina, McDonald, Alcamo, Palermo, McInerney, Birch, and Fitzpatrick. They represented a unified group who consistently voted against Bernardo Morales. They were led by Alderman Dryad, who, on good days, rallied up to half of the city council on his side against the Hispanic mayor. The votes were so consistently split down the middle during council meetings, that the media had dubbed them "Council Wars." Alderman Dryad and his group were generally all white males while Mayor Morales' half had blacks, Latinos, and women. I started to read.

The meeting began at 10 A.M.

Alderman Dryad: "The mayoral primaries are just three months way. We've watched our great city change under Bernardo Morales in the last four years. Some say for the better; others say for the worse. I say things are not good. And I believe you all agree with me."

I pictured the other aldermen nod in approval.

Alderman O'Hara: "Bernardo Morales has to go. Four years in Chicago is more than enough time for that man. We really need some new blood to steer Chicago. Someone with experience in handling this city the way it's meant to be handled. Tradition has a lot going for it."

He was a big, hefty, rotund man, part of the Old Guard. He used to be chairman of the Finance Committee. His face was usually red and bloated, and he was always coughing and wheezing. He was either digging into his pocket for his handkerchief or wiping that big white cotton square across his face. I had seen him in action in City Hall, and when he spoke, people around him nodded to his face. But they glanced at one another in a way that allowed their eyes to roll just a fraction of a millimeter. He was a powerful figure once, but he had gotten old. I think he was pushing eighty. I looked back at the minutes.

Alderman Dryad: "I won't beat around the bush anymore. You've heard the rumors. Now here's the facts. I'm entering the race for mayor, and I need your support."

Alderman O'Hara: "Elections don't come cheap, you know. And your ward isn't known for its generosity in contributions. Just how do you plan to let people know you're serious?"

Alderman Dryad: "Thanks for asking me that question. You've probably heard me say I would run for mayor if I had financial backing. As you all know, I come from a poor family that couldn't possibly afford to finance me. But, as it turns out, I now have a wealthy backer. We've been friends for years. He has recently offered to help. He is very unhappy with the present mayor."

Alderman O'Hara: "Who's your big backer?"

Alderman Dryad: "Edgar Sheldon. In fact, he's right here."

I wondered where he was hiding. He probably made his appearance with a fat cigar sticking out of his mouth. I pictured him lunging toward Dryad with his wide grin, grabbing his right hand in his two-handed clasp. The minutes reflected applause.

Mr. Sheldon: "Thank you, everyone. You are all too kind. I believe I am backing a winner. Alderman Robin Dryad is a fine candidate. And a very shrewd politician, I might add. He's certainly stacked the deck in his favor."

Alderman Messina: "What are you talking about?"

Mr. Sheldon: "Dryad has been studying his opposition carefully. So carefully, in fact, that he has uncovered very interesting information. Information so powerful it will help him win."

Alderman Dryad: "I was saving that for later. But I guess now is as good a time as any to bring it up. I've hired an undercover investigator to watch Morales. I've had a hunch he's not as moral as the name he bears."

Alderman O'Hara: "We've all known that, Robin. We just haven't been able to prove it. What have you got?"

The minutes reflected he had a coughing spell.

Alderman Dryad: "Calm down, Alderman O'Hara. You're getting too excited. And with my news, you'll get even more excited."

Alderman O'Hara: "What?"

Alderman Dryad: "He regularly calls an astrologer. Up to three times a week."

Alderman Chiappetta: "An astrologer? Jesus Christ! If that don't beat all!"

Alderman Dryad: "Yes, it's true. We have reports of him meeting her at her home in Bridgeport. They also meet at the Stouffer Riviera. In any event, I don't know which is worse. The fact that he's got a mistress or the fact that he runs this city based on the positions of the stars, the fullness of the moon, and the cycle of the planets."

I could just picture this group rubbing its hands together.

Alderman O'Hara: "Robin, that's the best piece of news I've

heard in a long, long time. This will ruin him. Job well done. Just like the old days. Congratulations!"

I pictured everyone clapping and patting each other on the back.

Mr. Sheldon: "Congratulations are in order. And I believe we have champagne?"

At this point, my mother was probably handing out the glasses and pulling the chilled champagne out of the refrigerator.

Mr. Sheldon: "This is a very special occasion. To a new future for Chicago."

Alderman Dryad: "Thank you. Thank you. Now the real work begins. Tomorrow I officially launch my campaign against Mayor Bernardo Morales. We have less than three months."

Mr. Sheldon: "A lot can happen in that time. We have to work fast. For starters, I'd like each of you to be at my New Year's Eve party at my new restaurant, The Crystal Palace."

I remembered the gold-trimmed invitation I received with the gold tassle in its center fold. Inside, my invitation read:

"It's a New Year's Eve Party, and You're Invited!

Where: The Crystal Palace

When: December 31

Cocktails at 7 P.M.

Dinner at 9 P.M.

Entertainment: The Big Band Boys

Alderman Dryad: "Who are you inviting?"

Mr. Sheldon: "Everyone. I want all the aldermen there."

Alderman Dryad: "And Mayor Morales?"

Mr. Sheldon: "Especially him. That party will be a stand-off between the two of you. We'll have the opportunity to study which aldermen socialize with which candidate. We'll gather plenty of information on who is on whose side."

Alderman Dryad: "And on who is betraying who. Very wicked."

I couldn't believe these types of points were strategized among men running for office. I thought all they talked about were issues and how to best accommodate voters.

I thought back on that New Year's Eve party. Why didn't I pay more attention to what was going on? I wasted so much time wishing I could go home, when all along, I could have been....Oh, hell. It wasn't even worth trying to turn the clock back. *Just move forward. Read the minutes.*

Mr. Sheldon: "And what about that skull?"

Alderman Dryad: "What about it?"

Mr. Sheldon: "Did you know that the mayor has taken a shine to it?"

Alderman Dryad: "Yes, I've heard. Not surprising he has a taste for the occult, though. Is it?"

Mr. Sheldon: "I guess not. But I think we should have the skull play a more prominent role in your campaign."

Alderman O'Hara: "What the hell does that 'numbskull' have to do with us?"

Alderman Fitzpatrick: "My daughter wants to spend all night with that skull. For God's sake, she's even praying to it! She says all her friends visit it too. We have to remove that crazy wizard and his damn skull."

Mr. Sheldon: "Listen very carefully. The mayor is in favor of saving the skull. Tomorrow, everyone will hear he's into astrology. Once he's ruined because of that, he'll be discounted for his alliance with the skull. It's very simple. Skull equals Mayor Morales. No skull equals Mayor Dryad. Your message, Dryad, is that the skull will ruin the city. It'll brainwash our children. It'll cause people to...to...act funny."

Alderman Dryad: "Even if I go along with this, Sheldon, I have no control over the skull. How am I supposed to launch a campaign around something that's not even in my hands?"

Mr. Sheldon: "I have a plan. I'm going to get that skull and keep it—at least through the election."

Alderman Dryad: "And just how do you plan to do that?"

Mr. Sheldon: "The way I do everything. With money. I'm going to ask the wizard if I could display his precious skull before a big audience—in my restaurant."

Alderman O'Hara: "What makes you think he's just going to give it to you?"

Mr. Sheldon: "I'm going to offer the wizard so much money, he won't say no. Works every time. And once I have possession of it, Robin, you can revolve your campaign around it."

Alderman Dryad: "Don't you mean *our* campaign? After all, I think you know everyone in this room is here, principally because you've agreed to finance me."

Mr. Sheldon: "That's probably true. But, did I forget to mention my one condition?"

Alderman Dryad: "Condition? What condition?"

Alderman O'Hara: "There's always a condition."

Mr. Sheldon: "I want my support to be anonymous. I would like this to remain a secret."

Alderman Messina: "There's about a dozen people here. How do you expect this to remain a secret?"

Mr. Sheldon: "I realize this is a difficult request, but I assume everyone in this room wants Mayor Bernardo Morales out. For this to work, Morales must not find out about my role. At least not until New Year's Eve."

Alderman Messina: "Why? What's going to happen then?"

Mr. Sheldon: "I'll give him the shock of his life. I'll put my arm around him, then tell him I'm removing my support for him. That should knock him dead. But I have another appointment now and I must leave."

The minutes reflected Sheldon left at 11:25 A.M. The meeting continued.

Alderman Messina: "Congratulations, Robin. I guess you'll be our next mayor."

Alderman Dryad: "If everything goes according to plan, I will be. And I promise you all one thing. I won't forget who supported me in my early days."

Alderman Messina: "You can count on all of us in this room, Robin. You know that."

Alderman O'Hara: "That's right, Robin. Don't you worry about a thing."

Alderman Messina: "There's just one other detail we should iron out to make your campaign run as smoothly as possible."

Alderman Dryad: "What's that?"

Alderman Messina: "The cigarettes."

Alderman Dryad: "What about them?"

Alderman Messina: "There was another raid in Pilsen. It's the second one in two months, and they're becoming a nuisance. The whole market is going to be affected."

I looked up from the minutes. Taxing cigarettes even higher was a pet project of Mayor Morales. Was this group of aldermen involved in the distribution of tax-free cigarettes?

I was getting a headache. My car was still going. I would have turned it off, but it was too cold outside. I needed the heat. I was also getting hungry—despite all the potato chips I had eaten earlier that day. I looked in my gym bag. I still had some water left. There was also an energy bar. That may have been the only time in my life that I ate one of those things when I really needed it for energy.

Alderman John McDonald: "Any theories on who's doing the raiding?"

Alderman Chiappetta. "It's gotta be somebody from the mayor's side. Nobody else can get in and out of the neighborhood so easily."

Alderman Palermo: "Yeah, the raids are very neat and methodical. Very clean. Very professional. Very quiet. Three factories are down, and nobody in the city is saying anything."

Alderman Chiappetta: "You mean our little Bernardo Morales is authorizing city employees to raid respectable tortilla factories in the Mexican neighborhood—the barrio that got him elected?"

Alderman Palermo: "Yes. That doesn't make him look good, does it?"

The minutes stopped abruptly. The meeting officially ended at 12:05.

But I'm sure it unofficially continued for much longer.

I looked up. What did this mean? Most in this group were Italian and Irish. They represented the Old Guard. They once dominated City Hall. In some ways they still did, despite the Mexican mayor. The Mexicans, on the other hand, wanted more control and were frustrated things weren't going their way. Could it be that most of those involved in this Nicotine Ring were at this meeting? Could this be the Nicotine Ring?

I still wasn't sure where I was headed with this line of thinking, but some sort of a germ of evil conjecture sprouted. The mayor got wind of this Nicotine Ring and raided the establishments in Pilsen that housed the tax-free cigarettes. The irony, however, was he had to raid Mexican businesses, the ones that supported him in his first election. How did he get into that mess?

I would have killed for a cup of coffee.

It was one thing for this group to want to remove the Mexican mayor. But would any of them kill him? How could I double-check any of this information? Where were the cigarettes stored?

My mother had handwritten notes on the last page. They stated:

Edgar—always the manipulator—politics is just another sport. He's betraying Bernardo. Wants skull for Palace.

Frank—involved in cigarettes. Tortilla King factory in Pilsen.

John O'Hara—fading fast.

Crystal Skull—Dryad must remove.

Chicago Tribune—Call ASAP about Maria de la Cruz.

Chapter 18

My car was still running. It was near four o'clock. I was debating with myself whether I should go ahead with it. *If I wanted to, I could still do it.* My heart beat faster.

I looked over my mother's notes again. There was one aspect of this story I could probably double-check now. Right this minute. I reread that passage.

"Frank—involved in cigarettes. Tortilla King factory in Pilsen."

What if I drove to Pilsen and checked out the Tortilla King Factory? What if I found cigarettes stored there? That would be the first major break for me. I was meeting with my editor tomorrow, and I still hadn't collected any concrete information. I had to do something.

Jesus. What if it was my mother's boyfriend? Could I rein myself in? Stay cool. Even if I do find something suspicious at the Tortilla King Factory, that doesn't necessarily mean it's linked to the mayor's death—Deep breath in. Deep breath out—But maybe it does.

Where the hell was Pilsen? My new rental had an auto PC that I hadn't had a chance to use. I wondered how the navigator worked. I grabbed the quick tips card that was in the overhead visor. To wake up the unit, the card indicated I had to say "Auto PC," then give the command "Navigation." I read how this "toy" had a Global Position Satellite antenna connected to it. That's how it always knew where I was.

In a commanding voice, I said, "Auto PC." The unit responded with a barra ba beep sound. Then I said "Navigation." The navigation screen came alive in the dash screen. It was where the radio was in the old days. The LCD displayed a map of where I was. *Wow, this thing was neat.* I found the Point of Interest screen, selected "business" and then said, "Tortilla King Factory." The system immediately went into calculate mode and then outlined the map and gave me verbal instructions on how to get there.

"Start off by going straight for point five miles, then turn right." I previewed the directions to get a clear picture of where I was going. In another few seconds, I learned that I'd have to take Lake Shore Drive up north to Balboa Drive and turn west, which is just what I did.

I crossed Michigan Avenue until I hit State Street. I took a left, and drove four blocks to Roosevelt Road. I drove west about a mile and a half to Blue Island Avenue, then hung another left. That was one of those diagonal streets that would take me straight to 18th Street.

I wasn't alone. I shrugged it off. Maybe I'll teach these guys something.

My gas light turned red, and my auto PC's voice kicked in. "Fuel is low," said my car computer. "Where was I going to find a gas station now?" I said aloud. Then the computer answered, "The closest gas station to your present location is in point three miles. Would you like directions to that gas station?"

Wow! Can I get it to cook and clean for me too? "No, not this time," I answered. I figured I could go a few more miles before I really had to worry.

I drove a few blocks west, past Ashland Avenue, past a building with a bright mural of an eagle with a wing span of about fifty feet. A little further to my left was a white, three-story building with red windows and doors. The Tortilla King Factory. Rey de la Tortilla. I parked the car, got out, and looked around. I felt like I was in another country. Signs hung over buildings across the street: "Joyeria," "Farmacia," "Botanica Natural," "Curandera/Psiquica/Limpieza."

I stood in front of Rey de la Tortilla, which was huge, taking up maybe six blocks. I bet it was about 100,000 square feet of property. There was a double-door entrance, which was open. To the left was another single, red door that was closed. To the right was a window, and on the second floor were two windows. All three had red wrought-iron bars. There was just one way in: the front door. Once inside, I walked down a short corridor that led me into a waiting room, with an arrangement of couches set on a Mexican rug. Colorfully painted masks adorned the wall. A receptionist looked up and asked what I wanted.

"Que quiere?" she asked.

"I'm sorry?" *What was I doing here?*

"Can I help you?" she tried again.

I looked around the room and saw what looked like a son helping his father fill out an employment application.

"Do you have any employment applications?" I blurted.

"Yes, we are looking for help in the third shift," she answered, handing me a sheet.

"What's the third shift?" I asked.

"Midnight to eight in the morning," she said. "The factory never shuts down. We produce fifty million tortillas a month." She said it like she ran the company.

"Wow!" I said. *Who would have thought the world demanded so many tortillas?* I took the application and sat down in the waiting room, wondering what my next move would be. The receptionist stood up and left her desk. On the other side of the waiting room was a door.

Still holding my application, I opened the door, closed it behind me, and ahead of me saw a cement stairway, painted gray. I climbed the stairs. There were forty of them. Once I made it up to the next landing, I noticed another door. I walked through it. It lead to offices. Inside, I saw cubicles with people hunched over desks, working with calculators and computers. I'd say there were at least twenty people, maybe more. The employees had a lot of tortillas to keep track of, I guess.

It was almost the end of the day, as several employees were preparing to leave. A woman approached me and noticed my employment application. She pointed toward another door down the hallway, and instructed me to walk through it. I acted like I belonged here.

"Put a hair net on before you talk to the manager down there," she instructed.

I continued walking toward that other door, looking around. I noticed the fancy office to my left with a nice desk covered with family pictures. That was probably the president's office.

Once I walked past that other door, I saw a white box on a wall to my left, filled with hair nets. I grabbed one, and shoved my hair under it. Then I walked down a stairway that led into the plant. It was air-conditioned. I counted three tortilla presses and observed ten people operating each press that produced tortilla after tortilla after tortilla.

The line operators, dressed in blue uniforms and wearing hair nets, continuously monitored the dough. Sometimes, the tortillas didn't come out in perfect, flat circles, and they had to be discarded.

One of the operators looked at me, then approached me. His face crinkled like a spider web from age. His probing brown eyes squinted over his pug nose.

"Que quiere?" he asked, wiping his gloved hands on his blue pants.

"Do you speak English?" I asked, showing him my employment application.

He nodded. He took the employment application from me. The other employees looked up. He looked over my application, which I didn't even have a chance to fill out.

"It is empty," he said, waving it in the air. "What are you doing here?"

"I love Tortilla King tacos."

He stared at me.

"For years, I've been wanting to visit your factory to see where the best tortillas in the world were made. I was just in your neighborhood, and I thought, maybe I could get a job here?" I shrugged my shoulders, and blundered forward. "Maybe, you could give me a tour?"

The man looked puzzled, and shook his head.

"Fill out the form first. Did you talk to anyone about coming here?" He was eyeing me suspiciously.

"Uh, sure," I said. "There was a lady upstairs, and she told me to come down here." I wasn't lying yet. "She said you could give me a tour of the place." Now I was lying.

"No, señorita, I do not think so," he said. "That is very irregular. You would need special permission."

"But, I've come all this way. You don't know how important this is to me." I wished I could have just snuck in through a window. *How was I going to find out whether there were any cigarettes here?*

"You do not belong here, senorita," he said. "You must leave." He motioned for me to head back toward the door. I stayed firm in my position. I grabbed his hand. "Please, sir, I just wanted to see your factory. That's all I ask. One minute. Please."

The man scratched his head through his white cap. "First, I have to call my boss. You wait here."

He walked to the wall and picked up a phone. He looked at me while he dialed, then turned around.

The other employees watched. I walked up to one of the presses, nonchalantly, seeming interested in their work. This group had the process down to a science it seemed. I walked down the factory floor to get a better idea of how the tortillas were made. I was trying to look interested. I noticed how first the flour, stored in a huge silo, was pneumatically pumped, then automatically sifted and weighed into a mixer. I saw how the water and vegetable shortening was pumped into the flour from big tanks. Someone added some other ingredients. From the mixer, workers dumped dough into an automatic chain-hoisted trough that led to a funnel-shaped chamber. From there, another worker dumped dough onto another press line that automatically divided it and rolled it into balls. The employees let me watch, but I could tell they were hesitant. I waved to one of the women, and she waved back. I continued to watch.

Dough balls dropped down the funnel feeder onto a press that flattened them. My favorite part was how the tortillas traveled through a three-pass oven to bake. Then, they cooled for packaging.

The man on the phone turned around, I waved to him. By then I was at the entrance of another room and saw packagers dropping dozens of tortillas in boxes labelled "Tortilla King Factory." I waved to the packagers, trying to act like I belonged here. I looked around for anything unusual, but didn't see anything. *Where were those cigarettes?*

I felt a tap on my shoulder.

"I ask you to stay close to me, señorita," the man from the phone said. "Please." He was motioning me to go back.

"Of course. I'm sorry. I couldn't help myself. I hope it's okay."

"No. Not okay," he said. "My boss want me to ask you your name."

"It's Alexandria Vilkas."

He went back to the phone, and said my name. He turned around to look at me while he listened. "Yes, I show her out now."

He hung up. I was directly in front of him, just inches away.

"Why are you here?" he asked.

I decided to take a chance and tell him the truth. "I'm trying to solve the mystery of who killed Mayor Bernardo Morales."

"Bernardo Morales?"

"Yes, did you know him?"

"Ay, yes. He was a great mayor. We all loved the Mexican mayor." Then he narrowed his eyes. "You are the reporter with the skull, no? Who had the skull in her car?"

"Yes. But I didn't take the skull. Someone put it in my car."

He shook his head and took several steps away from me. He opened his eyes wide, then said, "I know that skull. I went with my family to see it. Even then, I knew it would bring much trouble. I told my wife, but she insisted." He shook his head. "And now you are here, causing trouble. Señorita, you must leave. That skull bring bad luck. I have bad feeling. Please, you go."

He began to walk away. I grabbed his arm.

"Please, I just needed to take a look around here."

"Why?"

"Because I think there might be something here that will help me solve the mystery of the mayor's murder."

"You saw everything. The presses are there. The packaging is behind there. The tour is over." He looked very frightened.

"You're scared of the skull!"

"That skull is very powerful. I know that skull bring me much trouble. Señorita, please go!" He trembled.

"Don't you want to help the mayor? Somebody killed him, and I'm trying to find out who."

"Ay, señorita!" He grabbed his head. "You are asking for much trouble." He turned and walked briskly back toward his press, and left me standing there.

I decided I should just quit. I walked back up the stairs into the offices. Everything was quiet. All of the employees had left. It was dark outside and after hours. I walked past some file cabinets, then past the president's office. I stopped to look at his office door. No lights shone. What was I thinking? I opened his door like I was another person. How could I do that? I had come all this way. It would be so nice to find some proof of illegal cigarettes being stored here.

The street lamp shined in from the window. I walked into this room, and shut the door behind me. On one of the walls, I saw a photograph of Alderman Frank Messina. He wasn't even from this ward. I walked to the desk. On top of it was an in-box with some papers, a writing pad, and a phone. I opened the top drawer. In it was a pack of cigarettes and a gun. I slammed the drawer shut, almost forgetting where I was. I'd have to be more quiet. I checked the other drawers in the desk. One had half a bottle of Tequila and two shot glasses. The other had pens, paper clips, rubber bands, glue, thumb tacks, and a small key, like a file cabinet key.

I tried to take stock. What kind of proof was I looking for? I didn't even know what I needed. Then I remembered walking past the file cabinets in the other room. If there was any information up here, it would probably be in one of those cabinets. I went back to the desk and took the small key from the bottom drawer, telling myself that I was doing the right thing.

When the phone rang, I almost jumped out of my skin. It rang four times, then stopped. I decided to look out the window. A police car drove by. A white Tortilla King Factory van rumbled behind. I started looking for information. I headed toward the filing cabinets.

There were three tall ones lining the wall. I tried the first one. It was open. Then I tried the second one. It was open too. What about the third? It was locked. I inserted the key and opened it. I leafed through folders. Oddly, they were labeled with names of taverns and bars. I opened one of them. It said "Jack's Bar, 6526 South Kedzie."

Inside the folder was a piece of paper with three columns. It was a list with dates, numbers, and dollar amounts. It looked like a tally of when this bar received shipments of something, how many boxes it accepted, and the dollar amount paid.

Was this a tally of the boxes of tortillas being delivered to these bars? I looked through a few more folders to figure this out. Soon I knew. The "Midnight Rambler" file made it very obvious. I read "5 cartons, $2,500." A week ago.

I did some math. If each carton had ten packs of cigarettes, and if each pack legally sold for $100, each carton was really worth $1,000. That meant that the legal value of five cartons of cigarettes should be $5,000, yet this bar was paying only $2,500 for five cartons. If this bar sold the cigarettes to its customers, one by one as was the custom in most places, this bar would make a $2,500 profit.

There were more than a hundred folders here. Were all of

these neighborhood businesses receiving shipments of tax-free cigarettes? So where were they? And how were they delivered?

I stuffed the Midnight Rambler folder into my bag. I looked out the window again. A police car drove by. Who could I trust?

Then I heard someone coming up the stairs. I remembered the gun. I scurried back into the president's room, closing the door behind me. It was very dark, but I fumbled from memory toward the desk, opened the top drawer and found the gun.

Jesus, I never used one of these things. Maybe this was a bad idea. I picked it up and felt its weight. It was small and flat and fit into the palm of my hand. I didn't even know how to check if it had bullets. I shook it to see if I could hear them rattle. That didn't reveal anything. Even so, I clutched it tightly and held it to my breast.

I heard the steps more clearly. This person walked slowly. I heard the door from the stairway open and close. I decided to make a move for the closet. Clutching the gun, I moved ever so quietly. As quietly as I could. Tip toe. Tip toe. Tip toe. I walked to the closet, opened the door, jammed myself inside, then closed the door in front of me. I was in the closet, practically kissing the door, clutching the gun and the Midnight Rambler folder. I held my breath, let it out very, very slowly. It was a small closet, maybe just four feet wide. I felt a vacuum cleaner in a corner. I was crouching down to fit under the rod holding the clothes. They felt like plant uniforms.

My heart thud-thudded. I felt a cold sweat on my forehead. This person moved toward the president's office. He opened the door, and turned on the light. Who was he? I didn't dare find out and just stayed in my crouched position, wondering how I would get out. What would I do with the gun? Was this story worth all this? Maybe I could just walk out, give myself up, and beg for freedom.

The light was shut off and the door closed. I didn't have a good idea of where the man went. I just assumed it was a man. How could I make it to the stairway that led to the front door? But then I realized the front door was probably locked since it was already after hours. My only other way out was through the plant. One of the hangers in the closet jabbed into my neck. I turned and felt a uniform brush against my cheek. A uniform! I put on a uniform. I'd act as an employee, and just sneak out. It was a perfect plan. As a back-up, I had the gun.

I tried to be very quiet opening and closing the office door. I tried to be quiet walking to the staircase leading to the plant. I walked down the staircase as fast as I could.

When I made it down the stairs, I looked up. It was then I realized my plan wasn't so perfect. At the top of the landing was a man. Rather, he was more like a shadow of a man. He had a black ski cap on, with holes for his eyes and nose, and was wearing black leather gloves. He was holding something that gleamed. A gun? A knife? I wanted to run for my car. At least get out into the street. He lurched down the stairs. I ran. I ran through the plant screaming, knocking over a bag of flour. My pursuer tripped over the bag.

"Stop her! Stop her!" he screamed. The other employees stopped working the presses and watched me run past them. The presses moved the tortillas along, but no one gathered them, and they started to pile up onto each other. I just kept running. If I could just get outside and to my car. Where was the door? One was just ahead of me. It was wide open. A truck stood nearby. Finally, I was outside. I whipped around, but didn't see the guy. I still had a chance to hide. The truck's back door was open. It was one of many trucks lined up in a row. I jumped inside and saw Tortilla King Boxes. I scurried into a corner and heard conversation outside.

"Hey! Did you see a woman run by?" asked a man.

I heard a bang against the outside wall of the truck. By this time, I was crouched down behind a wall of boxes. They were lined up in rows and it was easy for me to walk all the way to the back of the truck and surround myself with the boxes. Then I smelled cigarette smoke and heard men talking.

"Which bars are we going to tonight?" asked one of them.

"The usual round: Jack's, Tom's, Midnight Rambler. They each ordered about five cartons again."

Jesus. Christ. This was all falling into place. I grabbed a box nearby and opened it. It was filled with tortillas. I tried a box in another row. It was filled with cartons of cigarettes. This really was a cigarette silo, and now I had my proof. Those Tortilla King Factory trucks delivered the cigarettes to the taverns along with their tortillas. I had seen enough and wanted to leave. For evidence, I stuffed a few packs of cigarettes in my purse.

Someone jumped into the truck and walked toward me. He was banging the sides of the truck with a metal object as he moved toward me. I had nowhere to turn.

"Going anywhere?" he sneered, as he towered over me. Who was this man? If I was going to die, I wanted to know who he was and tried to pull his face mask off. But he grabbed my arm, and then whipped me around until my back was pressing against the front of his body. His arm clutched around my neck. I was forced to walk backward as he dragged me outside. He was taller and stronger than me. I just let him pull me out. He was squeezing me so tightly. Finally, we were off the truck. I tried to look around and saw no one else. The row of Tortilla King Trucks stood like mute witnesses. A long, gleaming blade swung past my eyes and was jabbed into my neck. Its sharp point punctured my flesh. Blood trickled down my neck. I heard heavy, fast breathing. Then I struggled and twisted. I couldn't give up without a fight. But my neck and shoulders were held so tightly. I tried to scream. I grappled for my gun. Where was it? Why couldn't I find it? I coughed and gasped for another breath, then felt the cold knife in a fresh spot on my neck.

I finally whipped out the gun and pulled the trigger. I fired my first shot.

The grip loosened. He released me. I turned around to watch the man run back into the plant, holding his knife high, like an Olympic torch, gleaming in the darkness.

I ran around the corner, clutching my gun like a nun grasping her rosary. "Thank you, God. Thank you, God." That's all I could say. I kept running. My car was still there. I fumbled through my bag and found my keys. I opened my car door and turned on the ignition.

"Fuel is low. Fuel is low." My auto PC had a female, sarcastic-sounding, annoying voice, like my mother's. I made a mental note to myself to change the computer voice to a lower male sounding one. Then the auto PC said, "The closest gas station to your present location is in two miles. Would you like directions to that gas station?"

"Hell, yes! Let's just go!" I screamed.

I looked in the rearview mirror and saw a Tortilla King truck coming toward me, its beaming headlights blinding me in the mirror's reflection.

I stepped on the gas and just drove. I couldn't think straight. Where was I going? Which way was home? How come the stupid computer didn't give me directions? Just then the computer responded, "Go straight for point eight miles, then turn left on Archer."

"Thank you, Jesus," I said.

"Fuel is low. Fuel is low." My red gas light flashed steadily.

I kept driving west down 18th street. I took a left somewhere, driving through a red light.

"In point five miles, turn left."

I just zig-zagged down streets, going in a general south and west direction.

"Fuel is low. Fuel is low."

I looked behind me and didn't see anyone. I slowed down at the Archer and Damen intersection. I looked up and saw Huck Finn painted on a huge, white-lighted sign revolving round and round. About one block further south was a gas station.

"You have arrived at your destination on the left hand side," said the auto PC.

I pulled in. Behind me, a police car drove up. Just as I had finished positioning my car next to the gas pump, an officer walked out of his car and came toward mine.

"You low on fuel?" It was Detective Joe Burke.

Chapter 19

"Where the hell were you?" I asked.

"I was following you all day," he answered. "You've had quite a day. And you just blew a red light." He opened my car door and reached down. I jumped when his hand grazed my left thigh. He pulled the lever to release the door to my car's gas tank. Then he pumped gas into my car, the cheapest gas.

"Feel like talking?" he asked.

"Not really."

"You're still a suspect in the mayor's murder," he said. "You can talk in the police station or over there at the doughnut shop. Your choice."

He finished pumping.

"How do I know I can trust you?" I asked.

"You probably can't."

"All right. I'll meet you over there."

It was close to six-thirty, but around here in winter, it was as dark as it was going to get at midnight. I pulled into the parking lot, taking the last open spot. This was getting as bad as the North Side.

When I walked in the diner, the hostess screamed.

"Oh my God! Are you all right?" she asked.

"No," I said, running to the bathroom. When I looked in the mirror, I almost screamed myself. Blood coated my neck and coat. I grabbed a paper towel, shoved it under running water, and tried to clean myself up. The wound wasn't too big. It was a gash, about the size of a thumbnail on the left side of my neck. The dried blood on the uniform I "borrowed" wasn't coming off. Next, I worked on the two black streaks of mascara that looked like tire tracks screeching down my cheeks. I tried to put on some lipstick, but wiped it off after I wasn't satisfied with how the shade looked. Oh, hell. I lubed myself again.

Deep breath. I walked out of the bathroom and spotted Detective Joe Burke in a corner booth.

I sat down, glanced at him, and grabbed a menu. This was a neighborhood diner—the first comfortable place I was in all week.

"How've you been?" Joe Burke asked, like we were two friends catching up on old times.

"It's been a bad year," I said, studying the menu.

A waitress came by and asked what we wanted to drink. Detective Joe ordered a Coke.

"I'd like a glass of red wine, at room temperature, please," I said. "Not from the refrigerator." She looked at me as if I ordered a warm beer.

"Sorry, no alcohol here," she said.

I sighed. "Fine. A diet Coke, then."

"Their hamburgers are great," Detective Joe recommended.

"I don't eat meat." I put the menu down, having decided on a vegetarian omelette.

I took another look at him. Still short and stocky with closely clipped hair. His cheeks were paunchy and pockmarked. I put him at thirty-five, but he was beginning to gray. I saw the wedding ring, and wondered what it would be like to be married to a cop. His fingernails were chewed down to the quick.

"You have children?"

"Yeah, a boy and a girl."

"How old?"

"Ten and seven."

The waitress came by with the drinks.

"So. You were following me today?"

"Saw you most of the day," he said, pulling out a notebook. For some reason, that notebook made me feel uncomfortable, like it was my book of reckoning, where every jot and tittle was recorded.

"You were at the gym by nine, then you went to visit the South Side Psychic at 10:30. At 12:15, you drove to the Field Museum. You came out at two in the afternoon, then sat in your car, reading something until about four. That's where you wasted your gas, you know."

He looked up momentarily from reading his notebook. I looked at the black scribbles on that lined, white paper like I was looking at the book of my life. *What other little secrets did he have in there?*

"Then you drove to Pilsen and parked in front of the Tortilla King Factory. The next time I saw you, you were running toward your car, waving a gun in the air, like you just saw a ghost. After which, you got into your car, blew several stop signs and a red light."

He flicked his notebook shut and looked up at me. "I should write you a ticket."

How did he miss the guy chasing me out of the Tortilla King Factory with a knife? "I can't believe you managed to miss the good part," I said.

"Which was?"

"Which was when I was being stabbed!" I practically yelled, no longer able to act like the calm and cooly collected journalist that I normally was. While flailing my arms in exasperation, I managed to knock over a glass of water. A pool of icy liquid spread across the table top like lies spreading on the Internet.

"You were stabbed?" he asked.

"You know, Joe, here's a tip," I said, taking a wad of napkins and padding them all over the table. "If you're gonna follow a girl, it would be nice if you were around when she was being killed—not when she was doing aerobics."

He raised his notebook high to save it from the flood. By

then, the waitress was there with a towel, clucking all the while.

"I'm sorry," I muttered to her. And to anyone else who was listening. I was really sorry. Joe's eyes connected to mine and he held my gaze for a moment.

"Why don't you show me your gun," he quietly said.

I pulled it out of my coat pocket and layed it on the table. I felt like a three-year-old who stole candy from the corner store and was forced to reveal my loot. Customers nearby looked over. Even in Chicago, it wasn't an everyday occurrence for diners to see a gun laid down on a table.

He let it lay. If I didn't know better, I'd think he liked all the commotion it was causing.

"Is this yours, by any chance?" he asked, pointing a knife toward it. I figured he didn't want to add any more fingerprints to it.

"Of course not! I had to steal it to protect myself." I crossed my right arm under my left.

"You're a suspect in the mayor's murder, you've blown a red light, and now you've stolen a gun." He was counting off his fingers on his left hand, using the knife in his right.

"I'm beginning to have a theory about the mayor's murder," I said.

He put the knife down and folded his hands together again. The table was again dry enough for him to place his notebook back down.

"I have evidence to believe that the Tortilla King Factory is a cigarette silo. A place where they store illegal cigarettes. They package them in Tortilla King boxes and deliver them to hundreds of taverns across the city in their vans." I looked around. "Maybe even to here. I don't know how yet, but I think Alderman Frank Messina is involved in this, maybe even with other aldermen."

"How do those cigarettes just show up in the Tortilla King Factory?" Detective Joe asked.

"My theory is that the cigarettes must be shipped straight from the manufacturing plant to the Tortilla King Factory."

I stopped talking and looked at him. He had a troubled expression.

"I also think the police are involved in this," I said. "I think the aldermen are in on the take."

Detective Joe continued to stare. He raised his eyebrows.

"It works like this. The cigarettes are manufactured, then sent straight to the Tortilla King Factory. From there, they go to hundreds of bars and restaurants in this city, where the owners don't have to pay any taxes on them. They sell them to the customers at a nice profit, and hand over some of the profits to the aldermen...and the policemen. Just the crooked ones, of course."

"Which screws over the federal government," Detective Joe said.

"Yeah. Everybody's heartbroken."

For the first time, Detective Joe cracked a smile.

"Most of what people pay for the cigarettes is taxes, so these contraband cigs would cost very little, maybe as little a hundred dollars a carton," I continued. "If the sellers add another hundred dollars for their profit, it's still a big bargain for smokers. If enough are sold this way, the governments—federal and state—could lose quite a sum. If they lose eight hundred dollars per carton and a million cartons are sold...this could threaten some lifestyles of the rich and famous. Why, think about taking eight hundred dollars per sale from cocaine dealers. It wouldn't add up to nearly as rich a cache as this scam."

He tapped his notebook slowly, drumming his fingers one at a time. "Do you have any proof with this theory of yours?"

I pulled out the folder I took from the Tortilla King Factory, and slid it over to his side of the table, making sure I didn't bump into the gun. By now that was as innocuous as a glass of water. He opened it and studied it.

"That's all I could get," I said lowering my voice. "There were many more, but that's when I noticed I was being followed." I described how I was in the lot behind the factory, how I noticed boxes of cigarettes loaded into the vans, and how I was attacked.

"Let me see your wound," he said.

I pulled down the left side of the uniform's collar and displayed my gash. He leaned over the table to examine it. I could smell his breath—icy Coke breath.

"I don't think he wanted to kill you," Detective Joe said, leaning back onto his side of the booth. "But he definitely wanted to scare you."

"Why do you say that?"

"The guy could have easily slit your throat, but he didn't. He showed a lot of self control by just nicking you."

"You call this a nick?" I asked, indignant at his belittlement of my near-death experience.

He shrugged his shoulders.

Our food arrived, and we stopped talking to eat.

"So what do you think about the Nicotine Ring?" I asked, after I finished about half of my omelette.

A pained expression crossed his face. "It's a very interesting theory, which I will follow up on. But if it's true that the aldermen and police are involved, I don't think you should hold your breath for any quick resolution. This will take some time." He had about half of his hamburger left, but he put it down on his plate. He wiped his hands on a napkin.

"So does this get me off the hook from the mayor's murder?" I asked. "You know, about the skull?"

"It's helping," he said. "But we still don't know how Crystal Skull got in your car and why the mayor died in your arms."

"I wanted to hear that I was completely off the hook, that I could go on with my life again."

"Sorry. There's a lot of people involved in solving this case, and everyone's impatient. The mayor's been murdered, and you're still the best suspect. In fact, here's our game plan: We'll continue to look for evidence to arrest you and blame the murder on you, so we could turn evidence over to the DA. I'm under pressure to throw a body in front of the DA by next week, if you must know."

I finished my glass of soda and as the waitress walked by, I asked for another. Then I turned to Joe. "That's the most forthright statement I've heard from you," I said. "Is it really all that bad for me?"

He bit at a fingernail. "This is politics. A lot's at stake. If you have any evidence to lead us in another direction, it would help. Otherwise, next week, you're in for a lot more questioning."

I pondered that for a moment.

"Have you heard any more news on the skull?" I asked.

"Yeah. We just had some strange pick-ups the other day. A couple of teen-agers were caught for committing crimes in your neighborhood."

"So?"

"One of them shot his eighty-five-year-old grandmother. Said the skull made him do it. And the other molested his two-year-old sister. Again, he blamed it on the skull."

"Did they see the skull?"

"Said they visited it at the South Side Psychic Studio after Thanksgiving."

"Jesus! Like the skull is the devil? That's their defense?" It made no sense to me.

"They certainly have a wild imagination," he said. "Regardless, if this gets out, it's gonna cause problems. I can smell it." He pointed to his nose. I agreed with him. That was very bad news for Crystal Skull. Like defamation of character.

The waitress walked by, and Detective Joe said to her, "Just put this on my tab."

"No problem, Joe," she answered.

He stood up, grabbed the gun and the folder, and said, "I'll have to take these for evidence."

"I figured as much."

He walked out of the restaurant and I finished my diet Coke.

Chapter 20

The next morning, I was getting ready for work. My first day back on the job. I wasn't exactly eager to face the commute or the rigamarole of looking busy in front of my boss. She always reminded me that she was running a business and it pained her to see people just sitting around—even creative types whose excuse was they were thinking.

I parked my car in an outdoor lot to save a few bucks and walked six blocks to work. The blustery January air couldn't penetrate my long, black wool overcoat. I entered the brightly lit lobby of a fifteen-story building on Ontario Street, and saw a group of about eight people waiting for an elevator. When one of the six elevators opened its doors at the lobby level, the entire group walked into the movable box.

It was going to be another Elevator Dance.

A hefty guy bumped into me and said "Excuse me." I took a step to the right until I felt the wall. The person in front of me moved two inches forward and the person behind me moved six inches backward. When the door opened on the second floor, an elderly woman with a cane walked out, and we all shifted to a new position until there was an even amount of space between us. We did this automatically. No one talked.

I moved three inches. By the time the elevator had reached the seventh floor, I had shifted my position five times, and was now standing directly in the middle of the elevator waiting for the doors to open.

Half of the seventh floor belonged to *Gypsy Magazine*, a three-year-old bimonthly that employed a full-time staff of ten and a scattered lot of local freelancers. I stepped out of the elevator and headed toward the editorial section, a cubicled group of three writers and a copy-editor/secretary. We were next to circulation, a cubicled group of two whose job I was barely aware of, but that I knew was crucial to my existence. All I knew was that their work involved getting people to subscribe to our publication and to keep renewing their subscriptions. Then in the middle of it all was my boss's office. She was the only one who had a real door, which was always open except for three reasons—hirings, firings, and reviews. There was also a fourth reason, which was when one of her staff walked in with a grievance that was supposed to be a secret.

On the other side of her office were the graphic designers, a group of two who layed out everything we wrote into beautifully designed pages with illustrations and photographs that perfectly complemented the copy we provided. Well, that was my fantasy anyway. The truth of it was that I often walked into my boss's office upset over how one of my stories was layed out. Once, a graphic designer forgot to place my byline on the story. Often, I suspected they never even read the stuff.

Such were the petty squabbles that we bore to get this magazine out.

I hung up my coat on the rack in the corner and walked to my office. Under my desk, I had about five pairs of shoes and had to decide which pair to wear. I slipped off my winter boots, wet from the slushy snow, and chose black, low pumps to go with my black slacks and black angora sweater. A yellow silk scarf hung around my neck for a little color. I pressed the "on" button of my computer so that it would load my programs. I looked inside my coffee mug, a tall white plastic container, and thought once again, that I should bleach this thing, maybe autoclave it, to remove the brown, ingrained, layered coffee stains. But I really needed a bolt of java right away, and instead, walked to the kitchen, just a few steps away, poured out the old coffee, swished the cup under some hot running water for about two seconds, and poured in the new, fresh brew.

One thing about Alyce Brownlee. She pampered us with top-of-the-line caffeine. Only the strongest, richest jolts for her staff. I walked back to my office and was just about to check my e-mail, when Alyce walked by.

"Are you ever going to make an appearance in my office?" she asked, arms crossed and foot tapping while she stood in my doorway.

"Hi, Alyce. Good to see you. Come on in. Door's wide open." All of us in our open-air cubicles let out our resentment with that joke.

She pivoted to the right and jabbed her pointer finger toward her office. "Now." She was very anxious.

I walked into her office and sat down in one of two chairs that faced her desk as she took the plush seat. I noticed how she pursed her lips and tensed her body.

"Why don't you close the door," she said.

There was a collection of paperweights placed throughout her office—several on the desk, on the window ledge, and in a book shelf. They were crystalline figures of animals, like ducks, elephants, horses. I usually grabbed one of them to hold and rub when I sat in her office to talk, but this time, I resisted the urge.

"So, how's your story going Alexandria?"

"Is something wrong? Why are you all uptight and acting funny?"

She placed her elbows on the desk and put her palms together in the prayer pose and then let her lips touch her fingers a few times.

"Alex, we need to talk." She paused for a moment, still trying to determine how to best break her news. "I'm behind you one hundred percent. I want you to know that."

"Is somebody not behind me around here?" I asked, as my mind darted through the names of my co-workers.

"The publisher, apparently, is getting very nervous about your story."

"Edgar Sheldon?" I asked. Even though he owned the publication, Alyce barely mentioned him by name, and he seemed an almost invisible presence, never interfering with story choices. "The man who trusts his staff to do their job? Since when is he so involved in a story?"

"Since he owns the magazine, Alex," my boss said, purposefully ignoring the obviousness of my question.

"You know what I mean, Alyce. He never interferes. What's the problem?"

"The problem is he's nervous about your story." She didn't continue.

"Am I supposed to fill in the blanks or what? Are we playing twenty questions?"

"Alex, Edgar Sheldon was a very good friend of the mayor."

I waited. I could see she was having difficulty mustering up her message.

"He's a little nervous about your investigation into the mayor's murder and is worried you might be asking the wrong questions to the wrong people." She blurted it out very fast, like she was ripping off a band-aid from a tender wound.

I still waited, containing my journalism speech about asking any goddamn questions of any goddamn source I felt like if it was going to reveal answers for my story. At this point, though, I feared the worst.

"So am I off the story?" I asked.

"Oh, heaven's no!" she exclaimed, almost in a relieved way. "You're still writing it. God, yes. You're still writing it. It's just that...well...we're not sure if it's going to be published."

"I'm sorry?" I said, like I was talking into a phone with a bad connection.

"Edgar wants you to write it, but he wants to read it before making the decision of whether he wants to publish it."

"What?" I asked, incredulous that such a request could ever

be made of a journalist, even indignant. "I'm not Mr. Sheldon's private investigator, doing this to rock my jollies. If I'm doing a story, I completely expect my publication to stand behind me and publish it."

"Alex, I totally agree with you, but this is different."

I looked at my boss and felt my attitude toward her shift. She wasn't the paragon of virtue that I thought she was. She was crumbling in the face of her boss and following his orders, pretending she believed in him, just to get me to follow through too. I knew I wasn't going to get her to admit any indignation over this. She would sit there and convince me Edgar Sheldon had every right to decide what would be published in his publication just because he owned it. She even started to try to convince me of the logic of his request.

"He's in a very delicate position, Alex," she said. "Try looking at it from his perspective."

I wasn't sure how to react anymore. My mentor was now someone I could not completely confide in. Again, I was being let down, disillusioned, even deceived. I had expected her to be more valiant, someone who would rally to my defense. Even if it meant her job. She could turn this around if she wanted to. Instead, she was taking the party line.

"Alyce, is this easy for you?"

She sighed. "No."

All I could do was mutter, "Okay, Alyce, let me think about this. I'm going to still keep working on this. I figure I'm too involved to just stop." I was thinking this through as I was speaking out loud. "I'm going to keep going with my research, and I'll probably organize my notes until this makes sense to me. Once I have it all together, I'll decide whether it needs to be written."

Alyce didn't say a word. Either she knew to stay quiet since she was getting what she wanted anyway, or she was embarrassed for herself, her publication, and her lot in life.

"Hey, kid, one more question."

I turned around.

"How's your wrist?"

"It's getting better." I walked out.

I continued back to my office in a stunned stupor. She didn't even want to review my story with me to find out how much information I had uncovered. She didn't ask about my visit to the psychic, and I didn't have the opportunity to tell her about my visit to the Field Museum, or my adventure at the Tortilla King Factory. I didn't realize how much I needed to tell her all of this until she never stopped to ask. Again, I told myself, I was on my own. I was faced with the death of another relationship, as I knew it.

I stared at the screen saver of my computer. I had chosen an image of a lotus flower to adorn my screen when it wasn't in use. I was thinking of the mayor's death again, and was trying to figure out what I should do next, what my purpose was here at this magazine.

The philosophy at the magazine was that earth was a classroom and we were here to learn lessons. Most of the sources I talked to held this philosophy as well, so it was hard not to absorb it. What lesson was I supposed to be learning now? Why did the mayor of Chicago die while dancing with me? I tried to analyze this and was faced with confronting the very painful subject of death.

Here I was, twenty-nine years old, thinking I would live forever, as would everyone else around me. And then... Bam! I had a corpse on top of me. I had been so dizzy over this fact that I couldn't even properly mourn for the mayor. In fact, I had to admit, I was angry about this. It wasn't fair. There were a thousand people in that room, and he had to die on top of me. Why?

Then I thought about my job. Most stories concerned the afterlife or the beyond-life. Death, I knew, was avidly studied by occultists. They were a group who seemed to embrace the subject with their arms wide open. Everyone else tried to run away from it, including me. But here I was. Stuck.

Maybe I was asked to confront a real death to have a better understanding of what I was writing about. Maybe I had to solve the mystery of this one man's death to remove myself as a murder suspect and to have a better understanding of my purpose in this life.

I had become even more worried about being the prime suspect in the mayor's murder. Wasn't Alyce a little worried about me too? Didn't she realize I have to write this story to get myself off the hook? Was she at all conflicted about relaying the publisher's demand?

God knows, I tried to be objective about my story's subject, to study it like I would research any other story. But it was hard to shove aside my fears and my internal demons.

My phone rang. It was Juan.

"Alex, I've been trying to reach you!" I already had several messages from him, on my home phone, on my car phone, and my work phone, as well as my e-mail.

"Hi Juan, how are you?"

"What does it take for you to return a phone call?" he asked.

"Juan, I don't really feel like talking right now." I was upset he had left the other night, without saying good-bye, without being around. But Juan was a whole other project for me to work on, and frankly, right now, I didn't have time.

"When will you feel like talking?"

"It's hard to predict, Juan." We let a silence build up. Both of us were reporters so this could go on forever.

"Do you want to get together?" he finally asked.

"Juan, it's my first day back to work in over a week. I've got a lot of catching up to do."

"How about if I come over tonight?"

My place was a mess again, and I wouldn't have time to clean it up before he came. "I'm going to be working late tonight."

"How about tomorrow night?"

"Juan, I don't know..."

"I've only got another week left at City Hall before I'm out of a job," he said. He had a bit of an edge to his voice.

"Is that supposed to be my fault?" I asked.

"No, Alex. I didn't mean it that way. I know you didn't kill the mayor."

"You're sure about that?" Maybe he was holding an unconscious resentment toward me.

"Yeah, you're a vegetarian."

I laughed. "I'd still like to see you again," I finally said. I looked over my schedule. "I've got interviews scheduled with Maria de la Cruz, Frank Messina, and Edgar Sheldon, as well as a luncheon at the Crystal Palace with my mother. How about your place in three nights?"

"Okay, see you then," he said.

"Bye, Juan."

I hung up and looked at my schedule again. My interview with Maria de la Cruz was at 1 P.M. today. I still couldn't type, so I took out a yellow, legal pad of paper and started to take some notes.

I was recalling a previous lunch I had with Juan, the day it was discovered that the Chicago mayor was using the services of an astrologer. Actually, it was my first date with him. That was the day the news was published in the *Chicago Tribune*, and the day that Maria de la Cruz was interviewed on a news show on television. I remembered the day very well.

Chapter 21

It was Monday morning, after a long Thanksgiving weekend.

"Alexandria, get an interview with the mayor and do a story on him," said Alyce, holding a copy of the morning edition of the *Tribune*. She was standing in my doorway, chewing gum, and staring at the paper like it was a treasure map that would lead her to a big pot of gold.

"Oh sure, right after I talk to the pope," I said.

"This is really, really big," said Alyce, shaking her paper back and forth. "Imagine! A mayor of a major metropolitan city, a lawyer, a conservative Catholic. And he has an astrologer! This is beautiful."

The beautiful part, I knew, was that this was a great story for our magazine. A story filled with irony, mystery, and validation. My boss wanted me to interview the Chicago mayor about his belief in astrology because it would legitimize the New Age field, and most especially, her magazine.

"Just listen to this," said Alyce, rereading the story head-lined "Mayor's Lucky Star Just Fell." "Before Mayor Morales makes a move in his political or personal life, he calls his astrologer for a confirmation, according to Alderman Robin

Dryad, who officially entered the race for mayor last night. Alderman Dryad admitted to hiring a private investigator to follow the mayor, when he began to suspect that the mayor relied on a celestial forecaster to make his decisions."

She looked over at me as if she were in love, with a shine in her eyes and a glow on her face that editors have when the perfect story crosses their path.

"And how do you propose I get this interview with the mayor?" I asked. "I mean, I'm sure he's not going to be dying to talk to me."

"You've got connections, kid," she said, snapping out of her reverie. "Use them."

I regretted the day I mentioned my mother's job with Robin Dryad to my boss. I considered whining and protesting some more, but I saw that Alyce was determined and would not waver. This was going to be one tough assignment, I thought, the toughest part being to land the interview. My best connection to the mayor was Juan Guerrero, the mayor's press secretary. I knew him from my journalism school days and we still kept in touch. I always sort of had a crush on him.

"You *will* get this story, kid," she said, turning to head to her office. "I know you will."

I turned back to my "black hole," my nickname for my computer. Then, I heard a voice from behind, coming from the other side of my partition.

"Aren't Mondays great?" asked Tony Catania. He was another reporter for *Gypsy Magazine*. He sat on the other side of the six-foot high partition that separated his office from mine. His head bobbed over the partition. At six-feet-six inches, he was tall enough to stand up and peer over the divide. As I looked at him from the neck up, I knew I wasn't seeing his best feature.

"Shut up, Tony," I said. "I don't need you to rub anything in my face."

"Awwww, I feel sooo sorry for you," Tony cooed to me. "You always get the great stories, and then you complain about them."

"Look, I don't need this from you," I said, reaching for my

ringing phone. I rolled my eyes as I listened to the caller.

"Yes, you've got the right place," I said, trying to find the voice that sounded like I was smiling. "Our classifieds cost one hundred dollars for ten lines, or one hundred twenty-five dollars if you want a confidential box number. Yes, I'd be happy to take your order."

I hated this part of the job. I had the responsibility of coordinating the classified advertisements, a task which I always thought belonged to the advertising representative. But he didn't want to deal with it either, saying he couldn't pull in enough commissions to cover his time. So it was delegated to the writers because we were the cheapest labor. This was the part that made me want to freelance.

By this time, Tony was sitting in the chair in front of my desk with a big smirk on his face, holding a golden-gilded invitation. I hung up with my caller.

"Look, Tony, I'm really busy now," I said. "I've got to figure out how to interview the mayor. Unless you have any ideas, I'd like to be left alone."

Tony waved the invitation in the air. "Are you going to this thing? I heard everyone on staff got one of these."

"What is it?" I grabbed the invitation out of his hand and examined it. The paper was heavy and the design showed a lot of shiny gold. Its weight, for an invitation, was appreciable. Inside, there was a thin-twined, gold rope with a tassle. We were invited to a New Year's Eve Party, hosted by Edgar Sheldon at the Crystal Palace. "I still didn't have a chance to open all my mail." I wondered if Juan was invited. I wanted to get closer to him, maybe as a way for me to get closer to the mayor.

"Seems like a mandatory experience," Tony said. "I'm sure Alyce Brownlee would be highly offended if we weren't all there."

"I'm sure she would," I said, wondering when he would leave, so that I could go through my mail.

"You like me, don't you?" he asked. "I'm handsome, talented, and at the moment, available." He leaned back into his chair, so the chair's two front legs lifted off the floor, while he sat balanced on the back legs. He crossed his hands behind his head and rocked back and forth, like he owned everything around him.

"I've got a boyfriend," I said. I was already starting my fantasy over Juan. I mean, it wasn't actually true yet. But at the moment, it was convenient for me to say that.

"Yeah, who?" he asked, letting the chair fall back into position.

"Juan Guerrero," I said. "Know him?"

Tony scowled. "The mayor's press secretary? He's an asshole. Can't ever get any help from him. He's the only PR person I know who runs in the other direction when a reporter approaches him."

"Don't take it personally," I said. But Tony had stood up and skulked back into his office.

I was looking at my computer screen. This story assignment meant I had to call Juan. *Shit.* He was the only one who could get an interview with the mayor for me. I wondered how I should approach him with this request.

I dialed the mayor's press office and my heart beat faster with every ring. After three rings, Juan picked up.

"This is Juan Guerrero."

"Juan, it's Alexandria Vilkas. How are you?"

"Life sucks," he said. "But I'm glad you called."

"Um, listen, I was wondering if you're busy for lunch today," I said. "I want to talk to you about something."

"Does it have anything to do with your mother's boss leaking something to the *Chicago Tribune*?"

"Leave it to my mother," I answered as lightly as I could. "But please don't take it out on me. Okay?"

"All right, all right. I need to get out of here anyway. Where do you want to meet?"

"Well, I haven't been to Berghoff's in a while. How about an early lunch, so we can beat the crowds. Say 11:30?"

In the next hour, I tried to shove Juan out of my mind and continued my research on crystal, adding more notes to my file on the subject. I was rereading a passage from a 1991 book on crystal healing by Phyllis Galde.

"It is possible for someone who is very adept at programming and using crystal to put a message into a crystal that another person owned. It is possible that just by holding it in their hand for a few moments, they could program their thoughts into the crystal, and those thoughts, in turn, would be rebroadcast to the inner body, inner consciousness, subconscious memory bank and all of the body cells of the person who owns the crystal. So, if someone were antagonistic to you and wanted to touch your crystal, you might want to cleanse it later and clear it because you might not trust their intentions."

I wondered if someone could take Crystal Skull and program messages into it. I continued adding more nuggets and tidbits of information to my file on crystal. At 11:15 A.M., I grabbed my coat and headed for Berghoff's.

Juan was already waiting for me at the bar, swirling a celery stick around in a Bloody Mary. This was the side of the restaurant where everyone stood around the bar to eat their lunch. There were no chairs, so that the clientele would revolve through faster.

"How long have you been here?" I asked, standing next to Juan, noticing that he looked like he already had a couple of drinks.

"About fifteen minutes," he said. "The office is going crazy with the latest scandal. I figured if I came here, I might be inspired with a miracle." He continued to swirl his Bloody Mary with his celery stick.

"Are you hungry?" he asked, sipping down the last of his drink.

"Starved. The weinerschitzel looks good, but I guess I'll go for the potato pancakes."

The bartender walked by. "Sir, can I have another please?" Juan asked, waving his empty glass. He turned to me.

"I'll have a Diet Coke," I said to the bartender. Then I looked at Juan again.

"Aren't you overdoing it? It's not even noon yet."

A dark shadow seemed to cross his face. "Work is miserable. I'm a spin doctor, you see. And it's my job to make this whole fiasco look okay. The phones are ringing off the hook. Someone even spotted the mayor at the hotel last night."

"What!" I gasped. "Last night?"

"That's the least of my worries, though. This will never be fixed. Morales' political life was charmed, and now the spell is broken. It was like he could do no wrong with the support of the entire city. Now look at him. He's a flake. Looney tunes. We answer questions like 'How could a star-gazer be capable of running a city of three million people? It's like I could feel those questions seeping up through the City Hall building and flooding my office. You know what I mean?"

His eyebrows knit together tightly and the creases on his forehead wrinkled in angst.

"You're very overwhelmed, Juan," I said, patting his hand.

He responded to my gesture by looking at me. I remember how flushed my face became. I looked down at his hands, long shapely fingers, perfectly manicured nails. I brushed my hair behind my ear. He lifted his hand and followed my stroke, helping me push my hair back.

"Juan," I said breathlessly. "I...I...didn't expect this."

"Neither did I," he said. "Can I see you tonight, after work?"

I remember scrawling my address to him, giving him directions to my apartment, writing down my home phone. From that moment, we were involved.

Then Juan relaxed.

"I shouldn't even be out of the office," he said, "but... We just heard that Maria de la Cruz is going to grant an interview on the *Noon News* to give her side of the story." He looked like he was about to burst into tears.

I was still searching for my moment to broach the subject of garnering an interview with the mayor, but decided to wait. Things were happening too fast. The bartender came back with Juan's drink. A line already formed for the food island.

"You go first," Juan said, tilting his head in the line's direction. "I'll save our spot."

I dropped my purse to the floor after removing my wallet, and pointed at it, making sure Juan would pay attention to it.

Then I stood in line to get some food. Looking through steamed glass, I had a choice of a variety of German-Bohemian dishes, but since most involved pork or beef, it was easy for me to settle on the potato pancakes. I paid for my lunch at the cash register and went to stand next to Juan.

"I should have gotten that for you," he said.

"Don't worry about it."

"Hey, bartender. Do you mind if we watch a little TV?" he asked. "I need to see the news at noon."

"Sure, no problem," said the bartender. He searched for the remote control under the bar and then aimed it above at the TV. In the meantime, Juan left to get his lunch. By the time he came back, the news program had begun.

Maria de la Cruz was being interviewed by a reporter. Most of the noise in the bar quieted down, as the lunchers realized what was being aired.

"Yes, I've been providing consultations for the mayor for about ten years and with very accurate results, I might add," said Maria de la Cruz to the reporter. She was sitting in a chair facing him.

"Many in the city find it incredible to believe that the Chicago mayor was relying on an astrologer," said the reporter.

"It's not so far-fetched and unusual as you might think," she said. "The mayor hasn't used me for every decision in his office. He just wanted the odds in his favor. And that's what I've been able to do. If he was able to reschedule a meeting, a press conference, an interview at a more convenient astrological time—sometimes only hours away, he did. But he never jeopardized his responsibilities. By using an astrologer, he's been able to enhance his chances of getting the job done the right way the first time."

I turned to observe Juan's reaction. He was shaking his head back and forth. The entire bar fell silent as the restaurant patrons listened.

"Mayor Morales has had a remarkable three years in his term as mayor," the reporter said to Maria. "Do you attribute his success to the consultations he had with you?"

"Mayor Morales is a man with deep convictions. He is very charismatic, benevolent, and kind. He is also very powerful with many responsibilities."

Juan groaned loudly.

"He could probably be successful without me, but I have helped him. I can't take a poodle and turn it into a labrador. But I can take a healthy, vibrant hunting dog and help the dog return with a prize. Mayor Morales is his own man. Sometimes he follows my advice. When it's not convenient, he follows his own."

"Do you have other famous people who use your services?"

"Yes, but I'm not at liberty to disclose their names. It's like a doctor-patient relationship and the client has a right to privacy."

"Yet, you have no problem talking about your relationship with the Chicago mayor," the reporter pointedly said.

"That's true. But I'm here talking to you about the mayor because the whole country has found out he has used my services."

"Yeah, and now you'll get a lot of free publicity," Juan yelled grandly to the television. The other patrons chuckled.

"Does the mayor know you're doing this interview?"

"Yes," she said.

"Will the mayor continue using your services?"

"I'm sad to see a client go. But that's the nature of my business. Astrology is not well understood and is not openly accepted. To be fair, there are a lot of charlatans who give the good astrologers a bad name. You would be surprised at the number of people who secretly visit fortune tellers. There is a great need to find out about one's spiritual and mental health, which unfortunately, is not being addressed in our more scientific arena."

"Well, as fascinating as this is, we've run out of time," the reporter said, turning away from Maria and facing the camera. "We've been talking to Maria de la Cruz, Mayor Bernardo Morales' astrologer for the past ten years."

I looked around the room to see people's reactions. Some were shaking their heads in disgust. Others were deep in thought. I decided to canvass the room to find out people's reactions, taking notes as customers responded to the question of "What do you think about the mayor using an astrologer?"

– "Hey, if it works for him, why not? Where's the harm?"

– "He's a devil worshiper. And that astrologer is the devil's concubine. I'm not voting for him again. He'll lead us to Hell."

– "She seems okay. I think I'm going to visit her. Do you have her number?"

– "I'm totally disillusioned. I thought the mayor was logical and straightforward."

– "Astrology is just another tool to understand ourselves and our world. I hope he'll be okay without her services."

– "He's weak and he's crazy. He'll lose the election big time now."

– "He's been the best mayor this city has ever had. I'm going to keep an open mind about him."

I came back to Juan and read my responses to him. I was trying to cheer him up.

"That's four to three in favor of the astrologer," Juan agreed. "It's not as bad as I thought."

"See? Aren't you glad you were here? Out in the streets, so to speak, instead of in your office? Now you had this opportunity to see for yourself what regular people are saying."

"That's true," Juan said. "But I'm still worried about the mayor."

"Look. People are beginning to reach out for something more in their lives. Like we need an individual communion with God, or the universe. More people are willing to explore this kind of stuff now. That's why our magazine is doing so well."

"What's your circulation?" Juan asked.

"It's up to 650,000 now," I responded. I was feeling so good, I put another pat of sour cream on my potato pancakes. I felt I could even defy fat.

"Listen," I continued. "I have an idea."

"What's your big idea?" Juan ordered his third drink.

I took a deep breath and said, "I want to do a story on the

mayor. I normally don't do this, but I promise you, Juan, he can have complete control of his quotes. We have an appreciative audience for what he has to say."

Juan had a puzzled, pained expression.

"Everyone knows he used an astrologer," I blurted onward. "This is not going to go away before his election. He can't just bury his head in the sand over this. He has to be proactive. The story could be ready for the February issue—just in time for the primaries. He could tell the rest of the press he's granting an exclusive interview on this topic with *Gypsy Magazine*, that he has given his word to us that he won't talk about the subject with anyone else."

"That would really give a lot of publicity to your magazine," Juan said, snidely, stirring his drink while raising his right eyebrow.

"Yes, it would help the magazine," I admitted. I patted his hand again. "I don't deny it. But it helps the mayor too. He gets a couple of months reprieve on the story, while at the same time he doesn't look like he's ducking the issue. His response will be that he's talking to the press, and he has no control over their publication date."

"Hmmmmm...." Juan mused. "What do I say to reporters who keep hounding us for the story, especially since they know the mayor is spilling his guts to you?"

"You tell them the truth," I beamed. "We're the perfect publication to hear the mayor's side of the story. Half of our readers are Chicago-area subscribers. The mayor has given this a great deal of thought. He wants to follow his convictions and his beliefs, and he wants to be open about it. Until now, he has kept this aspect of himself very private. He is now willing to share his viewpoints, but he wants to do it in his own way."

"The February issue," Juan said, putting his drink down.

"Whatever you want," I said, knowing that Alyce would be cringing if she knew what kind of latitude I was providing to the source. But I was trying to land an interview and needed to be as accommodating as possible to put my source at ease. It was one thing to be in the throes of dealing with the tangles of a story. It was quite another to deal with the anxieties of an editor and a publisher.

As I looked back on that lunch, I realized it was also quite another thing to start dating your source.

"Okay, I can't promise anything," Juan said. "I have to talk to a few people. I'll call you."

"Thanks Juan. You won't regret this."

Chapter 22

Lunch with Juan had been two months ago, and now as I bit into my tuna sandwich, I pondered how it connected to what I would be doing next.

I contemplated my upcoming interview with Maria de la Cruz. To prepare myself, I wrote some questions down on my yellow legal notepad. This exercise was a like a runner doing stretches before a race. In-person interviews were always more complex than over-the-phone ones. For one thing, I had to be groomed. I couldn't sit in my comfortable office at home, wearing pajamas. For another, my relationship had to be warmer with the source. This involved a lot of smiling and eye contact. Instead of just focusing on her words and voice, as I would on the phone, I would have to notice my surroundings, her facial expressions. And worst of all, I had to go through the trouble of getting there.

I continued writing down my questions. How long have you known the mayor? When did the mayor first approach you for an astrology session? What do you know about the mayor's death? I understand you are the sister of Christopher Warlick. Can you tell me about your relationship with him? What do you think about the Crystal Skull?

That reminded me. There was an oval piece of rose-colored crystal somewhere on my desk. It was a memento given to me by Mayor Bernardo Morales after I had interviewed him on New Year's Eve. I decided to take it with me on the interview. After I found it wedged under my in-box, I tossed it in my purse next to my tape recorder.

Then I drove to Bridgeport, where she lived.

By the time I pulled up in front of her house, it was five minutes to one. A quick survey of the block revealed a pretty ordinary neighborhood for an astrologer. I didn't know what to expect, I guess. Maybe a fat telescope shooting out of her roof?

She had a typical red-brick bungalow with an old, weary octagonal face adorned with stained glass windows. There was a big, oak door protected by a brown wrought-iron storm door. Its rails were arranged in a sunburst pattern.

I rang her doorbell and listened to the chimes. When she opened the door, she looked even more beautiful in person than on television. Her long, brown hair draped over her shoulders and cascaded down her breasts to her waist. She wore a leopard patterned body suit that was tautly hugging her slender figure. Black opened-toed and open-heeled pumps completed the animalistic outfit. Her skin was alabaster, her eyes were brown, and her face had a balanced symmetry as if it were sculpted by a careful artist who didn't make mistakes. Even if she was older than fifty years, her energy was fresh. Her full lips parted to a smile as she opened the door.

"Alexandria Vilkas, I presume?" she said in a voice that lilted.

I stepped in past her threshhold, and shook her hand with my right, good one. She was taller than me and slimmer too. A dart of envy shot through me as I acknowledged my familiar assessment of other women. They either weighed more or less than me, and my relationship with them started from there. If they weighed less than me, they had the advantage.

I felt clumsy in my rubber-bottomed black winter boots and felt even more vulnerable when I had to walk into her living room in my stockinged feet. Her home was richly decorated with red velvet drapes pulled back by big red cords. Her furniture was French provincial. And her hardwood floors gleamed like just-polished chrome on a well-cared-for car. I smelled furniture polish. She had modern artwork of abstract colorful splashes adorning her white walls. Every corner had green plants with spiky leaves.

Her living room was unexpectedly large. So large, it had three groupings of furniture organized in conversation-inducing arrangements. She directed me to the arrangement near the windows. A crimson love-seat faced two regency-style carvers with red and gold striped seat covers. They surrounded a low coffee table.

"Would you like some tea?" she asked, in a way that told me coffee wasn't an option.

"Sure, I'd love some."

She walked into the kitchen and left me alone to continue my assessment of her surroundings. I sat in one of the chairs and pulled out my notebook and tape recorder. Behind me was a fireplace that looked like it hadn't been used for years. What was that on the mantelpiece? Several bottles of Imprimatur cologne? There were three round glass globes topped with gold crosses. I'd have to ask her about those later.

To my right were the windows and to my far left was the adjoining room that Maria walked through to get into her kitchen. I walked across the expanse of the living room into the dining room. Its walls were lined with book shelves that overflowed with books. One shelf had nothing but videotapes. Maybe that special videotape of her and the mayor was there? I scanned the videotape spines but didn't see anything labeled "Maria and Bernardo Do the Nooky-Nooky."

Another shelf had photo albums and one of them was labeled "Clients." I probably shouldn't have done it, but I grabbed that album and flipped through it. Inside were several photos of Maria next to lots of famous people in Chicago. There was an opera singer, a radio announcer, a news anchor, a divorce attorney, a doctor, a university professor, and the former mayor. One photo was rather faded, showing the mayor at a wedding, sitting at a table with his wife, brother, and Maria. I became so engrossed in the photo that I didn't notice Maria walk in carrying the tea.

"I see you've been keeping yourself busy, Alexandria," she purred. The cups and saucers didn't even rattle on the tray.

"These photos are amazing," I said, ashamed I was caught. "Some of your clients... well, I just would have never guessed." I closed the album and put it back in its place.

"This is confidential information," she said sternly. "I hope that the names of my clients will stay only in this room. They certainly are not for publication, and if they are, we can end this interview right here."

She stood facing me with her tray of two cup-and-saucer sets, two bags of chamomile tea, two teaspoons, a small pot of boiled water, and a container with sugar. She was ready to head back into the kitchen.

"Oh, no. I wouldn't dream of it." I cursed myself silently for having this start off so badly.

Maria set down her tray on the low coffee table and busied herself serving the tea with swift, graceful movements, while I fumbled with my notebook, pen, and tape recorder.

"The police were here not too long ago," she said, raking me with her eyes. She threw me off guard with her directness. Usually, sources were nervous, wanting to make a good impression on me, and it was my job to calm them down, ease their uneasiness. This dance was different.

"Oh?"

"They told me I was a suspect in the mayor's murder." She slowly sipped her tea, eyeing me over the rim of her cup.

"Join the club." I shrugged. We eyed each other suspiciously.

"I was wondering if we could start off by you telling me about how you met the mayor and how your relationship with him began."

"Do you have specific questions, or do you just want me to ramble?"

"Feel free to talk, and I'll stop to ask questions along the way."

"Can you explain the basis of your story again?" She put down her tea.

"Of course, I'd be happy to. It's a story about Crystal Skull, its effect on this city, and how it's linked to the mayor's death. At *Gypsy Magazine*, we strongly believe that the disappearance of the skull is associated with the death of the mayor. In any event, as you know, the mayor himself had a fascination for crystal and astrology, and I'm here to explore that aspect of him."

I kept to myself the fact that I needed to find the mayor's killer so that the police would stop following me, so that I would finally have a private life again.

"Do you think I killed the mayor?" she asked.

Now that was a direct question.

"Frankly, I don't know. To be honest, you're on my list of suspects."

For the first time, she sat back, relaxed and belted out a hearty laughter.

Again, I was disconcerted.

"You know why I'm doing this, don't you?" she asked.

Truthfully, I couldn't believe she granted the interview, but I hadn't taken the time to analyze why. I guess I figured she wanted the publicity.

"I want the whole world to know that Bernardo loved me. Our passion was deep and furious."

I was taking notes.

"We met on his wedding day, fifteen years ago. I was the date of Bernardo's best friend, Arturo de la Cruz, who was the best-man at the wedding. After he returned from his honeymoon, we started to double-date. Bernardo and his wife. Arturo and me. About a year later, I married Arturo. All four of us continued to see each other often. Eventually, I read Bernardo's chart and told him he would be a powerful man in the city. I offered to read the stars for him on a regular basis."

She poured herself more tea, and stood up. Pacing slowly in front of me, she recounted her story as she sipped her tea.

"We continued to meet periodically. When he ran for alderman, he asked for my advice. After he entered the race, his campaign ran like clockwork. He called me about once a month to synchronize his political plans with my astrological calendar. Soon, we were meeting in person. By that time, I was divorced."

"But you kept your former husband's last name," I said.

"I hate the name Warlick," she said. "People often confuse me with a Latina anyway. I think there's some gypsy blood in our family."

She paced slowly with smooth, cat-like steps, looking over at me for assurance. I nodded my head, not daring to stop her with another question that would break her emotional momentum.

"Bernardo told me that I reminded him of his grandmother—otherworldly, regal, exotic. We were in his aldermanic office ten years ago, when we first kissed. He opened the door to his office to greet me. He held the door open for a few seconds and was speechless. I walked through the door, and he kissed me on the right cheek, as is the Hispanic custom. I love that custom. Then he grabbed my chin, and kissed me on the lips. We stared at each other, trembling. 'We cannot do this,' I gasped. 'Yes, it's bad for both of us,' he sighed. 'You have bewitched me with your magical powers.'"

Maria set down her cup and saucer on the cocktail table, and sat back down on the sofa. Her voice lowered.

"The door was closed and we were alone in his small office. He walked to the door and locked it. He went to the phone and told his secretary not to interrupt him for half an hour. He approached me, and removed my coat. We embraced and fell on his old, burgundy leather couch....Ever since then, he has been promising to divorce his wife and marry me. He was only waiting for his children to graduate from high school."

She shrugged her shoulders and looked at me, as her eyes filled up.

"It must have been so difficult for you," I said. I thought my love life was bad.

"Life is like an amusement park and sometimes you end up in the Tunnel of Love with someone who you have no business being in love with. It was like the ride had stopped in the dark and it wouldn't move forward. Our feelings increased for each other, but then the Tunnel of Love turned into the Haunted House. The twisted ride finally ended."

I let her be silent for a moment.

"Why don't we talk about your brother, Christopher Warlick," I said gently. "I understand you visited him the night before the mayor's death."

"Yes, it's true," she sighed. "We had been estranged for many years. It was all because of the skull too." She laughed, waved her hand as if she were shooing away a fly.

"More tea?"

"No thank you."

"How about something stronger." She looked at her watch. "It's a little early, but I think I could use a drink. Do you mind?" I shook my head.

She scratched the back of her head. Then she stretched her arms out fully, like a cat. With a quick movement, she stood up and walked into the adjoining dining room. She came out with a thick bottle of cognac and two small cognac goblets.

"Are you sure?" she asked, waving the two goblets that she held in her right hand.

If I refused, I could make her uncomfortable. If I accepted, she would feel more confident talking to me. This was a tough job. I didn't know much about cognac, but I loved the shape of the round goblet and imagined the two of us looking elegant swirling the caramel-colored liquid.

"Okay, just a little," I conceded.

Slowly, she poured the liquid into each glass, filling them up about a third of the way.

"So you must be European," I said, as I accepted a goblet. I mimicked her motions before taking a drink. First I smelled the liquid, then I swirled it around, and took a slow, sensuous sip.

"Yes, my brother and I were both born in the old country."

"Which one?" I asked.

"It was an East Block country, a small one. It doesn't really matter. We still have relatives living there, and there is considerable traffic between my old country and Chicago."

"My father was born in an Eastern European country too," I

said, pushing away the inner pang of loneliness I felt as I thought of him. "Vilkas means wolf, I'm told." My cheeks were probably flushed by then as the cognac's potency seeped upward to my head.

"Yes, you are right," she said, nodding slowly. "You are a wolf."

I didn't really like how she enunciated the word wolf, like it was a mean, wild creature of the night with fanged teeth that couldn't be tamed. To me wolves were observant, watchful, and careful, but I needed for her to get on with her story.

"So where did the skull come from?"

"It's a long story, one that has taken me my whole life to forget," she said. "Only to come back to me, filled with memories, memories that will not go away." She looked out her window, perhaps searching for a floating postcard that would give meaning to her origins. I wrote her words down in my notebook.

"That skull has been in our family for generations. My father received it from his father, who received it from his father, who received it from his father. My father handed it down to his son, Christopher, shortly before his death. All of the men who owned that skull have died a tragic death."

I looked up from my pen and notebook. She was holding the cognac goblet close to herself, with both hands crossed over the glass that she caressed against her breast, rolling it back and forth.

"My brother and I both witnessed the death of our father over that skull. The government outlawed it. But my father had become possessed by the skull, as all of its owners have before him. Crystal Skull became the mistress of men, the concubine of their innermost passions. Personally, I think that skull is cursed, and its curse has followed my family for countless generations."

"How did your father die?"

"He should have just given it to the authorities. But he refused. Soldiers walked through our house, searching for it. Spies in the neighborhood had informed on us. Oh, don't look so surprised. It was a common practice there. My father gave readings to people in the neighborhood using that skull. He could tell them about their health, their wealth, and their death."

"Where did he hold those readings?"

"In our kitchen. We had a very small apartment. It was so small, my father would hide the skull in the kitchen oven, when it wasn't in use. In the winters, though, it was constantly in use. Winters in our country were so cold, with much snow. We had very little heat, even when it was turned on. Then one winter, we had no heat. The government just shut it off. Some nuclear reactor accident, they said."

"You think the government turned off your heat on purpose?"

"Of course. It was a way to get to my father, to have him relinquish the skull. It didn't weaken him, but we watched my mother die of pneumonia."

"I'm sorry." I put the glass down on the table. "Why didn't they just take the skull away from him, using force, instead of punishing him and your family?"

"It was always a game with them. They wanted him to relinquish it freely and publicly, so that the rest of the neighborhood would be enlightened. You understand?"

I wasn't sure, but I nodded.

"The day after my mother died, the heat was turned back on again. About a week later, my father began acting very strange. He paced in the apartment, back and forth, and kept looking out the window. Finally, he pulled me and my brother to the side, saying that we would have to live with his sister in a city that was about two hours north of us. As he told us the news, he threw all of our clothes in a bag while his sister waited outside in a car with her husband."

"What about the skull?"

"Oh, the skull was safe. He had already sent it ahead of us to his sister's house days earlier. He told us where it was hidden in her backyard, and he instructed us to leave it there. Then he told us to leave the country at our earliest chance and to take the skull with us."

"How old were you then?

"I was ten and Christopher was fifteen."

"So what happened?"

"Two soldiers walked into our home and shot him in the back of his head. They turned to us, and one of them said, your father didn't give us the skull. So we took his."

"They killed your father right in front of you?"

"Yes. To them, it didn't matter."

"So then you went to your aunt's?"

"Yes. We stayed with her for several years. But Christopher and I kept fighting over the skull. One night, I was so upset, I tried to kill him."

"Because of Crystal Skull?"

"You don't understand its powers. Whatever is inside of you, the skull will amplify it, and bring it to life. We all have a dark side. If we don't have it under control, the skull wedges itself inside the dark side and then gets to work on extracting it."

"On extracting the dark side?" I asked, trying to understand.

"I have been thinking about this for years," she continued. "This is difficult to explain. It extracts the dark side by bringing it to light. Sometimes those dark thoughts will burn under the bright light of truth and freedom, but sometimes.... well, those dark thoughts will thrive and multiply."

"How did you try to kill him?"

"With a knife, while he was sleeping. But he woke up, and turned that knife around on me, and cut me here."

She pointed to her right upper breast.

"I have a big five-inch scar here. Our aunt woke up and thought we were crazy. Which we were. She threw us out of the house, and my brother and I went our separate ways. He kept the skull. I kept my scar. I never saw him since then...until...."

"Until the night before Mayor Morales died?"

"Yes."

"Why did you seek him out then?"

"I felt compelled to see him again. Crystal Skull has drawn us together once again, you see."

I waited for her to continue.

"I was having dreams about Bernardo, and I feared for his life. I thought the only ones who could help me were my brother and Crystal Skull. But I was too late." She sighed wistfully.

"What was your dream?"

"I was sitting in a balcony of city council chambers, looking down upon the proceedings. Aldermen were shouting at each other and order was disrupted. They were emotional. I couldn't tell what they were talking about. Then the lights suddenly went out and everybody was screaming. I only saw darkness but felt fear everywhere. I sat gripping my chair feeling useless. Then lights came back on, and Bernardo was gone."

"He was leading the proceedings in your dream?"

"Yes, it was a city council meeting. When the lights went out, he disappeared. His chair was empty. Then I walked out of the chambers and walked slowly up two flights of stairs to the mayor's office. Dread was everywhere. Underneath me was a black carpet, strewn with white rose petals. I came to his office. The bronze, life-size statue of George Washington stood across his doors. George had a mocking grimace, as I walked past him into the mayor's office. Inside, the office was draped in black, and the security guard was wearing a black jacket. The carpeting, usually a light grayish blue, was charcoal. Slowly, I turned left and looked at the wall covered with black and white portraits of the past mayors, all of them dead. Mayor Bernardo Morales' photograph was hanging there in the last position. In front, where a bronze plate of the City Seal normally hung, I saw a picture of a skull and crossbones."

I sat transfixed, listening to her describe her dream.

"And did you ask your brother, the wizard, about this?"

"Yes, that's why I needed to see him. To get his opinion. He confirmed my worst suspicions. He told me the mayor was in very grave danger and will lose his life. Somebody was intent on killing him."

I wasn't sure how much of a confirmation her dream was, but it matched my hunch.

"Who?"

"Somebody close to him. Someone he cared about. Someone like a family member."

I waited for her to give me a name, but she sat silently caressing her goblet, close to her chest.

"Who do you think killed the mayor?" I asked, with some persistence.

She took a drink.

I shifted in my chair and then looked at the fireplace behind me. Again, I noticed the cologne.

"Why do you have three bottles of Imprimatur on your mantle?" I asked, as I walked over to the fireplace and reached for one of the bottles. The shape reminded me of a round crystal ball, and the bottle filled the palm of my right hand. The glass was thick and mottled with a rough texture. The cap was shaped as a cross, almost three inches high. I knew Imprimatur was created by a priest who was ex-communicated for his beliefs in reincarnation. After he was thrown out of the Catholic Church, he became a playwright who wrote steamy blockbusters with New Age themes. I took off the cap and sniffed, then dabbed some on my neck. The liquid was a dark amber color, like the cognac we were drinking. Its scent had a tinge of citrus fruit and was mild, but distinctive. Promotions for the product revolved around a spiritual quest: "Seek the center of your soul, and ye shall find...."

"Imprimatur was Bernardo's favorite cologne," Maria told me. "Those bottles and the smell remind me of him. It's my way to keep him alive."

I replaced the cap and set the bottle back in its place. Staring at the three bottles, I wondered if I knew the ex-mayor any better for having tried his favorite cologne. Juan liked that cologne too, I thought. Him and every third man, it seemed, as that smell was ubiquitous, almost an obsession.

I couldn't stand it anymore. I needed to know.

"Who do you think killed the mayor?"

She shook her head and shrugged her shoulders. Her cognac goblet was empty and was held between the palms of her hands. By slowly moving her palms forward and backward, she caused the empty goblet to roll between her hands.

By this time, I had resigned myself to the fact she wasn't going to talk much more. It was time to conclude the interview.

My most difficult question was saved for last.

"Where's the videotape of you and the mayor that you used to bribe him?"

She turned toward me with a sudden, jolted movement, as if an electric shock had coursed through her body. The glint in her eyes was sharp and fierce. She stood up, towered over me, and then hurled her goblet down at me.

"How dare you!" she shouted. "How dare you!"

I tried to duck out of the goblet's way, but it smashed into my right shoulder, and the glass shards lay strewn over my chest. Slowly, I picked the pieces off my chest, one by one, and layed them down on the coffee table. I wasn't even angry with her.

The steely glint in her eye shook me, as if to ask how I even knew about the tape.

"The mayor's press secretary told me about it," I answered, as I continued to search for pieces of glass on my chest.

"That bastard! That bastard! I really wish I were the one who killed him. He deserved to die!" She sat back down and crumpled into a ball, holding her knees by crossing her arms over them, and she rocked herself back and forth. Still sobbing, struggling to control her grief, she wiped her cheeks. Finally, she quieted herself. "I loved him so much. I wanted to do anything to keep him." She looked over at me with her bloodshot eyes. By this time, I had cleaned myself up.

"Even kill him?" I asked.

"I didn't kill him," she whispered. "I wanted to, but I didn't do it." She shook her head back and forth. I wanted to believe her, but I wasn't sure. My own feelings were confused as I empathized with her role as a woman in love with the wrong man.

"Where's the videotape?" I asked again.

"I don't know," she sighed. "It's gone."

"When did you last see it?"

"I had it in my machine the night I went to visit Christopher. When I came back it was gone."

"Did someone break into your house?"

"Yes, the place was ransacked when I came back. At first, I

couldn't figure out what was stolen. All of my jewelry and money was still here. But then I figured it out."

"Did you call the police?"

"No, they don't know about the videotape. Nobody does. At least, that's what I thought. It's not something I wanted to report."

I noticed her blush. She looked down at her hands.

"What was on that tape?"

"It was one of our nights together, taped here in my bedroom."

"Can you show me?"

She looked puzzled.

"I meant could you describe to me what was on the tape, and perhaps show me where you taped yourselves," I said.

"I don't know what this has to do with your story."

"It might help me find the killer."

She stood up to lead the way. We walked through her dining room, down a hall, and into the master bedroom, which had a big, oak king-size bed. At the head was a sleighboard. Her colors were pink, lavender, and gold—very feminine.

"When did you tape it?" I asked, trying to figure out where Bernardo might have set up the camera.

"About a year ago," she said.

I shook myself and thought, *God forbid anybody should ever investigate my love life.* Then I asked, "How could the mayor of Chicago allow himself to be taped with you?"

She strode across the room, and then sat on her bed. "He did it as a reassurance to me. We had a big fight that night. About his wife. He promised me again he would leave her. But I told him I didn't want to wait anymore. He begged me, but I was really going to break up with him that night. Then he said he would prove his love to me. He set up my camera here in the corner, then hooked it up to the VCR and TV over there." She turned around to point at the mahogany armoire in the corner. I nodded.

"But after it was over—when he broke up with me just after Thanksgiving—he changed his mind."

"Now, this was a year later, you're saying?"

She nodded. "He asked for the tape back. By then, I decided I liked having this insurance around, so I made a copy of the videotape for myself. I returned the original."

"Did he know you had a copy?"

She shook her head. "No, not until a few weeks ago."

"How did he find out?"

"I told him."

I looked up at her bedroom ceiling and wondered, *Why am I in the middle of this?*

Chapter 23

I was back in my car. Now what? I needed to sit for a minute and absorb what just happened. Maria de la Cruz, the former lover of the mayor of Chicago, tried to bribe him with her videotape, but failed. She wished she had killed him, but says she didn't. I had all but practically crossed her off my list of suspects.

Where was I in my investigation? I decided to take stock and review my suspects. A police car drove by.

First, there's Alderman Robin Dryad, arch nemesis of the mayor. Candidate for mayor. He had the most to gain from the mayor's death. He was also cunning and had no fear in treacherous dealings—like stalking the mayor until he dug up his fondness for astrology.

Then there's Alderman Frank Messina, close friend of Alderman Dryad and close enemy of the mayor. Not to mention that he's my mother's lover. I had a bad feeling about him and wondered how I would confront him.

Broadening my list would include the Nicotine Ring Boys, any number of aldermen who were making good money from the sale of illegal cigarettes and would resent a current mayor sabotaging their booty. If I took this further, I'd have to think about the small business owners who sold the illegal cigarettes and the cops who protected them. This category was huge and it unsettled me to think I might have to interview hundreds of people connected with this aspect of the story, and who conceivably were suspects in the mayor's murder. I fingered the dried blood on my throat, resisting the impulse to peel off the scab.

My next suspect was Irene Vilkas, executive secretary for Alderman Robin Dryad, otherwise known as my mother. I hated putting her on my list, but I was trying to be objective. She wanted everything for her daughter and would do anything to put me in a better position. Her plan would go something like this: She'd kill the mayor, position her boss to be mayor, and then get me a great job in City Hall. She'd look good for raising such a dutiful, productive daughter.

Next, there's Edgar Sheldon, billionaire tycoon, publisher of *Gypsy Magazine*, the boss of my boss. I didn't even let my boss know her boss was on my list. But the mayor did die in his restaurant, the Crystal Palace. And now he was very jumpy about my doing this article. Plus, he was Alderman Dryad's financial backer, and that put him in a bad light with the dead mayor. I wondered if he were connected to the Nicotine Ring. And why did he want Crystal Skull so badly? He'd be tough to interview in person, though, and I couldn't think of a way to deal with him. Oh well, something will turn up.

Another suspect is Christopher Warlick, owner of Crystal Skull, and somewhat of a spiritual advisor to me. The mayor wanted to take the skull away from him. Christopher resented that, had gained the mayor's confidence, and was in a position to kill him. Well, he was at the restaurant that night. I really didn't think he did it, but I didn't feel confident about crossing him off my list yet either.

There's also Bernardo Morales' wife. She was upset he had a lover, embarrassed that her husband was caught in an affair, perhaps even humiliated. How was I supposed to talk to her? Maybe Juan could help me. This all was overwhelming.

With the thought of Juan, my hand shook. I mean, I just

watched it shake. There's no way that he did it. It was a dreadful thought, one that was easier to deny than to scrutinize. Shit. I'd be seeing him in two days. I did put him on my official list though. Juan Guerrero, mayor's press secretary, otherwise known as my boyfriend. The thing is, though, that he loved Bernardo Morales and was so proud to have a Mexican for a mayor. With him, I didn't see a motive.

It started to snow again. I turned on the radio. "Another Chicago snowfall is in progress," the announcer stated. "This winter is one of the worst in two decades." I sighed. *Tell me about it.*

The radio reporter was talking to a representative of the mayor's Snow Command – located on the seventh floor of City Hall. Juan had given me a tour of the place, and I knew that room was filled with radar equipment, radios, televisions and about thirty employees monitoring the weather and coordinating the 250 trucks on the 1,700 square miles of city streets. There would be another four inches of snow tonight. That meant Snow Command would be in full operation.

In Chicago, everything was political, and snow could be a disaster if it weren't handled correctly. The one year a Chicago mayor took a nap during a bad storm, the city took its revenge by promptly removing the guy from office. If he can't remove our snow, he can't be our mayor.

Anyway, it was 4:15 P.M., and I needed to get home. I called my editor to let her know I'd continue working at home. After three rings, she answered.

"Alyce? Hi, it's Alex."

"Where the hell are you, kid?"

"I'm in Bridgeport, outside the home of Maria de la Cruz. I just interviewed her for my article."

"Where's your beeper?"

I rummaged through my purse, my coat, and found it in my glove compartment.

"It's in my glove compartment."

"So how is someone supposed to reach you, Alex? Huh?" Her tone was a little huffy.

"Why? What's the problem?"

"The problem is I've been trying to reach you for the last goddamn hour, and you were nowhere!"

Big whoop-dee do. A whole hour went by and the city went without its occult phenomenon reporter. "Sorry, Alyce. I won't let it happen again. What's the problem?"

"There's a riot forming over Crystal Skull. Do you think you might want to be there to cover it?" She was talking to me like I was five years old, asking if I wanted to dress up as Cinderella.

"Where?"

"The South Side Psychic Studio. I've already sent Tony to help you."

"Tony!" I groaned. "Alyce, I can't deal with Tony now. Couldn't you have sent someone else?"

"I need photos."

End of argument. Our magazine's graphic designers wouldn't drop everything just to shoot something exciting happening live. Only a reporter felt the heat of the moment, and Tony could take pictures too.

"Okay, I'm there."

Chapter 24

I drove down Archer Avenue and saw a three-block long line of people waiting to view the skull. I took a right and parked my car on a side street, deciding it would be safer there. By the time I reached Archer again, I saw a few paddy wagons idling on the street corner. The snow continued to drop from the sky, like down feathers muffling Chicago's brassiness.

Up ahead, there was a commotion. Where was Tony? I walked past a long line of people waiting to view Crystal Skull. "Are they going to let us in?" someone asked. Several young women were pushing strollers with babies bundled in bulky blankets. An elderly matron, wrapped in a three-inch-thick fur coat, was negotiating her way up the line with a walker, with her husband, I presumed, holding her elbow.

I walked past a young couple sharing a cigarette. When the young girl drew the final puff, she stamped the cigarette out forlornly. Her boyfriend, keeper of the cigarette pack, pulled it out of his parka pocket, showed it to her, as if to reassure her, and then slipped it back out of sight.

Most of the crowd was made up of teen-agers dressed in a hodgepodge of boots, scarves, floppy hats and parkas. They stood like a group waiting to meet a rock star. Radios rested on several shoulders, blaring musical cacophony.

When I was half a block away from the studio, I could see people jostling each other. They were chanting.

"No! No! No! Keep the skull! Keep the skull!"

Police officers raked through the crowd. People shouted, "Pigs! Don't remove that skull! Don't remove that skull!"

The sky dumped its snow on the milieu. Some in the crowd began to run away as the police neared them. But one young man ran forward and knocked a policeman down. A few others joined in the fight. Just then, about five policemen came forward with billy clubs and began to beat crowd members. It was hard to tell whether they were soaked from snow or their own sweat. This was a full-fledged riot.

I needed to see what was happening better. I craned to view the studio, as I was just steps away from its front door. There was no skull in the wizard's window display. Was it taken down again?

"Keep the skull! Keep the skull!"

Two paddy wagons pulled up in front of the wizard's studio. Policemen opened the wagon's doors and started shoving people into the vehicle. The floor of the van was a puddle of water from snow that had melted off boots. I walked past the van.

A gaggle of reporters and TV crews were outside the studio, jamming their way in. This would be on the evening news: "Chicago's South Side Snow Job."

I was still looking for Tony. Two policemen were guarding the studio's front door. Only reporters with press passes could get in. Finally, I saw Tony making his way toward me. He was carrying two cameras and a shoulder bag full of camera equipment. He kept wiping the flakes off his expensive equipment.

"This is ruthless," he said. "This is the story you're working on?"

"I don't understand," I said while nodding. We were both digging for our press passes to get inside.

Once we got past the door, we saw the room stuffed with a ton of reporters and cameras. Alderman Dryad had called a press conference. A few feet away from him stood Christopher, holding Crystal Skull, almost shielding it from onlookers. He looked like he was going to burst into tears. I tried to make my way to him, but nobody would budge. Most especially, the camera people.

"You're print," some broadcaster growled. "You don't need to see anything."

I decided to take the long way around. I edged myself along the wall, turned the corner, edged along that wall, excusing myself along the way, until I finally was only a few feet from Christopher. I called over to him.

"What's going on here?" I asked, after I got his attention. He leaned over toward me.

"Alex, I have so much to tell you. This skull is making all of the events speed up. I saw all of this coming, but I couldn't stop it. Destiny must run its course."

"What are you talking about?"

Alderman Dryad walked over, beamed me an eerie smile, and tugged at Christopher's arm. He motioned for him to stand next to him as he spoke. Poor Christopher obliged, making himself look like a forlorn puppy that was just about to lose its bone. The room began to glow from all the camera lights.

"This skull is causing a great deal of consternation in the twenty-third ward, and I feel it is incumbent upon me to remove this blight from this city," Alderman Dryad said, reading his prepared statement. "Ever since this skull has been displayed in the South Side Psychic's window, gang activity has increased and crime has been on the rise. Four murders have been committed, besides the murder of our great mayor, and two babies have been found in our garbage dumps.

"Police have indicated that two of the individuals charged with crimes claimed the skull made them do it. Apparently, they said the skull is evil and transmits terrible messages, forcing them against their will to commit heinous deeds. One molested a two-year-old girl. The other shot his eighty-five-year-old grandmother in a wheelchair.

"A few days after viewing and touching the skull, these

criminals went out and committed their atrocities. They remind me of the teen-agers standing outside today to view the skull. Let me reiterate that I don't believe the skull was the cause of the crimes. The problem is other people find this skull disturbing, and it's my duty to remove any hazards—perceived or real–from my ward."

He stopped reading from his paper and looked up. "I'll take questions."

"Has it been confirmed that these criminals came to view the skull?" asked one of the reporters.

"Yes it has been confirmed." He turned to Christopher and motioned for him to step up to the microphone. He just hugged Crystal Skull and nodded. Alderman Dryad turned to the microphone again.

"This information has been very difficult to come by, but it's all true," Alderman Dryad said. "I have received these reports from the police, who can confirm this information. Privately, I will add, the police are worried about what this skull is doing to the community. I have been given a copy of a police record, which indicated that in the month of December—which coincides with the time that the skull was displayed here—burglaries rose five percent, murder one hundred percent, rape fifty-two percent, and vandalism two hundred percent. Imagine what could happen in a few more months!" He pointed to a reporter in the front row. "Yes."

"How can you blame this skull for an increase in crime?" the reporter asked.

"According to these reports, the perpetrators blamed the skull, saying it made them do it." I looked over to the wizard. He was shaking his head back and forth.

"What will happen with the skull?" asked another reporter.

"For now, this skull must be removed from this window," said Dryad. "And the wizard has agreed to do this. Tomorrow, we are convening a city council meeting to discuss the matter further."

"What does the wizard have to say about this?" asked the reporter.

Christopher seemed stunned to have been asked and walked toward the microphone as if in a stupor.

"I never intended any harm to come as a result of this skull." He shifted his weight to his other foot as he shifted the skull to his other arm. "But this skull has been handed down in my family from generation to generation and has been hidden from public view for centuries. It was put on display because I thought its time has come, but maybe I was wrong. In any event, it must be understood that Crystal Skull has great powers and holds much potential for our civilization. It can amplify our energy and help advance our culture, our civilization. Unfortunately, those with more evil tendencies can also be affected by having their misdirected energy amplified as well. But if it is Crystal Skull's time for public viewing, the positive forces will prevail, as they always have. I have faith."

He stepped back from the microphone and sat back down on the chair. Some of the bright camera lights began to switch off, and the conference seemed to end. Then another reporter asked, "Alderman Dryad, Alderman Dryad, can you tell us some more about the city council meeting tomorrow? And as a follow-up, how is your mayoral campaign going?" There was a rumbling laughter. The camera lights turned back on, and Alderman Dryad stepped to the microphone.

"As you know, Chicago's City Council has been divided lately. Part of that division has been stemming from this skull. Half of the city is in favor of keeping the skull, revering it, worshiping it. The other half wants it removed. Currently, I believe this skull is turning into a danger in this city, and it needs to be removed. But I believe in the democratic process, and will bow to the wishes of our esteemed governmental body." He paused to look around, then continued.

"The meeting is tomorrow at ten. As for my mayoral campaign, I must say I'm receiving a great deal of attention. I believe the people of this city know where I stand. At the moment, we're trying to solve the murder of the former mayor, and after that, it's up to this city to heal itself."

Then a light shined in my direction and a reporter shoved a

microphone into my chin. "Aren't you Alexandria Vilkas, a prime suspect in the mayor's murder?"

Jesus, not again! "Yes," I mumbled.

"Wasn't the skull found in your car the day after the mayor died?"

"Yes. But I don't know how it got there."

"Weren't you working on a story about that skull?"

"Yes."

"Maybe the skull planted evil thoughts in your head and made you kill the mayor!" the reporter shouted. "Like those teen-agers who killed innocent people!"

"No," I said. "No, that's not true. I did not kill the mayor. I know it looks like I did, but I didn't do it. Why can't you just leave me alone?" I turned to face the wall, shielded my head, and cried. Let them see me cry. I don't care.

The lights turned off for good this time, and the media crowd dispersed. Alderman Dryad shook my hand on his way out.

"I'm sorry about this, Alex," he said to me, handing me a tissue.

I wiped the tears off my eyes. "I'm going to find the killer you know," I said, looking right into his eyes. "No matter who it is."

He walked away.

The crowd outside chanted, "Keep the skull! Keep the skull!" It was almost five o'clock. Snow continued to fall. I looked outside. A city snow plow drove by, shoving snow from the street to the curb with its front side and dumping drizzles of salt rocks from its back side.

Chapter 25

I decided to stick around and asked Tony to stay with me. Within half an hour, the wizard's studio was empty. It was just me, Tony, Christopher, and Crystal Skull.

I felt a sharp jab at my side.

"I'm hungry, I'm sleepy, and nobody can pay me enough to endure this," Tony hissed. "Why are we still here?"

"I'm not sure," I said. "I'm digging for a little more information on the skull and the mayor's death. I'm under a deadline by the police to find some evidence about the mayor's murder. Otherwise, I'm headed for the DA's office. Crystal Skull is my best link. I don't think we'll be here much longer. Please stay a few more minutes."

He looked over and smirked. "That's the first time you ever begged me to do something for you, Alex. Does that mean anything?"

"Shut up, Tony."

He raised his hands and sighed. He leaned back into the couch and hoisted his right ankle over his left knee. He began to inspect the damage the salt on the ground had inflicted on his cowboy boots.

"I've got to bring these boots in for repair and a good polish," he said. "I just bought them three months ago, but I guess they're just not made for Chicago winters. Man, I can never find a cool pair of boots that can make it through this city snow. It's almost embarrassing to walk around the office with these." His boots were supposed to be black, but they had several alternating thick and thin layers of grimy, white salt up to his ankles.

"You should do what most women do," I said. "Wear rubber boots with fake fur inside, and then take them off at work and put on a decent pair of shoes for the office."

"Yeah, and then I'll be tripping over ten pairs of shoes every time I try to sit down at my desk. In fact, I'm surprised you haven't broken a leg trying to get to yours."

It would have been fun to continue this argument, but then Christopher walked over to us, holding Crystal Skull in his arms, like a father holding his infant son.

"Will you meditate with me?" he asked. "I need to make some decisions."

Tony looked at me, and I answered for both of us. "Sure."

Christopher brought over a chair to place next to us, and placed Crystal Skull on the couch before us. We followed his lead. He sat straight with his spine erect, palms up, and looked at Crystal Skull. He breathed slowly. I tried not to look over at Tony because that would have broken my concentration. The wizard closed his eyelids. I did the same.

Breathe in. Breathe out. Breathe in. Hold breath. Breathe out. I felt a warm, peaceful feeling that urged me to believe in the skull's powers despite my misgivings. I concentrated on the white light between my two eyes and at times, saw this white circle take the shape of a white skull, growing larger and smaller, losing its shape and taking its shape again.

When I opened my eyes about twenty minutes later, Christopher was looking out the window, watching the snow fall. It was dark outside. The street lights illumined the continuous supply of flakes falling from the black sky.

"I'm hungry," Christopher announced. He walked into the

backroom, and came back out with a jumbo-sized bag of sour cream and onion potato chips. He offered some to both of us. Tony and I each grabbed a fistful.

Christopher began to pace in front of us, holding his bag of chips, alternately crunching chips and dipping for more.

"Why were people drawn to Crystal Skull so much?" he asked. "What did they gain from touching it? I ask myself these questions all the time."

He looked at us for an answer, but we munched on our chips and watched him like we were watching a football game with our home team getting creamed.

"Am I just using this skull to legitimize my life, to give a greater importance to the meaning of my life?" he asked. "Does Crystal Skull have more to reveal to me?"

He continued his pacing, and a snowstorm of chip crumbs fell to the floor. I took out my tape recorder and began to record his self-examination, thinking it might be good for my story.

"Mr. Warlick," I asked. "Can we talk about the mayor's death for a second?"

He momentarily paused, then continued his pacing.

"If this crystal has any great significance, why did I own it?" he asked. "What's in store for me? So far, this skull has brought me nothing but trouble. Was I being tested? Was this my destiny?"

"Was it my destiny to get accused of killing the mayor?" I asked him.

Suddenly, he stopped his pacing and looked over to me.

"Juan was here."

"When?"

"Just before the press conference."

My heart skipped a beat. "Why?"

"He wanted to visit Crystal Skull."

Juan never showed a deep interest in Crystal Skull.

"He said he was looking for answers."

"Did he find them?"

"I don't know. He asked to be alone with Crystal Skull."

I wondered what this meant.

"But he agreed to adopt my cat," the wizard beamed.

"He took your cat?" I asked. "Juan? I didn't know he wanted one."

"I asked him if he wanted it," the wizard said. "My wife has been begging me to give it away. Juan seemed to get along with it, and I just had a hunch the cat should go with him."

"When was this?" I asked.

"About noon."

"So boyfriend was here," Tony jeered. "And he didn't wait for you."

"Shut up, Tony. And anyway, he didn't know I was coming."

"Why are you all flushed and ga-ga over this guy anyway?"

"I am not! Leave me alone. You're such an expert, aren't you? Is your camera loaded?"

"All set to go. Just say the word."

"Just take some shots of the wizard and Crystal Skull. I'll see you tomorrow in City Hall."

I grabbed my coat and left.

Chapter 26

The next day I was in City Hall early. It was about an hour before the meeting. City employees were getting ready for a full council meeting. Secretaries made last-minute photocopies, aldermen milled about each other's offices to lobby for their points of view. Coffee gushed from Mr. Coffees like oil in Kuwait. A sign outside city council chambers announced all of the upcoming council and committee meetings. Nineteen committees were formed among the fifty aldermen, but on this morning, the entire city council was convening.

There were also a ton of blue uniforms swirling around. I'm sure they weren't all here to follow me, but it felt like it.

I decided to visit Alderman Frank Messina. I grabbed a cup of coffee and headed for the second floor aldermanic offices. I bypassed the front entrance of city council chambers where I would have to pass through a metal detector. Instead, I entered through a side entrance. Then I passed through an annex furnished with a long table and red carpeting. Often referred to as the "back room," this long room was the site for many special deals, concessions and new legislation. While the public sees what occurs in city council chambers, many of the debates between the aldermen were really solved in this back room, where for the sake of expediency, aldermen promised each other favors and voted for each other's pet legislations in return for similar favors. All of this I knew from my mother, who had been in this room often with Alderman Robin Dryad.

I wasn't at all surprised to see Alderman Frank Messina here, drinking a cup of coffee and talking to Alderman John O'Hara. My stomach did somersaults as I approached him, but I knew that I had to talk to him, to confront him about his role in the Nicotine Ring, and somehow get him turned off to my mother.

"Alderman Messina," I interrupted. "I almost didn't recognize you with your clothes on."

He turned on his heels and faced me squarely. Fury flashed across his face, and he snarled at me.

"What do you want?"

"I have evidence indicating you're involved in the Nicotine Ring, and I'd like to talk to you about this."

He turned to his colleague to excuse himself. Then he grabbed my arm and forcefully ushered me out of the annex.

"Let's go to my office."

"Thought you'd never ask."

"You remind me a great deal of your mother."

Except for the fact that I'd never touch your slimy body! "In what way?"

"Your looks, your straightforwardness. Your questions. You have a knack for being in the wrong place at the wrong time." He squeezed my arm tightly.

"Ow! You're hurting me!"

"Your questions are going to get you in a lot of trouble," he whispered slowly. We walked past the press room, which was filled with reporters drinking coffee, typing, or comparing notes. Then we walked past the office of the vice mayor, who was now the interim mayor.

Across from the vice mayor's office was Alderman Messina's office. For some reason, he had the only alderman's office in this wing, as compared to the rest of the aldermen whose offices were located in the opposite wing.

"What the hell do you want?" he asked, slamming the door behind me. He strode to his desk and sat in his chair. I took the chair opposite him.

"Do you like to smoke?" I asked.

"It's not illegal, you know."

"I was at the Tortilla King Factory two nights ago."

"Really?"

"I found some interesting information there."

"Like what?"

"Like a folder with the names of thirteen aldermen involved in the illegal sale of cigarettes to about a hundred small businesses in the area."

I studied him closely for a reaction, but he was shrewd. He didn't flinch. Not even a muscle. We were practically in a stare down, and despite my having the upper hand here, my nerves were on edge, and I wasn't sure I could sustain the momentum of my attack. But I could tell he was trying to come up with a response. I was getting close to nailing him. If I could prove he was connected to the Nicotine Ring, perhaps even running it, I could make him a strong suspect in the mayor's murder. He had a lot of money and power to lose if the mayor tried to shut down his cigarette operation.

"What names?" he asked.

"You should know. Your name was one of them."

"My name is part of many lists," he answered cooly, inspecting his fingernails.

"I saw cigarettes at the Tortilla King factory. Being packaged. I also saw your photograph hanging in the president's office."

"Manuel Jimenez happens to be a good friend of mine."

"Yes, I can see why," I said. "You protect him from paying any taxes on cigarettes he sells to hundreds of taverns and stores across the city."

"You have no proof of such a preposterous accusation," he said. He opened the top drawer to his desk. I flinched as he took out a nail clipper and began to clip, clip, clip his nails slowly and deliberately. When he finished his left hand, he looked up and challenged, "On that list, did you see the word cigarettes anywhere?"

I had to think back. That list was now in the hands of Detective Joe Burke. "I...I....I don't remember."

"On that list, did you see the label Nicotine Ring?" he asked.

"No, but it was obvious what was going on."

He laughed lightly and shrugged his shoulders. "Like what? You're just upset I happen to be dating your mother. You were shocked to see me in her home, weren't you?"

"Let's just leave my mother out of this, shall we?"

He stood up, looked at his watch, and said, "Alexandria, you're upset. And that's understandable. But really, I think you have an overactive imagination. You're making connections where none exist."

He was trying to confuse me, make me believe I had made the whole thing up. Oh, he was good. Very well practiced. What was I trying to prove?

"Where is that list now?" he asked.

"I gave it to the police."

He tilted his head to the side, then smiled and spread his hands out. "You did the right thing."

Now I was worried.

"Are you here to cover the proceedings about Crystal Skull?" he then asked brightly.

"Yes." We both stood up. "I'm not done talking to you."

"Maybe somebody should remind the council that the skull was found in your car the day after the mayor died."

"Oh, I had forgotten all about that," I said. "Are you trying to scare me?"

"Perhaps I should be the one who's scared. After all, I could be facing a shrewd killer. You're the officially suspected murderess in this case. If you killed the mayor, you wouldn't flinch at killing a mere alderman, one who was dating your mother nonetheless."

How did he turn this all around so fast? I wanted to be the one asking the questions. "So, you deny being involved in the Nicotine Ring?" I asked, intent on making this interview go my

way. I knew he was a part of it, but I still needed more defini-
tive proof. I looked around his office, but didn't see anything
that would help me.

He clasped his hands together and almost clicked his heels.
"Yes, I deny being a part of the Nicotine Ring," he said.

"Did you know somebody tried to kill me at the Tortilla
King Factory?"

Again, he took a moment before he answered. "No."

This was when I hated my job. It was rough talking to someone like Frank Messina, who I knew damn well was lying to
me. But I had no way to prove it. All I could do was quote him.
I had to widen my net of information. I had to talk to someone
who might know about his involvement, who might talk to me.
Alderman John O'Hara was just talking to him. I thought he
had a worried expression on his face when I interrupted their
conversation. I knew he was on his last term as alderman. In
the next election, he would be replaced. He would be a good
source to check up on since he wouldn't have much to lose by
telling me the truth. In my job I learned that people often
answer questions if they're asked the right ones. When I left, I
had already decided that an interview with Alderman O'Hara
was in order.

Chapter 27

By ten o'clock, the aldermen took their places in their assigned chairs in the oval-shaped room. Many walked in with a doughnut in one hand, a cup of coffee in the other, and a manila folder stuffed with papers tucked under one of their arms.

The red-carpeted city council chambers filled up. Its long tables were covered by green felt and the burgundy-colored leather chairs squeaked as the aldermen took their seats. The mayor's chair stood behind a long table facing the aldermen's table. To the mayor's left stood the city clerk's chair, flanked by cabinet member chairs.

I took a seat in the press section, also to the left of the mayor, as the vice mayor walked over to his seat. The TV camera crews plugged in their equipment. We print reporters sat with our open reporters' notebooks. Some members of the public took their seats in the balcony. I noticed how people stared at me, pointed at me, and then murmured about me to a partner's ear. I imagined what they confided.

"Isn't she the one who's accused of killing the mayor? They found the crystal skull in her car the next day, you know. I hear she's about to go to the district attorney's office for an interrogation."

I took a deep breath and tried to act natural.

By 10:05 A.M., the clerk called the meeting to order. He stood and said, "The council is now in session."

I looked over at Alderman Messina and caught him glaring at me. I met his eyes, felt my pulse accelerate. This was a cat-and-mouse game, I decided, and the dance of this story was turning as complex as a political strategy session. With all the political tension in the air, it was a wonder everybody kept their manners and restrained themselves from having a scrappy, knock-out brawl. Here, political punches were part of the everyday fabric.

Alderman Enrique Diestro, alderman for the 22nd ward, stood up and said, "Mr. Mayor and respected council members. There is a very grave matter occurring in our back yard, which needs to be addressed immediately. I want to show you what is happening in my neighborhood."

Alderman Diestro lived in Pilsen. It was the first Mexican community in Chicago, and it used to be the poorest Hispanic area that was fertile for crime, poverty, and desolation. But with Bernardo Morales' rise to power, Mexicans accumulated the means and wherewithal to clean up their neighborhood, build new plants, and energize industries. Tortilla King Factory would never have been built in that neighborhood until recently. I also knew that Alderman Diestro was campaigning to be the next mayor of Chicago, hoping against hope the city would elect another Mexican.

He took out a cigarette, ran it between his thumb and forefinger, slid it under his nose, as if it were a cigar, and lit it. He began to smoke it and sent two perfectly rounded smoke rings floating into the air.

"Mr. Mayor, I have a question for you," continued Alderman Diestro. "Why are the tortilla factories in my neighborhood filled with cigarettes?"

I turned around to look at Alderman Messina. His face glowered.

"You are out of order, Alderman Diestro!" shouted the clerk. "Put that cigarette out now!"

He held the cigarette between his thumb and forefinger and began to wave it around. He turned to look where he could extinguish it. He took his coffee cup and dunked his smoking cigarette into it with a hiss.

The photographers snapped their cameras, and I scribbled notes as fast as I could. I heard Alderman Diestro describe the tortilla factories in his neighborhood and how he recently inspected two of them.

"Why are these cigarettes being stored in our tortilla factories?" he repeated. "I'll tell you why. One day I took a walk down my barrio and saw kids on the corner smoking cigarettes. I asked them where they got them. Do you know what they told me? They got them at school. They could get a pack for twenty-five dollars, or one-fourth of the market price."

He flailed his arms and shouted. "So here we have a product that is illegally distributed to the Hispanic youth in my neck of the woods. I believe some of our esteemed council members are involved in this scam. Their purpose is to deliberately corrupt Hispanic youth."

Alderman Dryad sprang out of his seat.

"I'll tell you who's corrupting your youth!" shouted Alderman Dryad. "And it's not any members from this council. It's someone right next door to my office in my ward, and that man has more teen-agers from your ward coming to visit him than you've ever seen on one street corner. Why don't you direct your energies against this crazy wizard and his blasphemous Crystal Skull instead?"

Aldermen Diestro crashed his fist down on the table in front of him, knocking over the cup of coffee with the extinguished cigarette, spilling its contents over his legs.

"That's enough!" shouted the clerk. "That's enough! This is a city council meeting, not a wrestling match. Alderman Dryad, please sit down! You're completely out of order! We can talk about your problem next. And Alderman Diestro, your accusations are extremely inflammatory, serving no purpose but to further divide this council. On top of it, you have not proposed your solution."

Still wiping the coffee from his trousers, he said, "I would like this council to determine who are the true owners of those cigarettes being held in my ward," answered Alderman Diestro. "And furthermore, I would like this city to conduct a full investigation. We can't let this stand."

Then Alderman John O'Hara cleared his throat and lumbered into his microphone.

"I am tired of Alderman Diestro and his kind continuously asking this city to spend money in their neighborhoods, inspect all kinds of allegations that do not exist, just because he's paranoid. Does he think his ward is the only one in this city that has teen-agers smoking cigarettes? If that's his only criteria, then every alderman on this floor should be asking for money."

More aldermen asked for recognition to speak at their microphones, and another hour passed. When the matter finally came up for a vote, fifty-five percent of the council voted for providing funds to investigate the Chicago cigarette scandal. When the final vote was announced, a loud cheer emanated from the floor. Alderman Diestro waved his coffee-stained white handkerchief as several other members came up to him and patted him on the back. The vice mayor stood up and waited for the commotion to subside. "This is a great moment in this city. I promise you a full investigation into this cigarette scandal will be conducted."

I looked over to Frank Messina who was sipping his coffee. He lifted the coffee lid and blew on his brew.

The city clerk introduced the next order of business.

Alderman Dryad spoke into his microphone. He wore a subtle gray tweed suit, black polished shoes, and a white crisp shirt with a red tie. The room fell silent. He scanned the room, made eye contact with several aldermen while smiling and waving.

"I've been a council member for fourteen years now," he said, clearing his throat and shifting his weight like a fidgety boxer. "And I've seen a lot of things happening in this city."

He closed his eyes and paused for two seconds. "But today, it's time to declare that our city is under siege," he thundered. "We have an abomination sitting in the twenty-third ward. It's an object that was quite harmless at first. You all know I'm talking about Crystal Skull."

Several heads turned to look at me. A camera swung in my direction. A photographer snapped a picture of me. I tried to shrink in my chair.

"It's up to us, esteemed council members, to harness this object, take control of it, and smash it," Alderman Dryad continued. "I want to tell you about this skull, and I promise you, it won't take long."

He took off his brown-framed half glasses with one hand and pulled out a white handkerchief to wipe them.

"This skull has become a powerful, evil influence in my ward," he continued. "The owner of Crystal Skull is a wizard, a man who at first looked like any other psychic setting up shop on Archer Avenue, but this one was different. He has been using this skull to brainwash the people, to make them believe things that aren't there. There's anarchy in my ward and I can see it spreading throughout the entire city. We need to get rid of it before it gets rid of us."

He placed his hands on his waist and scanned the room, ending with a nod toward the city clerk.

Alderman Carlos Garcia spoke into his microphone. He was a long-time supporter of Mayor Bernardo Morales and a key player in the city's Hispanic politics.

"I too know of this skull," said Alderman Garcia. "In fact, I have seen it myself, being in the ward next door to Alderman Dryad. What he sees and what I see, however, are two different things. The skull is harmless. At the most, it is a part of a powerful legend. At the least, it is just a piece of glass. If authentic, the skull is millions of years old, and has been a catalyst to all of the major technological advances in this world. My grandmother, a curandera in the neighborhood, told me the ancient Aztecs used to pray to this skull. She's convinced of it. She's not the only one. As many of you know, for Mexicans, politics and religion are intertwined. The removal of the skull will not bode well for residents in my ward."

A few cameras were on me to catch my reaction. I sat tall in my chair, brushed my hair back, masked myself with my poker-face. I took notes. Inside though, my familiar green bile of fear began to rise. It heated up first in my stomach, then slowly spread throughout the rest of my body. I resented being the center of so much ill attention. It wasn't my fault. Even now, I'm just trying to write a story on Crystal Skull, to go on with my life. But I can't. Everything has changed.

Then Alderman John O'Hara asked for recognition to speak into his microphone.He righted his three hundred pounds with effort. Once he was in position, he took another moment to catch his breath. He was sweating like a sumo wrestler in a sauna. He loosened his tie, then straightened his jacket.

"Jesus Christ!" he shouted into the microphone. His nostrils flared and cheeks turned violet. "What is going on around here? This city's mayor died because of this skull. And that woman over there—sitting with the press—probably had something to do with it!"

He was pointing at me. I stopped taking notes and looked up. All eyes were upon me. All cameras swung in my direction. I wanted to flee. If the council members had rocks, they'd stone me. *It wasn't my fault. It wasn't fair.*

"When are we going to solve the murder?" he barked. "When are we going to throw somebody in jail?"

My press colleagues threw me sideway glances. One of them patted me on the shoulder. I grimaced. I began to face the fact I'd have to meet the D.A. tomorrow. This town needed a guilty party, and I was it.

"You are out of order, Alderman O'Hara," thundered back the city clerk, wiping his brow. "We are now talking about the skull, and if you don't have anything to add to this discussion, PLEASE be quiet!"

Alderman O'Hara stood up and spread his legs wide, as if he could dig his heels into the floor. He clutched the microphone with both hands, as if were strangling it. He let go with one hand, and pointed toward the clerk.

"Charlie, you're a damn traitor, and you know it," he bellowed. "There was a time we could all count on you, but you're just as bad as the rest of them. And as for that skull, I'll talk to you about that skull. God save me, but the skull is an abomination. A sacrilege to the Catholic Church and an insult to my people. And if the former mayor and his kind want to rally behind this skull, thinking it's their God damn savior, we should do them all a favor, and just smash it before they get anymore delusional over it. In the meantime, we should take that witch and burn her for killing our mayor."

He waved his fist, punctuating every other word with a jab in the air. *What did he have against me?* I stopped taking notes and rubbed my temples. Tomorrow's the D.A. deal. In just one day, it'll all be over. I felt like crying. I needed a strong shoulder to lean on. I took another deep breath and closed my eyes. I vowed to find the killer.

Alderman Garcia stood and walked toward Alderman O'Hara, but was out of O'Hara's sight. When O'Hara turned around to say something, he noticed Garcia inches away from him. Seeing him unexpectedly, he startled, then whacked Garcia across the face.

"You crazy sonofabitch!" he yelled to Garcia, watching him fall to the floor. Then he bent over him. I couldn't tell if he was trying to help Garcia back up or kick him back down.

"Order! Order!" yelled the city clerk.

It didn't matter anymore. Council members brawled, pushed and shoved each other. Pandemonium reigned. Confusion mounted. The cameras were off me.

Then O'Hara fell on top of Garcia. Messina shouted "Somebody help Alderman O'Hara! Call 911!"

I couldn't tell what happened to Alderman Garcia.

"Get this gorilla off me!" Garcia shouted.

Lights flickered off and on. Silence blanketed the room. The city clerk announced, "Everybody just be still. We have called for help."

Two aldermen shifted O'Hara's body off of Garcia's. Garcia stood up, adjusted his suit, ran his fingers through his hair and staggered back to his seat.

We sat transfixed. Nobody moved. Security guards urgently whispered into their walkie-talkies. Four paramedics rushed into the chambers with a collapsible bed. They carried it up high to get through the crowd. Finally, they reached O'Hara, lifted him onto the bed, then carried him out.

The city clerk announced, "The meeting is adjourned."

Chapter 28

We were all in a state of shock. Alderman John O'Hara was declared dead. Looked like a heart attack. I called my boss to let her know what just happened. None of this made any sense to me, I told her. No, they didn't even have a chance to vote on the skull. Plus, he blamed me for the mayor's death, calling me a witch.

"Listen, kid," Alyce said. "Come to the office. Edgar Sheldon's here, and he wants to talk to you."

"Right now?"

"Yes."

My car was parked about two blocks away, but with all the commotion, I figured it would take me forever to get to my office, less than ten blocks away. I took a cab.

What did O'Hara mean by accusing me? What did he have to gain? It was hard for me to leave the chambers with all the reporters surrounding me. I just kept saying, "No comment." One reporter asked who my lawyer was. *Did I need one?* Maybe I'd talk to Alyce about this.

By 11:45, I was in *Gypsy Magazine's* offices.

Alyce's door was open. When I walked in, Edgar Sheldon

stood up and took two steps forward to clasp my hand.

"Alexandria Vilkas, so we finally meet," he said. "You know, I know your mother. She often talks about you. Now I can see why she's so proud." *How did he know my mother?*

Alyce pursed her lips and tensed her body behind her desk.

"How kind of you to say so," I said. "Is there anything I can do to help you?"

We both sat down in front of Alyce's desk.

"Yes, I understand you're working on a story about Crystal Skull and its connection to the mayor's death. The skull has certainly captured my curiosity. Now I can't stop thinking about it."

"It does seem to have that effect on just about everybody," I conceded. Normally, I never discuss details of a story with anyone. But Sheldon owned the publication. I told him how the skull was probably worth millions of dollars, how if used correctly by a skilled practitioner, it could be even more powerful and exert more energy than all the arsenals on earth.

"Very interesting," he said.

"I understand you offered the wizard some money to display the skull at your restaurant." Alyce looked like she wanted to fall off her chair.

"Is that part of your story?" he asked.

"I don't know yet. It's hard for me to tell what goes in and what doesn't, until I collect all the facts. So, again I was just wondering why you were so interested in renting Crystal Skull."

"I have a fascination for ancient artifacts, if you must know, and I have quite an impressive collection of archeological finds. I can show you my collection someday, if you wish."

"And you wanted to include Crystal Skull in your collection?"

"Yes."

"Were you upset when the wizard wouldn't sell the skull to you?"

"How did you know that?"

"I interviewed the wizard."

"Hmmm. In answer to your question, I would say I was disappointed."

"Disappointed enough to steal it so you could keep it, and then have some remorse and plant it on one of your staffers?" I asked. "Or have the mayor killed since he wanted to have the skull displayed at the Field Museum?"

"Alex!" Alyce yelled. She turned to Edgar. "She's been under a great deal of pressure lately. You know. Being accused over the mayor's murder, and all. Tomorrow's her interrogation at the D.A.'s office. She doesn't know what she's saying anymore. Isn't that right, Alex?" She had this fake smile.

"Is that what you think happened?" Sheldon asked.

"It's a possibility."

"Do you like your job?"

"It's okay."

"Do you realize I own your job?"

"Yes sir, I do."

"Then cut the journalistic crap where you think you can ask anyone any question in the name of doing your story. Especially me. There's no journalistic justice with me. I want my magazine to make money. This is a business venture. Do I make myself clear?"

"Y-yess sir," I said.

"That means, that if you step on any toes doing this story that makes my life difficult, you're out of here. This isn't one of those investigative magazines, one of those do-good, make-the-world-better, no-matter-what magazines. I want to make money. Do you understand?"

I looked at Alyce. She nodded. "Yes," I said.

"And furthermore, the focus of your story is just the skull. Your job is to write about that skull, not murder and politics. Stay out of politics."

I sat, too stunned to speak. *I was just trying to write a story. Besides, my boss assigned it to me.* I looked at Alyce. Her eyes were on her toes.

"Is there anything else?" I asked.

"Mark my words. Cross me, and you're through!"

I looked at Alyce again. She didn't look up.

I walked back to my office and stared at my black hole.

Where's my story now? How was I supposed to stay out of politics? The skull is smack in the middle of a political investigation. Crystal Skull and I were both involved in politics, murder, and a gone-crazy city council meeting, topped off by O'Hara's heart attack—if that's what it really was. Trying to separate the skull from politics would be like trying to separate water from rain.

Furthermore, where does that leave me? I'm still the number-one suspect, nowhere closer to finding anyone else to take my place.

My one solace was that the city agreed to a full-fledged investigation into the illegal cigarettes being stored in Pilsen tortilla factories. I was no longer the only one who had the scoop on the Nicotine Ring. If everything went well, Alderman Messina would be found out soon enough. Some of this story's burden lifted off me. The outer world caught up to my inner revelations. With patience, maybe I really had to do very little. If I could just stop worrying, though.

Edgar Sheldon's speech disconcerted me. Alyce must have been protecting me from his money-grubbing, weasly attitude. Or was she just as shocked as I was? After all, she asked me to cover all types of stories that were controversial, that could stir the occult world's cauldron. In fact, it was her idea that I let the skull lead me to the mayor's murderer. I guess it was safer for me to exploit witches and goblins than it was to investigate city politicians.

A surge of bilious resolve crept up from my stomach and clenched around my heart. If it was the last thing I'd do, I was going to solve this murder. Screw Sheldon. Screw *Gypsy Magazine*. This was my story. If Sheldon wouldn't print it, I'd sell it somewhere else.

I looked at my watch and remembered that in half an hour I was supposed to meet my mother.

Chapter 29

By 12:20 P.M., I had arrived at the Crystal Palace to have lunch with Mom. We had scheduled it over a week ago, as a kind of a reconnaissance after my big ordeal on New Year's Eve. As a waiter led me to my table, I noticed the crystal ball spinning slowly at the top of the ceiling. Its light accented the painted shimmering stars, glistening moons and gleaming planets. Telescopes of various sizes were scattered throughout. A pointed wizard's hat hung in a corner.

I sat down alone. A waiter dressed in black came by to take my drink order. My thoughts wandered to my mother. I wondered about the relationship I had with her, and my feelings that ranged from confusion to repulsion to adoration. I think my mother saw me as an extension of herself and had high, perhaps even unrealistic hopes of where I should go, which people I should meet, and what I should do.

She could pack a programmed punch with me. Using her powers of organization and acute atunement to society's proprieties at any given moment, she thought it was her job to maneuver me into just the right position for the most optimal outcome. I often thought she would make the perfect wife for a politician.

But would she commit murder for me?

Perhaps that was why my father was so successful in his career as a violinist. He was able to concentrate on his art while my mother tended to organizing the concerts—the fees, the expenses, the marketing, the invitations, even dry cleaning. As much as I missed my father, I was grateful he provided amply for us, leaving us a generous insurance policy.

There were times I resented the fact that my father died. I remembered, when I was ten, how frightened I was that my mother would die too. I'd get on my knees at the side of my bed and pray to God, pleading with Him to let me keep my mother because I didn't want to be alone. I'd have nightmares about this, and Mom would rush into my bedroom, hold me tightly in her arms and then rock me to sleep. The nightmares eventually subsided and I would ask Mother endless questions about Dad—what he was like, who he knew, what he could have become.

I knew he loved me. Whenever he entered the house, I would drop whatever I was doing and squeal with delight, rushing toward him with joyous desperation, shouting at the top of my lungs, so that the whole world would know, "Daddy's home! Daddy's home!"

But he was only truly happy when he played the violin. He performed with such emotion and frenzy that his facial expressions revealed a soul wracked with the pain of drawing out music from a point of deep concentration. It was only when he finished a piece that his body and face relaxed in a pose of peace and contentment. It was as if he would wake up from a trance, astonished that he was conscious to hear applause. Then he would start his next selection, and it was as if he would enter another realm that he could only see with his eyes closed, that he could only reveal and share with others through music. But his agony was that his music revealed only a fraction of what he felt and saw behind his closed eyes, and the frustration of failing to reveal the universe to the audience at once became apparent in his body language that was filled with twists, bends, shakes, and other erratic movements. He died on a concert tour in Europe, my mother had told me.

The waiter offered me a menu to look over while I was waiting. My mother was late. At the bottom of the menu, I read about how the fortune-telling works here. Private readings start at $25 and go up to $100 for a full hour. Depending on the evening of the week, customers have a choice of meeting privately with a psychic, an astrologer, a channeller, or a hypnotist who could help them recall past lives. There's even a match-making service for single customers on Fridays and Saturdays. If I were willing to pay for the computer astrological analysis, I could meet someone that night who would be considered to be my "psychic counterpart." Just as I began to fantasize about that, Mom arrived.

She wore a smart thick wool suit with a tweed print in dark colored threads that intertwined in autumn colors – brown, burgundy, beige and forest green. She pulled her hair back into a tight coif at the back of her head. Her brown, flat purse matched the leather of her high-top boots. I, on the other hand, wore a plain, black business suit with a white blouse.

She kissed me on the cheek and sat down. For appetizers, we had summer squash squares and clam-stuffed shells.

"I could make these," she declared, biting into a square. She thought her cooking was marvelous.

"So what does Dryad say about O'Hara dying?" I asked.

"He thinks it's a political ploy to gain the sympathy of voters before his election," she said cooly, although it was obvious she was kidding. "Have you gotten anywhere with your investigation?"

Her tone of voice seemed to mock me in my attempt to do something difficult. This is what I hated about my mother – the mixed signals. On the one hand, she pushed me to accept new challenges, and on the other hand, she criticized me for trying to do something she thought could be fruitless.

"You think it's a waste of time, I suppose," I said, defensively, beginning to regret that I ordered a lunch.

"It's somewhat out of your range," she said. "After all, the entire police department is baffled, the mayor's staff is clueless, and all of the big-shot reporters are chasing their tails. Besides, I thought you were swamped with all kinds of stories about crystals and psychics and skulls. Are you sure you have time to solve a murder mystery on the side?"

"If I don't solve it, I'll be charged with it."

I really resented it when she turned so sarcastic, directing her venom to place blockades in front of my plans. I also regretted telling her how busy I was. It seemed that every time I admitted a weakness or some difficulty in coping with a situation, she stored the information to use at a later date, saving the data for ammunition to shoot with twisted aim. Her purpose was to disorient me.

"Oh dear," she said. "Is it really all that bad?"

"The police are following me all the time. In fact, there's one of them now." I pointed to the cop drinking coffee.

"Oh, don't be ridiculous. You're just being paranoid."

"I have to solve it. It's clear you wouldn't lift a hand to help if I were charged with the murder!"

"Alex, dear. That's ludicrous! Of course I'd help. Do you need a good lawyer?"

"I think I do."

"I know who you should have."

"Can I see him tomorrow morning, before my interview with the D.A.?"

"It's a woman, actually. And yes. How's your investigation going?"

"Well, for your information, I happen to have some leads and ideas that I don't think anyone else has put together. I'm working with Juan."

"Oh, Juaaaan," she said in mock admiration. "Well, then, there's nothing to worry about, is there?" She wrapped the corner of her napkin around her right index finger and dabbed the right corner of her mouth.

"What is that supposed to mean?"

"Oh nothing."

At this point, I was stymied. Should I take the bait that would lead into another vigorous argument about my choices in career, in men and in clothes? I let the moment subside.

"So what are those special clues and leads you have that nobody else could find?" she asked, as if nothing had transpired between the two of us.

"Well, to be truthful, you're on my list of suspects," I said hotly. "You're very ambitious and would do anything to advance your own career. All you want is for Robin Dryad to become mayor and for you to run his show. So you'd kill the mayor." There, I said it.

My mother took the last bite of her cantaloupe, delicately laid her fork and knife over the plate, wiped her lips purposefully with the white napkin, and pursed her lips. Then she nodded her head slowly up and down.

"Honey, I have something to tell you, and it could be a bit of a shock to you."

"Did you hear what I just said to you?" I screamed.

"Dear, please calm yourself," she said. "Yes, I heard. But you're upset. You're under a lot of pressure, and you're saying things you don't really mean."

I marveled at how she switched from one subject to another as if they were purses of a different color, tossing the other one away because it didn't quite match the occasion. I braced myself for a whopper.

"What could be a bigger shock than my accusing you of killing the former mayor?" I asked.

"Oh dear, don't be silly. Of course, I didn't kill the mayor."

Of course she didn't.

"And I'm sure you didn't either."

"Well? What? Or am I supposed to guess? No, wait, don't tell me. I already know. You're going to marry Frank Messina."

She smiled. "Nooooo, actually I'm planning to break up with him."

"Ooooh?" Now it was my turn. "When did you figure out Messina was a scumbag?"

"I'm planning to do it this afternoon, if you must know."

The waiter walked by. "A bottle of your finest champagne," I said to him. "We're celebrating."

My mother stopped him before he walked away. "Please, don't. She's just kidding."

I rolled my eyes as the waiter shrugged his shoulders.

"That wasn't my news, dear."

"So if that's not the big news, what is?"

"I'm not exactly sure how to bring this up," she said, hesitating in an uncharacteristic fashion. "I've been seeing someone else." She paused to gauge my reaction.

I looked at her as if she were a stranger. I tried to penetrate into my mother's thinking with a daughter's vision to find out which connections in her brain were responsible for her attraction to men other than my father. If I could just figure out which brain cable was out of sync, I'd pluck it out so she could think straight. But after about thirty seconds, I gave up. If only daughters were granted radiographic insight into their mother's brains.

"I probably should have told you about this earlier. I've been seeing this man for quite some time now."

I tried to be nonchalant. "Oh, Mom, don't worry. I know how it goes. It takes a while for things to warm up. Nobody really expects you to talk about someone until a relationship is fully established. Why several months could go by until that happens." I was a real expert on this.

"It's been longer than a few months," she said.

"Okay, how much longer?"

"A few years."

"How many is a few years?"

"Twenty. Maybe even longer. Things were getting difficult for me with your father at the end, and this man was very kind to me, and even to you, although you never really knew him."

My world turned topsy turvy. My mother had been dating someone even before my father died, and I never knew it.

"Do I know him? It's not Alderman Dryad, is it?"

"No, no," she laughed, shaking her head back and forth. "Edgar Sheldon."

"Edgar Sheldon!" I cried emphatically. "Edgar Sheldon!" I said again, this time incredulously. "You've been seeing him for twenty years and I never knew about it?"

"Yes, dear. I really didn't know how to bring it up."

"Twenty years? I only knew Daddy for ten."

"Um, there's more for you to know, dear," she continued, stretching her lips out horizontally into something that resembled a smile, but looked more like she was enduring gas pains.

"Geez, Mom, I don't think I could take much more."

"Daddy didn't really leave us any money. In fact, all he did leave us was a big debt. Edgar, on the other hand, was very generous and has been providing for us ever since Daddy died."

I kept looking at the ceiling in disbelief. I slapped my hand down on the table and fidgeted.

"I told you that it was Daddy's insurance plan because I thought it was important for you to have a good image of your father," she continued, like a train at full speed and unable to stop. I felt as if my mother were betraying my father. Who was that woman behind that face? "Your father, dear, never really left us anything. In fact, he just left us debts. Apparently, he had mortgaged our house twice without my knowing about it. I know all of this is coming as a shock, but you had to know the truth sometime. Besides, you're an investigative reporter, and you probably would have dug up this information on your own."

The joke fell flat. I looked at my right hand, and rubbed my face with it, trying to wipe out the news I had just heard. I kept pushing my hair back.

"Edgar got you your job. I told him you needed something new, about how bad you were feeling working on the weekly paper near home."

This was not happening to me.

"You what! That's not true! I got that job all on my own. You had no help in that. You're just saying that to have more control over me, to prove that I can't do anything on my own!" I began to sob. This, I couldn't take. I so wanted to prove to myself that I could go off in this career world on my own, that nobody held my hand. That I was independent.

My mother looked at me, confused and perplexed.

"I thought you killed the mayor!" I tried again. That actually made more sense to me. Maybe she set me up with Sheldon's help. If she betrayed my father, she could betray me.

"Perhaps I should leave you alone, dear. I'll talk to you later."

When she left, I sat very still. The waiter came by three times to ask if I wanted anything, and three times, I told him no. The fourth time, I said I wanted some coffee. My table was cleared. I looked at my big, black bag, and pulled out my notes from this story. I decided to go through them, from beginning to end to reconstruct that fateful New Year's Eve when the mayor died.

Chapter 30

I looked at my notes to help me recall what happened on December 31. Only two weeks ago.

As usual, my day started at home. Looking outside my apartment window, I saw how several inches of glimmering snow weighted down the evergreen tree branches. The nearby mature oak tree branches dangled icicles like delicate spears that shimmered in the bright sunlight.

I was on my way to interview the mayor, scheduled for 10 A.M. It was going to be in his home. I took the Stevenson, guessing it would be cleared. Snow plows first swept the expressways, then the main thoroughfares, and finally the side streets. As I drove, I noticed how the salt gleamed on the wet streets, like diamond jewels on asphalt, sending chemical heat to melt the insidious ice. I was counting on the fact that it was New Year's Eve day and that most workers would be taking the day off, leaving the streets open for me to cruise.

I was anxious about interviewing the city's top politician. In my short career, this was the biggest story of my life. My strategy was to feel my way along with questions. With any luck, the mayor himself might bring up the topic of the astrologist.

If he didn't, I'd have to come right out and ask.

He lived in a penthouse suite in The Chicago Towers on Chicago Avenue, just west of Michigan Avenue. Constructed a few years ago, the building was touted as an architectural wonder, partly financed by Edgar Sheldon. It stood in a part of town known as the city's Gold Coast, an area that attracted well-to-do city-holics—that breed of people who snub suburbia and embrace the metropolis for its cultural qualities. If you were mayor, it probably wasn't a bad place to live.

At 9:55 A.M., I walked into the lobby and announced myself to the doorman. He instructed me to take the elevator up to the top floor. It whisked me up seventy flights in less than a minute. I was still trying to unpop my ears while walking toward the mayor's suite, when his door opened. I expected a servant.

"Juan!" I said. "I didn't know you'd be here."

"Hi Alex."

He took my coat, after he kissed me on the cheek. Blushing, I walked toward the living room through a short hallway, convincing myself it was no big deal Juan was here. He was the mayor's press secretary. Of course, he'd be here. Funny, he never warned me though. The last time we talked, just a couple of days ago, he made me fax him my list of questions. I hated doing that, but if I wanted the interview, it was part of the deal.

I looked at some photos of Chicago history that hung on the walls. Then I entered the living room.

"Hello Alexandria," Mayor Morales said effusively. He was as charismatic in person as on television. After we shook hands, I scanned the place. Seated on a big couch was a burly man reading the paper. He was dressed in a black business suit, and I figured him to be a bodyguard. Nobody introduced him.

The living room was adjoined to the dining room. Both rooms were surrounded by picture-sized windows. I was looking east and had a view of the Water Tower. Lake Michigan was a sheet of ice as far as the eye could see.

The dining room table was made of marble, and that was

where Mayor Morales indicated our interview would take place. The table was set with a pile of pastries.

"Where are your wife and children?" I asked.

"Oh, they're out shopping."

Juan walked out of the kitchen with a tray of coffee, sugar, cream, spoons, napkins, and mugs. He shot me a smile that beamed as bright as the sun. I had to look away.

"Can't get enough of this stuff, I always say," Juan said. He set down the tray. "You want me to stick around, boss?"

"Do you mind if my press secretary joins us?"

Once I saw Juan's face, I knew he'd be part of the interview. Press secretaries like to do that, make their clients feel protected. But did the mayor know anything about me and Juan? I was trying hard to conceal my discomfort at having my pseudo-boyfriend here to witness this.

"No, I don't mind at all."

The buzzer buzzed. Juan walked behind me, brushing my back on his way to the front door. He was into all these secret moves in public. We were waiting for Tony. We agreed he'd take the pictures. Juan ushered Tony in. Meanwhile, I helped myself to a cup of black coffee, and debated whether I should eat a bear claw in front of the mayor. I decided to skip it.

Tony entered the living room, hoisting three bags of equipment. Juan was right behind him, introducing him to Mayor Morales. Tony and I mumbled a hello to each other. I was anxious to start.

Tony slung one of his camera bags onto the table, just missing my coffee mug. He busied himself setting up his equipment.

I looked out the window again, and had to squint from the glare of the sun as it peeked through the floating clouds.

"That's one of the hazards of living so high in the sky," the mayor said. "Lots of sun. You gotta love it!" Then he looked straight at me. "Ready when you are."

I looked at Tony and Juan. They looked ready too.

"First of all, I want to thank you for agreeing to this interview," I began. "*Gypsy Magazine's* readers are curious about your views on astrology and crystal. In light of the recent revelations about your use of an astrologer, I'm happy you chose our publication to share your views."

"Fine, fine," he said.

"I wanted to talk about Crystal Skull, if you don't mind."

"Go ahead."

"You've become very interested in the South Side Psychic's crystal skull. What does the skull mean to you and why is it important to the city?"

"I'm glad you asked that question," he said, looking like he was carefully choosing his words. "This isn't the only skull of this kind in the world, as you know, but this particular one may be the most precious, according to the latest expert analysis. Its craftsmanship is exquisite. A skull with this level of workmanship could not be reproduced today."

"What experts are you talking about?"

"I asked Christopher Warlick if a representative from the Field Museum could analyze his skull. He decided it was priceless and that it was revered very highly in ancient civilizations. I'm not sure that even Mr. Warlick realized its true worth. Few people know the history, or any of the myths, surrounding Crystal Skull. Even fewer know it's a valuable treasure. A piece like this belongs in a museum. That's where I want to put it."

"You mean you want to take away the wizard's skull?"

As I reviewed my notes, I realized that was the first moment I heard of that plan.

"I wouldn't put it in so many words. First of all, he would be compensated for letting go of his skull. Second, the skull is controversial. The wizard is not equipped to handle the responsibility of allowing the public to view it while it's in his possession. I've told him that."

"You have?"

"Yes."

"And what did he say?"

"He told me he already sold it to another man."

"Who?"

"Edgar Sheldon."

"What did you say?"

He took a deep breath. "I told him I thought the Field Museum could outbid Edgar Sheldon if he was worried about money."

"So then what did he say?"

"He said not everything is about money." The mayor looked a little tired.

I waited.

"He said he would think about my offer. In the meantime, he told me he agreed to lend the skull to Edgar Sheldon for his big party tonight."

"You mean Crystal Skull is going to be at the New Year's Eve Party at The Crystal Palace?"

"Yes." He turned toward Juan. "I understand this handsome guy is going to be your date."

Juan cocked his head and smiled. Reddening, I wanted to crawl under the table. Why was this revelation such a big deal? Everybody is a grown-up. Juan and I are having a date. Big deal.

Luckily, I wasn't the one being interviewed about my love life though, so I decided to move forward.

"Why don't we begin talking about your views on astrology."

Mayor Morales took a sip of his coffee and stared at the liquid as if he would find the answer there. He exchanged a look with Juan.

"Yes, it's true. Maria de la Cruz was my astrologist. I don't pretend to have all the answers, and like many people, I'm searching for the meaning behind it all. I think the universe provides us with clues, but they're not always so easy to read. For the record, I didn't always take Ms. Cruz' advice. Although I probably should have."

"Is she someone you would go back to?"

"Probably not soon. It's still not politically acceptable to turn to such sources of information, and as a product of my times, I need to be sensitive to how far I can go."

"Can you share an example of when you didn't take her advice, and what the end result was?"

"She warned me about the bombings in Pilsen. Maybe not

in so many words. But she had a good idea of who was behind them. That I had enemies. Of course, I still have no concrete proof."

I looked up from my notes. I had handed over the concrete proof to Detective Joe Burke—the file folder of the aldermen and policemen involved in the Nicotine Ring. Pieces of the puzzle were falling into place.

The mayor inspected his fingernails.

"Was there any other time?" I asked.

"She doesn't want me to go to the party tonight," he said. "She had a bad dream about me. She consulted her charts. She's quite upset." He laughed nervously. "But of course, it's just all silliness. Isn't it? I guess by the time your article comes out, we'll all be laughing over this."

Smiling, I nodded my head.

"I couldn't possibly take her advice about tonight. Everybody is expecting me to be there." As I recalled, he seemed nervous about going to the party that night. I remember wanting to ask him more about this dream.

But Juan pointed to his watch. It was already eleven o'clock, and we'd gone fifteen minutes over the scheduled time. I decided not to push it. I'd push for follow-ups over the phone.

"Well, Mr. Mayor. I certainly appreciate your taking all this time to talk to me."

"It's been my pleasure." He smiled grandly.

Juan shot me a look to remind me of our deal, which was to show him the story before it got published.

He stepped toward me and nuzzled my neck. "See you tonight, babe." He had his hand on my waist. I looked down, struggling to maintain professionalism. The others in the room stepped toward the window to look at the view.

"I'm looking forward to it," I murmured.

"Don't make me wait."

"I won't." I wanted the day to rush by.

Tony took a few more shots of the mayor and his crystal collection and then asked if he could go back to the office with me. We said our good-byes, agreeing to meet that evening at the New Year's Eve bash.

Once I was outside with Tony, I asked "So what do you think?" I was feeling pretty good.

"I thought everything was great—except for the fact that I had to look at Mr. Ra-Ra Siss Boom-Bah," Tony scowled.

"Are you referring to Juan?" I asked. "Don't worry about him. He's harmless."

The snow crunched loudly under our feet. "Is something going on between the two of you?" Tony asked, throwing me a sideways glance.

"It's nothing serious." I reshifted the bag on my left shoulder.

We walked about a block in silence, then "So it's confirmed? You're going to the Crystal Palace with Juan tonight?"

"Aren't we a thousand questions this morning. As a matter of fact, it's true. What's it to you?"

He held the door to let me walk into our building. "I guess I was still hoping we'd be going together. I mean, you know, as ...work buddies."

By now we were walking out of the elevator on our floor and heading toward our cubes.

"I'm sure you'll find a way to entertain yourself without me," I said, drawn to my computer like it was a magnetized black hole.

Chapter 31

I looked back up from my notes and scanned my surroundings. It had all happened right here, right in this room in The Crystal Palace about two weeks ago. In fact, I wasn't seated too far away from where I sat on New Year's Eve. The waiter returned to ask if I wanted more coffee. I was on my third cup. My table was cleared of food and looked more like a desk with my computer lap top, my spiral pocketsize notebook, several yellow legal pads of paper, pens, and tape recorder. I reminded myself to leave a humongous tip for taking up a table this long. At least it was slow.

Having just gone over the mayor's interview, I realized that much of what he said jived with what the wizard told me days earlier. I was beginning to make connections. Mayor Morales and Christopher Warlick met the night before my interview to talk about Crystal Skull. They had a verbal tug-of-war over it. News of its value was traveling. The stakes were getting higher.

I looked over where Crystal Skull was perched that fateful New Year's Eve. It was about fifty yards from where I was now. There must have been a thousand people here. Who would have stolen it? I still felt its disappearance was linked to the mayor's death. But who wanted to frame me? Who recognized my car?

My heart throttled. My fingers felt cold on my cheeks as the awful thought crystallized. The only two people who recognized my car and knew my door couldn't lock properly were Mom and Juan. Why hadn't I thought of this earlier? Was it my mother who dumped Crystal Skull in my car? Or was it my boyfriend?

Slowly, I struggled to recreate that evening one more time.

Chapter 32

I remember being on the Dan Ryan Ohio ramp headed toward River North by ten o'clock on New Year's Eve. Juan asked me to meet him at 10:30 P.M. He hated it when I was late, and I was hurrying to find a parking spot. Unbelievably, I found one just steps away from the restaurant. I smiled as I pulled in, thinking this was an auspicious beginning to a great year.

Finding that spot was so incredible that I talked about it to just about anybody who would listen. I greeted the wizard and his wife. I shook Alderman Frank Messina's hand, then Alderman Robin Dryad's. He was next to my mother. I walked over and hugged her.

"Mom, you'll never guess what happened to me."

She took a sip of her champagne and opened her eyes wider.

"I found a parking spot just steps away from the restaurant. It was right there, waiting for me. Can you believe that?"

She shrugged her shoulders and dismissed my comment, but was eager to tell me something. She gripped my arm and whispered, "Tonight's the night for Robin to make a good impression."

I jumped into what she wanted to talk about. "You'd do anything to have Robin become mayor, wouldn't you?" I whispered back.

"Anything at all, dear," she said. "The price is always high if you're in politics."

She turned to Crystal Skull. I followed her gaze.

"What do you think about the skull being here tonight?" I asked.

She shrugged her shoulders. "As long as it stays out of my way, I suppose."

"What does that mean?"

"You know very well what it means," she said, her eyes flashing. "That skull is causing problems for Robin. It's become a distraction in his campaign. It was bad enough when it was on Archer, in relative obscurity. But to put it here! Right in front of everybody! I don't know what Edgar was thinking."

I laughed at my mother, at how much power she thought she had over one of the richest men in Chicago. Little did I know she'd been dating him for years.

"You're going to tell Edgar Sheldon what to do?" I blew air out of my mouth in a not- too-pleasant sound. "Yeah, right."

She looked at me sideways, like an opera singer on a stage throwing a dramatic glance.

I needed a drink. "Whatever, Mom. I'm going to look for Juan."

Finally, I was at my table, but he wasn't there. Instead, I saw Alyce Brownlee and Tony Catania.

"You two are dates?" I asked.

Tony rolled his eyes.

"Oh, now, it's not so bad," Alyce jostled him. "Is it?" She reached for a bottle of champagne, filled my glass, and refilled her own and Tony's.

Tony leaned over. "You look beautiful, Alex."

"Thanks Tony," I said. "I almost didn't recognize you in your tux."

"Are you alone tonight?" he asked.

"No, Juan should be here any minute."

I looked around the room. Maria de la Cruz showed up with

a date. How did she land at the wizard's table? I still didn't know she was the wizard's sister. I continued to scan the Crystal Palace. Just about every alderman was here, as well as several top entertainers and business people.

"You know," said Alyce, "if it weren't for the fact that Edgar Sheldon, multi-billionaire extraordinaire, was throwing this party, half of the city's politicians wouldn't be here. They'd be afraid of running into the other half." She poured herself another glass and I was wondering how many she had. "If you think about it, his money helps all these city politicians transcend their preferences to show up as one big happy family."

She stood up and beamed at me and Tony. Then she looked around at the other guests at our table, and raised her glass in a toast. "Here's to Edgar Sheldon!" Everyone else at the table picked up their glasses too. "To Edgar Sheldon! To Edgar Sheldon!"

I looked over to my mother, a few tables away. She was in her element. I couldn't understand what fascinated her about the whole sordidness of running this city. Come to think of it, I never fathomed Juan's passion for politics either.

I just wanted to go home. I probably should have been working the crowd, asking questions about the skull, the mayor's astrologer. But my editor, just two seats down, didn't seem to mind the fact that I was just sitting there, pretending to enjoy myself. Tony kept me company, while Alyce continued to pour.

By about 11:30 P.M., Juan showed up.

"Where the hell were you?" I demanded.

"I was with the mayor in the limo," he said, taking the empty seat next to me. "He had another fight with his wife, and she almost refused to come. She was upset Maria de la Cruz was going to be here."

I took another sip. "So what happened?"

"We had to calm her down. I promised to be near her side while the mayor made his rounds. We have a deal he'll leave right after midnight."

"Near *her* side?" I shouted. "What about me?" I was fuming

he was an hour late, and now I realized we probably wouldn't even be together at midnight. But I squelched my anger. I changed the subject and told Juan my parking spot story. Then the mayor and his wife entered the restaurant.

Within a few minutes, they were headed toward our table.

I looked up from my notes. I didn't bother to relive the next fifteen minutes of that evening because they had been playing in my head over and over during the last two weeks, like an endless recording.

Chapter 33

By now, I was on my fifth cup of coffee, and most of my notes were in order. I was jittery too—and not just from the caffeine. Revelations about that fateful New Year's Eve thirteen days ago were unfolding fast. They rolled toward me, wave after wave.

I needed to see Crystal Skull again. Maybe I would rub the skull and a genie would appear with all of my answers. I packed up my belongings, left a huge tip, and walked out. Outside, I inspected the spot where my car was parked that deadly night. I imagined someone walking by with Crystal Skull, opening the car door and dumping it in my front seat. Who was it? Juan or my mother? They both heard me talk about how lucky I was to find that spot.

Tomorrow I would go to the District Attorney's office for questioning at 3 P.M. I looked at my watch. I had 24 hours.

Before I confronted either of my suspects, I wanted to ground myself with Crystal Skull. For strength.

I drove back to the South Side. Traffic was snarly on the Dan Ryan, but clear on the Stevenson. By 3:45 P.M., I was on Archer Avenue, looking for a place to park. There was an open space in front of the South Side Psychic Studio, but I resigned myself to keep looking. A couple of cops were behind me, itching to post tickets on cars standing on Archer from 4 to 6 P.M.

The air was cold and my skin was numbing. I told myself it was good to walk two blocks, to have my body in motion. If I were standing still, I would just burst from all the feelings swirling inside me. I noticed my mother's car. She was in Alderman Dryad's office.

Christopher acted like he was expecting me.

"Tea, Alex?" he asked. "I put in a dash of lemon."

"No thanks."

I plopped onto his couch and looked around, enjoying the calmness, which was like an elixir that brushed away my frustration. Suddenly, I don't know why, I started to cry. Tears kept streaming down my cheeks like fat drops from a leaky faucet. The wizard sat next to me and put an arm around my shoulders. I slumped and sobbed.

"It's alright. It's alright now," he said soothingly. "Come on. It can't be that bad."

"I've narrowed down my list of suspects to two people," I said. "There's only two people who could have taken Crystal Skull and dumped it into my car."

"Who do you think did it?" he asked gently.

"Either my mother or my boyfriend. How about that?"

He set down his cup and saucer on the table before us. He stood up.

"I'll be right back," he said.

He left me alone. *That was it? That was his reaction?* I walked over to Crystal Skull. I felt like I was greeting an old friend. As I touched it, I felt a surging current course through me, imbuing me with a tremendous amount of energy. My mood changed from surly apprehension to joyful anticipation. I closed my eyes and stood still, feeling Crystal Skull's hardness. For a moment, I thought I felt my hand fall into the skull as if it had turned into water. But when I opened my eyes, I saw my hand resting firmly on its crown. But I saw flames flickering behind its eye sockets. After I blinked, the eye sockets cleared. I faced it like I was facing a real person. My nose was inches away from its nose socket. I had the sensation I was standing in water. The air pressure felt heavier. To move a leg forward, I used all my energy to fight an undercurrent. I'm not sure how long I was there.

"What does the skull mean to you?" Christopher asked. I didn't notice him enter the room. I turned to face him.

"This skull is my destiny," I answered.

"You are the perfect person to be on this assignment," he said, handing me a report. "You are where you need to be."

"But why would my mother betray me like this?" I asked. "Why would she take Crystal Skull, dump it in my car, and frame me for the murder of the mayor?"

"It wasn't your mother," the wizard said softly.

"Was it Juan?" I asked, wondering how he knew.

"It wasn't Juan, either."

"Is there something you're trying to tell me?"

Christopher Warlick lost his composure for the first time since I met him. He crumpled to the ground, like a Raggedy Andy doll. He sat crosslegged in front of me and pounded the floor with his fists.

"I cannot take this anymore," he wailed. "I cannot take this anymore."

"Take what?"

"I cannot be the owner of Crystal Skull anymore. The pressure is too much."

"What pressure? I'm the one who's under suspicion for murder!"

"It's all my fault," he said. "It's all my fault."

"What's your fault?"

"This whole mess."

"Did you kill the mayor?"

"No," he said. He lifted himself up from the floor and took my hand. He invited me to sit on the couch. He looked into my eyes with a deep sadness. "But I took the skull and threw it in your car."

I looked at the man before me, the man who I had trusted so profoundly with my innermost spiritual worries, my confessions of self-doubt, my yearnings to solve this mystery. How could he, of all people, be the one to do this?

"How could you do this to me? Why would you?"

"It was just all a big mistake," he sighed. "That night, on New Year's Eve, I kept looking at Crystal Skull, thinking that I could not bear to leave without her. She has been everything to me, my whole life, the essence of my meaning. How could I sell her? Do you understand?"

No. But I said nothing.

"Then when all the commotion started and the lights went out, I just took it. I thought this would be a good chance for me to take my skull back. I had no idea you were with the mayor. I did not know that yet. I ran out with Crystal Skull under my coat. Outside, I panicked. Maybe this was wrong. My wife was following me. What was I going to tell her? I noticed your car. I tried your doors. One opened. It was a sign. The universe was telling me I was doing the right thing. I conceived my plan. You would find the skull, bring it back to me, and I would tell you what happened. But then, of course, everything went out of control. I could not face telling you the truth."

"Until now," I said. "Why now?"

"Because of that report."

I looked at what he handed me. It was the analysis of the Crystal Skull from the Field Museum.

"It doesn't matter anymore," Warlick continued. "I just called the Field Museum to come and take Crystal Skull. I am giving it to them."

"You're not taking any money for it?" I asked.

"No. Crystal Skull cannot be bought or sold. It must be found and shared. My grandfather handed it to my father. My father handed it to me. I have no children. So I must hand it over. Its time has come to be displayed in public, and it will not be stopped. This was all my fault. I tried to keep Crystal Skull safe with me. Then I tried to make money from it. Instead I created this big mess. It is time to let it go."

I flipped through the report's pages. I saw the same diagrams I had seen earlier with Jerome Gelding in the Field Museum. I knew this report would help me write my story, that it would give me the background on this skull, and the names of other experts—real experts—to interview. I stuffed it in my bag.

"So, you see, once I let go, telling you the truth was easy."

"So, let me get this straight. You took Crystal Skull, dumped it in my car, framed me for its robbery, but you didn't kill the mayor?"

"No, Alex. I did not kill the mayor. And I am sorry for having caused you so much trouble."

"I'm sorry too, Mr. Warlick. I still can't believe this happened. If that skull didn't land in my car, I would have never gone through this hell."

"Yes, Alex. That is true." He looked into my eyes. I looked away. Bitterness rose up my throat. I hated betrayal.

I took another deep breath. A paralyzing chill rambled up my spine as a new thought clamped around my brain. I'd been completely wrong about my mother.

Chapter 34

I walked next door, to Alderman Dryad's office and stood in front of his door, composing my thoughts.

Crystal Skull's disappearance had nothing to do with the mayor's murder. I had completely misunderstood my mother, ascribing thoughts and feelings to her that she probably never even had. I wondered how much of my life was just a false interpretation of what other people said to me. How much of my life was just one big fantasy, a huge distortion of innocent episodes blown out of proportion?

Like those looks my mother gave me. I just assumed I knew what she was thinking. I conjectured what she was feeling. As mother and daughter, I felt like the two of us were of one mind sometimes. I really thought her hurtful phrases were intentionally directed to cripple me, to keep me underfoot.

But once I saw the wizard was an unholy man who lied to me, I realized my mother wasn't to blame for everything that went wrong. There actually were some things in my life that were totally beyond her control.

I owed her an apology. I wanted to tell her so. I wanted to give her a big hug, stroke her hair and cheeks, and tell her, "I was wrong about you." I wanted to tell her she didn't deserve my emotional outbursts, that I was just purging my demons and that she was the closest person in my path.

I was ready to walk through that door and tell her it was all right with me if she wanted to date Edgar Sheldon, that it was all right with me if she wanted to spend the rest of her life in politics. Who was I to judge?

Chapter 35

My mother was sitting behind her desk. I pulled up a seat next to her, grinning from ear to ear. She looked up with a strange, pained look. She stood and wordlessly motioned with her hand, as if she were shooing away a fly.

"You want me to leave?" I asked.

She pressed her index finger against her lips. She was shh-hushing me.

"What's the matter?" I whispered softly. "Why do we need to be so quiet?"

A look of terror spread across her face. I turned to follow her gaze. Alderman Frank Messina stepped out from behind the doorway, holding a gun. It was black and shiny.

"Your timing is very bad, Alexandria," Alderman Messina said. He waved the gun in my direction. This gun was different from the one I found in the Tortilla King Factory. It was small, but not flat. It was a revolver. Its barrel was aimed right for my nose.

"Alderman Messina!" I said. "What's going on?"

"What's going on? What's going on? I'll tell you what's going on. Your mother is ending our relationship. And it's all your fault."

He took a step toward me, holding his gun steadily.

"Frank!" my mother screamed. "Please! Can't we just be adults about this break-up? You're acting as if nobody has ever broken up with you. What's the matter with you?"

"What's the matter with me? I'll tell you what's the matter with me. Nobody, and I mean nobody, breaks up with Frank Messina. Got that?"

He took another step closer. I looked at my mother's desk and spotted the phone. Could I lunge toward it and dial 911? My mind raced. Was he really meaning to kill my mother just because she wanted to break up with him? And she complained about my boyfriends? I locked eyes with her, wondering if she was transmitting a secret plan of escape to me. I couldn't translate her signal.

I looked over to Alderman Messina again. Beads of perspiration dotted his forehead, a tremor shook his right hand—the one holding the gun. He lifted his left to steady his grip.

"I have a double bonus here," he said. "A two-for-one."

"What are you talking about?" I asked. "You plan to kill both of us?"

"Yes," said Alderman Messina. "I'll kill both of you."

"You'd never get away with it," I said. "How could you kill two women and think you could get away with it?"

He had a sinister smile, one that made me realize how much evil was in this world.

"I'm an alderman of Chicago. I have connections."

"And protection?" I asked, stalling for time.

What could I do now? I had a tape recorder in my bag. If I was going to live, I'd want all this recorded for my blockbuster story. If I was going to die, I'd want all this recorded for the police. Either way, I had to turn it on. I reached into my purse.

"What are you doing?" he asked. "I hope you're not trying anything funny."

"I....I....I was looking for a cigarette," I said, as I clicked on the tape recorder. I touched a pack of cigarettes I took from a box on the Tortilla King truck two nights ago. "I wanted to show you something."

I whipped out the pack and flashed it in front of him like I was waving a cross before a vampire. "Do you know what this is?" I boldly took a step forward.

"I didn't know you smoked, Alexandria," he said, lowering his gun by a few inches.

"I don't. Do you know where I found this pack?"

He raised his gun back up.

"I found it in the back of a Tortilla King truck," I said.

He flashed his smile again. "I heard you were there," he said. "How unfortunate for you that I now have to kill you."

"Just like you killed the mayor," I said. "To protect your Nicotine Ring."

He shook his head back and forth.

"You've got it all wrong, Alexandria. If you're going to die now, you might as well die well-informed. I didn't kill the mayor. I had nothing to do with killing him. Don't get me wrong though. Nobody was happier than me to hear he died."

I shot my mother a look. If she could read my mind, she would have deciphered this: *How could you possibly pick this sore loser for a boyfriend?*

My mother slumped in her chair.

Alderman Messina continued. "In fact, if I knew who killed the mayor, I would go up to the guy and shake his hand."

"How are you so sure it was a man?" my mother asked.

"Come to think of it, I'm not," he said. He shrugged his shoulders. Somehow, the comment put him in a good mood.

I brushed the side of my purse to feed off the power of the two double-A batteries running my tape recorder. "I know about the Nicotine Ring," I said. "And about your involvement."

"I'm not worried," said Alderman Messina. "Whatever you know dies with you right here." He took another step toward me. We were about eight feet away from each other.

"I have a list of aldermen involved in the Nicotine Ring," I said.

Alderman Messina laughed. "Yes, you told me this morning. Whatever list you have, I'm sure it's out of date. Business is booming. Everyday, we get a new alderman recruited to our cause. We don't even feel guilty about it anymore. It's like we're part of a big joke with the federal government. The feds wants to show their muscle by imposing big taxes. Well, this is Chicago. We don't cave into the feds. We're doing an old-fashioned boycott by letting our citizens smoke nicotine at affordable prices."

"And of course, the aldermen made nice money from such a noble cause," I added.

He took another step toward me. "If you're your mother's daughter, you know what makes this city work."

"There's just one thing I don't understand," I said. "Why are you storing all the cigarettes in the Mexican neighborhoods when the Mexican mayor was against those untaxed cigarettes being distributed?"

He took another step. We were five feet away from each other. "You answered your own question. It was a beautiful plan. We were against Mexicans running this town, so we needed to find a way to cause friction among them."

"Divide and conquer?" I asked.

"Yeah, you got it." He turned toward my mother. "You raised some bitch here."

With that, my mother stood up with such fury on her face that I thought she would hop over her desk to slap Alderman Messina's face. But he turned toward her and fired a shot.

"Down whore!" he shouted. "Down!"

The bullet lodged into the plaster wall nearby. The sound of the gunfire was so loud we were now all in the moment. No other thoughts distracted us.

I was four feet away from Alderman Messina. My eyes were riveted to him. I dared myself to jump toward him and grab his right arm to disengage his gun from his grip. He pointed the weapon at my mother's direction, but his eyes darted back and forth between the two of us.

"You'll never get away with this, Frank," my mother screamed. Her voice was tremulous and I knew she held back tears.

"Nobody leaves me, bitch!" Frank shouted. He took another

step in my mother's direction and fired another shot. She ducked under her desk, a big heavy stainless steel version that looked like a relic from the last war.

Ping! The bullet grazed the desk. By this point, Messina and I were less than two feet away from each other. I lunged toward him, springing from my spot so that I landed on him with all my weight. I grabbed his right arm with my right hand, trying to protect my left one from another break. We were both on the floor. We wrestled for the gun. He rolled on top of me. I was on my back. My mother jumped on his back and clawed at his face.

Suddenly, the door from the street flew open. In walked Christopher Warlick. He bounded over and jumped on the three of us, like we were a pile of football players, grappling for the pigskin.

"Ugh!" Messina grunted in my nose as Christopher landed on top of him. I didn't even have the strength to grunt myself because I was on the bottom of the pile, underneath I don't know how many pounds of wriggling flesh. I thought I'd go unconscious.

My right hand gripped Messina's wrist. My left hand, still attached to a broken wrist, was free. A useless appendage wrapped in a plaster cast. I whacked Alderman Messina in the head and screamed from the pain. Finally, Messina let go of the gun. I grabbed it and pulled the trigger.

Two police officers arrived and dragged Christopher Warlick, my mother, and Messina off me. I sat up to catch my breath.

"He tried to kill us," I said to the officers, pointing to Messina.

"We know," said one of them, pulling out a pair of handcuffs and wrapping them around his wrists. The police officer turned to me. "Are you all right?"

"Terrific."

Chapter 36

After I was back home, I stripped off my clothes and stepped into my bathtub. I had a date with Juan in an hour. I turned on the water and listened to its rushing gurgles. I poured a generous amount of lilac-scented bubble bath into the stream and was soon surrounded by a mountain of white foam. I sank deeper and deeper into the hot water.

It was almost seven o'clock. Earlier, my mother and I had talked in my living room, where she and I exchanged information. I gave her my apology. She wept. She told me she was very happy to have me as her daughter.

Then I asked her about Frank Messina.

"Did you know he was like that? So jealous?"

"I knew he had a very protective streak in him. At first, it was an endearing Italian quality."

"Endearing?"

"Yes, I liked that he wanted me near him all the time, I guess."

I was getting more used to her being with another man, and was beginning to understand her need.

"But he had three other wives."

"Really?"

"They all disappeared."

"What do you mean?"

"He said they left the country."

I raised my eyebrows.

"They're all dead."

"His three previous wives are dead?"

"Nobody could prove it, but the police thought he killed them."

"How did he get away with three murders?"

"Who knows, honey. He's Italian. This is Chicago."

I sank deeper into my pile of white foam, and thought about my situation. I had to talk to the D.A. tomorrow. My two weeks were up.

I still didn't know who killed the mayor. I was so sure that following the trail of the skull would lead me to the mayor's murderer. Instead, I found grief, betrayal, and misunderstanding. I wallowed in the water.

But I had had quite an experience, I had to admit. While making the skull the focus of my life, I found redemption, hope, and a renewed spirit. I realized this whole case didn't depend on my solving it. My life would still continue if I didn't solve the murder. It wasn't up to just me to fix this city, to remedy its problems. There were a lot of good people investigating this case. I was just one of many inching my way along to help. Someone more talented, more skilled, and more experienced than I would solve it. It didn't have to be me.

But damn. If the cops didn't find the real killer, would they try and make me the guilty one?

What else was I supposed to do? I'd interviewed just about everybody on my list. I resigned myself to meeting with the D.A. tomorrow.

Shit.

I wanted this weight to be lifted off my shoulders. I wished it would just end so I could get on with the flow of my life. I was tired of being stuck in this case, allowing it to consume me day and night. When could I focus on something else? God only knows what else, but *something* else.

For one, I needed to figure out what I wanted to do with Juan. I took a fluff of foamy bubbles in my right hand and blew at them, letting them scatter across the tub, and watched them blend back into the bubblefold.

I realized I wasn't too happy with Juan. I was just holding on to him, thinking I needed a boyfriend in my life. I sat still in my hot water and let the feelings wash over me. I'd have to give Juan another chance. That was only fair. Besides, sexually he did turn me on.

My date with Juan was in fifteen minutes. I pictured his long, black mane stroking my body. I couldn't get the image of his face out of my mind—that masculine, square jaw. And those hands. I loved his hands.

Chapter 37

By 8:30 P.M., I was at Juan's doorstep in Bridgeport. He lived in an older red-brick building with six apartments converted into condominiums not too long ago. About ten years before, this neighborhood was blue-collar, beer-country. Then somebody noticed it wasn't too far from downtown. That's when builders rehabbed faster than a yuppie could ask, "How much for that?"

The funny thing about me and Juan is that we never went out on any official dates—no operas, no movie theaters, no fancy restaurants. We always hung out at my place or his. I didn't mind. I preferred being alone with him. Sometimes we just drove around to check out houses in the city.

I rang his doorbell. In a few seconds, I heard the buzzer to let me in. Juan was on the second floor. I took the striped carpeted stairway up to his condo. He opened his front door to greet me. He looked like he hadn't slept in days. He had dark circles under his eyes. His black hair was stringy and greasy.

"Come on in, Alex," he said listlessly, as he let me pass by. I walked over piles of clothes and crumpled styrofoam containers. I walked into his living room, sat on his wide, black leather couch and looked around. To my right was the adjoining din-

ing room, with his bamboo table covered by unopened mail. I
could see his small kitchen from where I sat. The L-shaped
counter- top had dirty glasses, an opened bag of ground coffee,
half-eaten bagels, empty beer bottles, and several round
opened tin cans that looked like they once had tuna fish. I
never saw his place look this bad.

"What's going on, Juan? What's the matter with you? You
look terrible."

He sat down next to me and dug the remote out from underneath some crumpled napkins. He pointed it toward the television, causing a videotape to rewind. It clicked to the starting
position and began to play.

"I've been watching this over the past few days."

"Really? What's it about?"

I looked around for the jacket to read about it. But I couldn't
find it. Then I started to watch.

Mayor Bernardo Morales was naked. He groaned over the
breasts of Maria de la Cruz.

"That's the tape? The one that Maria de la Cruz used to
blackmail the mayor?"

Juan nodded.

"How did you get it?"

He pressed the pause button and looked at me.

"Well?"

Juan slumped back into the couch and threw his legs on the
coffee table, crossing them before they landed. He crossed his
arms behind his back. "The mayor asked me to get it. He was
desperate for it."

"When did you take it?"

"It was the night before New Year's Eve. That was the night
the mayor went to visit the wizard. He asked me to wait outside in his limo. It felt like forever. I had no idea what he was
doing there so long. About two hours later, I saw Maria walk
into the wizard's studio. I thought they had a rendezvous that
night."

"A rendezvous?"

"Yeah, and the more I began to think about it, the more it

was pissing me off. The mayor was already in a lot of trouble over her, and he didn't need more. I needed to stop that relationship. I realized this would be a good time to look through Maria's house to find her tape. I took my chance and left."

"You took the mayor's limo?"

"He had police escorts who would take him home."

"The police let you take the mayor's limo?"

"I told them I had a family emergency. They said they knew where to find me, and that if the mayor got upset over his limo, I would have to deal with him."

I nodded. "But weren't you worried you'd be noticed on her block with the limo?"

"I drove the limo back to my house and switched to my car. Then I drove over to her house, snuck in, and stole the tape."

"Was it hard to find?"

"It was labeled 'Bernardo' and it was in her VCR."

"So then what happened?"

"I got home and called him. He said thanks, but then cut me off, saying he had other things to do."

"You say that like you were disappointed."

Juan shrugged his shoulders. "I expected him to be happy about my finding the tape, that he would be proud of me. I wanted him to make a big deal about it. But he acted like I got one of his suits back from the dry cleaners."

"Did he want the tape?"

"No, he said I should destroy it."

"So ever since then, you've been watching the tape?"

He nodded. "You want to see it?"

That was when I began to have an uneasy feeling about Juan. Something told me I should say no, but I was drawn to the idea of watching two people do something they both knew they shouldn't be doing.

Juan rewound the tape.

It began with Maria in her bedroom in front of the mirror. The mayor's reflection was behind her. He was holding the camera. A bottle of champagne was chilling in an ice bucket next to a dozen red roses in a white porcelain vase.

Maria was dressed in a transparent black gown with a low cut in front that revealed her round, white breasts. She admired herself and applied red lipstick on her full lips. She pursed them.

"You always knew how to take care of yourself," the mayor said.

Maria turned around and faced him. The mayor scanned her body up and down.

They sat on her bed. Maria undressed him. She kissed him on his forehead, his cheeks, his neck.

"Remember how much we enjoyed the show last time?" she asked. The mayor nodded, keeping his eyes on her. She laid back, pulling the mayor to her. He rolled on top of her, then she on top of him, their buttocks rolling in and out of the camera's range.

I looked over to Juan, wondering how many times he watched this. My stomach got queasy. I walked toward the bathroom, leaving Juan alone with his tape. When I came back, the tape ended. Juan was rewinding.

"You're watching it again?"

He ignored my question, allowing the tape to get into its starting position. He pressed play again.

"Is this what you've been doing over the past three days?" I asked.

He was mute.

Then I noticed the cat smell. I heard a meow. The sound came from Juan's bedroom.

"Is that a cat I hear?"

Juan nodded. "The wizard gave it to me," he answered, still watching his tape. "He said I would do his wife a favor if I could take the cat from him. She's allergic to cats."

"So I heard. I also heard you visited him the other day, to see Crystal Skull."

The white cat padded into the room. I called her to me. "Come here, kitty, kitty. Come here, kitty."

I turned to Juan. "What's her name?"

Juan shrugged his shoulders.

"You don't know her name?"

"No."

"Where's her litter box?"

"In the bedroom."

"Are you nuts? Nobody puts a litter box in a bedroom. You have to put it in the kitchen."

I stood up to begin rearranging.

"Did you ever own a cat before?" he asked.

"No, but I have common sense. A litter box goes in the kitchen. Everybody knows that."

"Nobody knows that."

"Juan, you're not yourself." I walked to his bedroom and opened his window to let in some fresh January air. The litter box was under the window. It was filled to capacity with kitty doo-doo.

I looked at his dresser and noticed six bottles of Imprimatur. He arranged five of the cologne globes around one, like five moons orbiting a planet. I took one of the moon bottles and splashed cologne around the bedroom to kill the cat smell.

"What are you doing?" Juan stood in the doorway.

"I'm straightening out your mess. I don't know why I'm even bothering, but you can't live like this."

I put the cologne back, then bent down to pick up the litter box and move it to the kitchen.

"What are you doing?" he shouted. He grabbed my good wrist.

"Let me go. I'm doing you a favor." I tried to step forward, but he didn't loosen his grip. The litter and doo-doo shifted back and forth in the box, as Juan and I struggled for control. But I wouldn't let go. He tried to yank it away from me. That was when the whole box fell, litter, doo-doo and all. Along with a knife.

I stooped down to get it, but Juan grabbed it first.

"What was that knife doing in the litter box?"

Juan brought it close up to my neck.

"Does this feel familiar?"

I couldn't believe this was happening.

"You killed the mayor!"

"Sherlock, you're not," Juan said, pressing the blade into my neck. He swung me around and gripped me with my back to his front. "But you have a knack for being in the wrong place at the wrong time."

I squirmed.

"You're not getting away this time. I trust you have no gun."

"Not like I did at the Tortilla Factory, the last time a man had me in this position."

I turned around and managed to push him on top of his bed. He held his knife and laughed, seemingly relaxed.

"What were you doing at the Tortilla King factory that night?"

"I was watching you, sweetheart."

"Don't call me sweetheart! Why were you there?"

"You were ruining my master plan."

I was looking around to see what kind of a weapon I could use. I glanced at the bottles of Imprimatur. They looked big and solid. I was about four feet away from them.

"What master plan? Establishing the Nicotine Ring in Pilsen?"

"Let's just say I played an important role in that. I had connections in the neighborhood."

"But why would you hurt your own Mexican mayor?"

"I had a vendetta. I wanted to hurt him the way he hurt me. I wanted to find a way to betray him the way he betrayed me."

Juan looked smug. I inched my way toward the Imprimatur globes.

"We had the perfect plan. Bernardo treated the Mexican businesses like they were his own children. When he found out that one of them betrayed him by storing untaxed cigarettes, he was torn."

"Did you help Frank Messina find a place in Pilsen to store the illegal cigarettes?"

"It was my idea," Juan said, looking proud of himself. "I spent a lot of time with Bernardo. This cigarette thing was his pet issue. He hated Robin Dryad and Frank Messina."

I puzzled this for a second. "So you knew Frank was the weak link?"

"Bernardo did background checks on Robin and Frank. Robin was clean. But Frank was filled with lots of dirty secrets. I knew I could convince him to start trouble against the mayor."

"So you approached Messina with the idea of helping him establish a Nicotine Ring in Pilsen?"

"Yes."

I still didn't understand Juan's motive. "The Mexican businesses trusted you. They thought they were helping the mayor by following your suggestions."

Juan nodded.

"But why?" I asked. "I still don't get what you had against the mayor. Why did you want to cause all this trouble for him?"

"Do you know what it's like to grow up with a father who won't even recognize you as his own son, as his own flesh and blood?"

"My father died when I was ten, Juan. You know that."

"Yeah, but he loved you. You know what kind of father I had?"

I inched myself closer to the bottles of Imprimatur. Juan sat with his legs hanging over the foot of the bed, his feet touching the floor.

"I grew up a bastard child. My father had a quick affair with my mother and then left her pregnant. He denied I was his son."

"Did he tell you that?"

"No, my mother did. She wanted me to know who my father was. I grew up watching every move my father made."

"Did you ever confront him?"

"Not directly, no. At least not right away. But I shadowed him. I built my whole life around him. I wanted to be near him, to win him over, and finally to have him accept me as his son."

The uneasy truth hit me. "You worked for him—as his press secretary."

"Yes."

By now, I was in front of Juan's dresser and the Imprimatur bottles were directly behind me. "Bernardo Morales never knew you were his son?"

"Not until the night I found the videotape. That was when I thought he would be so proud of me. I told him I found it for him. Then I confessed to him that I knew he was my father. I wanted it to be a big moment. I wanted him to bond with me. But instead, he just hung up."

If it weren't for the knife Juan pointed at me, I'd actually feel sorry for him.

"So that made you want to kill him."

"Yes."

I grabbed an Imprimatur and held it in my hand like a pitcher ready to throw a baseball.

"And you did it with nicotine poisoning. Traces of nicotine were found on his cheeks and the palms of his hands," I said. "As if he had splashed on cologne."

"Bernardo always liked to pour his cologne on heavy," Juan said, taking a step toward me.

"And everyone knew Imprimatur was his favorite," I said, remembering the bottles Maria kept on her mantel. "You gave him a bottle of poisoned Imprimatur as a gift."

"On New Year's Eve. Bernardo Morales was no longer worthy of being my father. If he would deny me, then I would deny him."

I stayed silent, still ready to pitch my globe.

"As soon as he splashed on the poisoned cologne, I knew it was just a matter of time before he would die."

"Did you plan for him to die in my arms, Juan?"

He smiled as he took another step toward me. That was when the cat walked into the bedroom. She stood in the doorway and stared at us. First at Juan. Then at me.

"No, I had no idea that would happen. But, as I said, you seem to have a knack for being in the wrong place at the wrong time."

"Just like now," I said, wishing I had a gun.

"That's right!" he said. He lunged toward me. I moved to the side, holding the round bottle high over my head. I took a step toward Juan and crashed the bottle over his head. It was solid and didn't shatter. Juan fell to the floor, but quickly stood back up.

"That cologne works much better as poison," he said turning toward me. I opened it and started splashing it over him.

Juan laughed.

"You don't really think I'd keep bottles filled with poison on my own dresser, do you?" I tried to turn away, but couldn't. The cat hissed. Juan jumped on my back and I fell to the floor. The bottle rolled away from me, spilling its perfumy contents. I was on my stomach, my face in the rug. Juan jabbed his knife in my back. I screamed loudly as the blade pierced me, hitting one of my ribs.

The cat hissed again and jumped on Juan's back. He screamed. I suddenly began to like cats. As he recovered, he stood up. Then he pulled the knife out of my back. He chased the cat. She scurried under the bed.

I got up on my right elbow and knees, trying to move despite my stab wound. I lunged for the bottle of Imprimatur just two feet away from me, stood up, holding onto the bed for support, and raised my globular weapon over my head. I smashed it into the side of Juan's head. There was a cracking sound. The bottle shattered.

"What the..." Juan shouted, feeling the bump on of his head. He stopped chasing the cat and went after me again. I jumped to the other side of the bed, leaving a trail of blood on his covers. He met me at the dresser, where I picked up another bottle.

He grabbed my arm, stopping me from smashing the new bottle onto his head. The cat leaped onto my back, propelling me to fall on top of him. He lost his balance and fell to the floor. I straddled him, holding him down with my weight. I raised my Imprimatur and smashed it on his skull. Then again and again. Panting, I watched his face scrunch up, his eyes open wide. I poured cologne over his forehead, his eyes and into his ears.

He finally stopped struggling. A trickle of blood dripped down his right temple. I heaved and rolled off him. I made it to his front door and ran down the stairs, terrified at what I had done. The cat ran behind me. I ran out into the street and pounded on the window of the cop car standing in front of Juan's apartment.

Chapter 38

It was April, a week after Chicago's mayoral election. I was standing in line at the Field Museum, snaking my way along to visit Crystal Skull. To get into the museum, I walked through a forty-foot plyboard skull. It was constructed to celebrate the museum's newest acquisition.

"A shatterproof glass encases the full-size replica of the human skull carved out of quartz crystal," I read in a brochure handed to me as I walked in. "The encasement has an opening at the top to allow a hand to fit through and touch the crown."

The line to Crystal Skull wound up the museum's south staircase onto the second floor. Crystal Skull's new address was Granger Hall, the hall of gems. Within an hour, I was inside it. The line moved slowly, but I used the opportunity to view several window displays of precious stones. One window showed jewelry made of emeralds, rubies, opals, pearls and lapis lazuli. The sign in the window indicated these precious stones could increase psychic powers, stimulate chakras, magnify telepathic thoughts, and attract others who are like-minded. Somebody turned up the New Age music of flutes, harps, and bells. It soothed me as I gazed through another window display of crystal bracelets that could help give or receive love. From a sign in the window, I learned that the wrist contains one of the main pulses connected to the heart and is metaphysically linked to the heart chakra. That's why cologne dabbed on a wrist retains its scent for a while.

I felt the pulse in my left wrist, which no longer had the cast, and I was grateful that I was here, that I was alive. I was one of thousands of visitors that day. As I moved up in line, I thought about the new mayor of Chicago, Robin Dryad. He won the Democratic mayoral primary in February in a closely contested race against two Mexicans, three blacks, and an Irishman. Having a Republican mayoral primary was just a formality in this city. Democrats always won the general election. In fact, the papers barely covered the event. What's the point of covering a foregone conclusion?

My mother was busy arranging family pictures on her new desk at City Hall. When she asked me if she should pull any strings on my behalf to get a job as one of the mayor's speech writers, I declined. I needed to make my own way, even if it was a tougher road than the one she would have me follow.

I took a few more steps and thought of Juan. He was in jail. It was a miracle I hadn't killed him. What did I ever see in him? Maybe it was that penetrating look that just made me want to take my clothes off. Unfortunately, my fantasies of being with him were richer than the times I actually was with him.

I thought of my job at *Gypsy Magazine*. I couldn't decide if I should move on. Covering the occult was much more exciting than I had anticipated. By writing that story on Crystal Skull, I became enmeshed in a political whirlpool—one that almost sucked me in. I typed out my story on the former Chicago mayor, his interest in astrology, and his untimely death. I interviewed aldermen who were involved in the Nicotine Ring and eventually, with the help of Detective Joe Burke, I found the names of other policemen who were in cahoots. Once the story came out in late March, I was amazed at how fast this city moved to clean up its act. City people were like trained stage hands who knew how to rearrange the props so that the show could go on.

I realized that covering the occult had a very deep effect on me. Most of my questions were still unanswered, but I still needed to search. Maybe dealing with matters of the occult would help me. I don't know. I always went back and forth on this. I mean, I still had a hard time believing in half the stuff I reported.

I was just a few feet away from Crystal Skull. I took a step closer, wondering how I should spend the rest of the day. I could just go back to the office and have a conversation with Alyce about my next assignment.

Or, I could blow off the afternoon.

Anyway, I was now an owner of a white angora cat, and its name, I learned from the wizard, was Saddharma. Even after I looked it up in a dictionary, I still didn't understand what it meant. Some Buddhist thing. Maybe it would be a good idea to keep Saddharma. Like me, she had a knack for being in the wrong place at the wrong time. Maybe we could help each other.

Mark Brown/ PhotoPro/Chicago

SILVIA FOTI lives less than one block away from Chicago with
her husband and two children. She used her Masters degree
in Journalism from Northwestern University, along with her
fifteen years of experience in reporting for magazines and
newspapers, and transmogrified them to her first mystery
novel. She teaches speech at St. Xavier University. Contact
her at lotusink@aol.com